Amy,

Love having you [as] company as a fellow parent. You're great :)

Take care +
Happy Reading

Becky
RFN
5/16/09

Midnight Veil

by
Rebecca Nolan

authorHOUSE®

AuthorHouse™
1663 Liberty Drive, Suite 200
Bloomington, IN 47403
www.authorhouse.com
Phone: 1-800-839-8640

First published by AuthorHouse 3/10/2009

ISBN: 978-1-4343-2705-5 (sc)

*Printed in the United States of America
Bloomington, Indiana*

This book is printed on acid-free paper.

Chapter One

"The Seed is Sowed"

Today is intolerably hot. August in New England offers only the utmost discomfort of humidity and bright blazing sun. The steam is visibly rising off of the debris-covered earth. Looking out my bedroom window on the second floor, everything on the horizon is covered by a thick haze, similar to the last few years of my life.

Despite the illuminating sun, inside my beat-up apartment is dreary. Gloom lingers within the neutral painted walls and matching tile floors. Even the ceiling has the same dismal and boring paint. I wonder why it wasn't painted white. At any rate it is an apartment of my own. No more sleeping on the couch, or during a weed fest, or waking up to screaming kids at an ungodly hour. Now I at least have the peace and quiet of the emptiness that surrounds me in this desolate apartment.

The unit is about as empty as I. The couch I own is still in storage, along with my dinette set and TV/VCR. The only piece of furniture settled in is my new bed. The deliverymen were kind to assemble the frame when they brought it in, because I am prohibited from moving heavy objects in my condition.

Being incapable is not a fact I am willing to accept, but compromising with limitations will suffice. It is a foreign concept for me to be dependent on another, and that will prove to be a major

1

obstacle to overcome. To make matters worse, my radio is one of my belongings locked up in storage. Music is my portable sanctuary. In this newfound silence I collect myself on the edge of my bed and stare at my trash barrel full of clothing that seems to shrink by the day.

On second thought, I might just miss the chaos and disorder from my lovely couch-stead! Haunting thoughts begin to clamor in my brain. They scream at me, making up for lost time, trying to clarify the circumstances that have led me here. How on earth did this party-girl Jezebel wind up suppressed, depressed, and slowly inflating? How the hell did I get myself into a situation where I have to face the responsibilities of being single and pregnant? What am I going to do now?

Sitting with legs crossed at the edge of my new bed, an elbow resting on each knee, I can't ignore the excruciating pain inside my skull. Tremendous surges of electricity form "Ys" and flash fiercely through my room, zapping my brain. I rub my skin long and hard, putting pressure into my eye sockets with my fingertips and pulling my cheeks down as my hands slowly fall back into my lap. I take a second to catch my breath and regain clear vision. Looking out of the bedroom window the sun's rays penetrate my pupils like laser beams aggravating the agony behind. My hands automatically rush back to my face. Exhaling a sigh, I see the blue Joe Boxer shorts and boring, black ribbed tank top. Is this the best I can do?

The Sound of Silence

Screaming ideas and yelling the facts
The sound of silence, it always attacks

Not an outside voice or songs of a bird
No twinkling stars could so be heard

From somewhere this silence continues to ring
Reminding me of what the future may bring

Wishing to ignore, but can't, this silence
Trying to refrain from thoughts of violence

The sound of silence, it is a creeper
Digging down a hole deeper and deeper

Turning visions to sights of black
Setting minds on a one-way track

They wonder why some are nocturnal
The sound of silence is eternal!

Memories of my childhood are vibrant with color and warm with the sun. Playing with my sisters in the lush landscape, picking golden buttercups and thistle for our mother, always made us proud to be well behaved. The rewards of smiles and hugs were more than positive reinforcements; they were the building blocks of our self-worth.

Racing the clouds down the long paved drive through the apartment complex in which we lived was one of my favorite activities. The noticeably quick-paced clouds were tough competitors, as I never won those races.

I am Reba, the middle of three daughters to my native New Yorker parents. Stacy is two years my senior and Amber is two years younger than me. We were friends as girlfriends would be. Even my rainy days were bright with adventure, making tent cities with our blankets throughout the apartment. Being the middle child often made me feel like the most popular in the group. I was old enough to comprehend a mature style of play and still elementary enough to play with Amber. No matter what our age I had the advantage to either bridge the gap or remain neutral playing with one and then the other.

I don't know how or when, but that all changed. By the time we were teenagers Stacy was in a world all her own and only on occasion was I allowed in it, which is more than I can say for the rest of my family members. It was no cause for concern for my parents, because she retained a solid 3.8 GPA. Amber, on the other hand, certainly had more freedom. Unfortunately during this critical time our parents were living in their own time of strife.

The demise of their marriage all began with the first fight. My sisters and I sat at the top of the stairs in the new house my parents sacrificed so much to buy for us—no one realized just how much even years later when my family was broken into so many pieces. My father's voice was very gruff, so his words were clearer than my mother's in her feminine tone. I remember hearing things I didn't want to and rapidly retreating to my bedroom blasting the music so I couldn't hear any more. Stacy and Amber remained at their posts, absorbing as much detail as they could.

The fighting continued for many months, with short bursts when my parents wanted to pretend we were picture perfect. It was frustrating trying to keep up with that kind of inconsistency. My sisters and I wanted to spend more and more time out of the house. Stacy got involved in academic activities after school while Amber and I hung around the neighborhood with our separate group of friends. Danielle and Casey were my closest friends.

Amber had only one girlfriend, whom she called Shonnie. She was a Puerto Rican girl who lived with her mom and her mom's drug-dealing boyfriend.

Amber and I needed a quick escape plan out of the house one weekend. Stacy was on a school trip for a few days to a foreign land. Amber and I couldn't take the tension at home and decided to work as a team. We concocted some story that allotted us several hours out of the house without having to check in, but in all reality we had nowhere to go and nothing to do.

After finding out that Casey was on punishment and Danielle had a family gathering to attend, we decided to walk across town to pick up Shonnie. We arrived unannounced and caught the household off guard. Our knock on the door had startled her paranoid mother, who was under the influence. Whispers and shuffling were heard through the door before Shonnie finally answered.

Her face was swollen and her eyes were red. "What are you guys doing here?" she said softly. The expression on her face was that of relief, although her uneasiness was recognizable.

"Well, we had to get out of the house," Amber started.

"What is the matter?" I inquired.

Just then a male voice shouted, "Shonnie, who is it?"

"It's for me; don't worry about it, jerk!" she replied as she shut the door and stepped out into the hallway of her apartment building.

"Who was that?" I asked.

Simultaneously Amber and Shonnie replied, "That's the perverted drug-dealing jerk!"

"Did he do it again?" Amber asked sympathetically.

Shonnie broke down into tears, and we sat on the steps furthest from her front door where she told us what had happened moments before we arrived. I came to learn that he would distastefully grab at Shonnie every chance he got. Her mother was usually in her catatonic drug trance when he attempted to victimize her. Any effort Shonnie made to confide this to her mother was futile. She never received the desired reaction of a protective parent. Amber already knew this was happening. I was completely mortified. This explained why Shonnie was never intimidated by our dysfunctional home life. Ours was refreshing to hers in comparison!

We allowed Shonnie to pour her heart out as long as she needed before we lightened the air.

"Man, you know where Stacy is right now? That bitch is sitting her ass in a cold cement shack with her seven strips of toilet paper for the week! And she calls that a vacation!" I digressed.

"Yeah, ain't Russia like always freezing and shit? Ya know like when Rocky fought the Russian guy in Part IV, and Paulie was all pissed 'cause he couldn't even walk in the snow it was so deep. Then he fell over like a weeble, but he didn't get up!" Amber added with giggles.

Shonnie chuckled a bit at the thought.

"Are you hungry?" I asked, imitating Rocky Balboa from Part V, holding out my M&Ms for Shonnie. It was one of the few phrases Amber and I chose to mimic from the favored films.

Shonnie shook the candy from the package onto her hand and passed the bag to Amber, who then did the same before handing it back to me.

"I don't know why she would want to go to a place like that anyway. They don't speak English, their government is cruel, they don't like Americans, and it's cold and blah looking."

"Poor people are everywhere, and so are the wealthy. I am sure a tour group of high-school kids will be treated well just so we don't think those bad things about them. You're just mad 'cause she missed your birthday," Shonnie suggested.

"She DIDN'T miss my birthday. She is a million miles away and *she* didn't forget to put the card in my top drawer. Everyone else forgot."

"I said I was sorry!" Amber pleaded.

"I didn't bring it up!" It was terribly upsetting that no one in my family remembered my birthday the day before. Our parents were focused on Stacy being in a foreign country when they weren't engrossed in their own problems. I wanted to forget it. I broke the uncomfortable silence. "Stacy saved her money for a year just so she would have enough toilet paper for the week and maybe some snacks. Although, I don't know if I would wanna eat what they got over there. You think they serve goat heads and shit? They grind up the horns for topping like Parmesan cheese!"

"Reba, where do you come up with this shit?"

"I don't know; maybe I watch too many movies!"

"Well, I never seen no movie like that. That's all in your crazy-ass imagination!"

"You know that shit is real. Memba when we went to the resort that time and they had some exotic meal night and that kid, Don, got the sheep's head?" Amber said.

"What?" Shonnie exclaimed.

"Hell yeah, I remember. How could I forget? I couldn't sit with him. He saved the fucking skull. His sister said it was in the bathroom sink soaking for the rest of the night. I would've slept in our room if I was her."

"What are you talking about? You're not really serious, are you?"

"Yes we are," we said in unison.

"He brought it back to the Bronx with him and tacked it on a mantle and even named it after me," I continued.

"He even sent her a photo of it with her name engraved on the plaque. I'll show you the next time you come over."

"Yeah, I will have to remind you when we're back at your house. But do you think they really eat that shit over there?"

"Well, we will have to ask Stacy when she comes back … if she comes back. They probably got them over there and now they are stuck. They got them all enslaved behind large stone walls with ugly mutha fuckas on guard holding big guns. Talking 'bout 'Nyuk shitsenzvodka!'"

"You're retarded! That's your sister. Why you even talking like that?" Shonnie said, laughing.

"I know. Let me shut up before I jinx it." I made an honest effort to contain myself.

"Hey, Stacy is smart. She'll get out of it," Amber stated once she was able to calm her laughter.

"Yeah, man, she's smart but not that way. She has no street sense. What is she gonna do, threaten them with a calculus equation?"

"She could be like McGyver and build a bomb with soap and hairpins," Shonnie said.

"There ya go! See, she'll be all right. We always are, girls! Anyways while Stacy is building bombs and drafting escape plans, Amber and I devised our own escape plan and now we need something to do. You down to get outta here?"

"You know I am!"

"One problem, we don't have much for cash, so what can we do without it?" Amber asked for suggestions.

"Hey, I got an idea," Shonnie whispered, urging us closer. "I can get a few bucks from the jerk's wallet."

"Alright!" Amber agreed enthusiastically.

"We might have to get our hands dirty though," Shonnie warned. "It's probably in his back pocket."

"Whatever!" Amber complied.

"Are you fucking mad?" I intervened.

"Don't worry; he's probably out of it just like my mother by now. I told you he hooks my mother up first and then preys on me before he takes his hit." She started back towards her front door with Amber two steps behind.

"I don't know Shonnie, I don't like this guy. I ain't trying to get stabbed or anything!"

"Reba, stand by holding the door open. Amber will come with me around to the kitchen. I will distract him while Amber grabs his wallet."

We all walked in together to scope the scene. Shonnie's mother was nowhere in sight, and the perpetrator, now prey, was slumped over on the couch. I grabbed Amber's sleeve and urged her towards front-door duty.

I motioned Shonnie to reach for the wallet in his back pocket while I stood in his view in case he came to. I had no plan if he awoke; I just knew I had to distract him so the other two could successfully escape. Fortunately I didn't have to do anything but stare at Shonnie's abuser; strangely, he didn't reflect one.

While focused on his relaxed eyelids the image of a middle-aged man magically transformed to one of a young boy. The disgraceful expression on his face melted to the innocence of a child. The goatee and sores vanished and were replaced with milky youthful skin. His chapped colorless lips smoothed out and gained a pinkish hue. I saw the split in his skin appear before my eyes and his blood slowly dripped from the opening.

Skimming over the surface of his full figure the hair on his arms thinned and lightened a shade, giving way to stick-like stems. The wounds from countless needle incisions faded as fist-sized purple bruises emerged. His clothes were simple with grass stains at the knees and mud on his sneakers.

"I got it; let's go," Shonnie whispered.

But I was frozen, captured by the boy I saw. Something shimmered from his eye that I hadn't noticed at first glance. It was a tear building up at the inside corner, but before it could stream down the side of his nose the vision of a drug-induced man was dominant again.

Still stunned, I followed Shonnie out of the house. She managed to retrieve thirty-three dollars from his wallet, and we left for the day. It was enough money to get us into the movies and away from life for a couple of hours. Once inside the cinema we hopped from theater to theater, prolonging our stay as much as possible.

When it was time to return home Shonnie came to our house. My dad worked nights and Mom was usually out. We were all sleeping before either one went in the room to check on us. Half the time they never noticed Shonnie was there. Sometimes she was with us a week straight before they sent her home for the night.

She and Amber caused a bit of ruckus with the local boys a block from our house. Every time I went to check up on Amber, she and Shonnie were in the midst of teasing the horny young kids. I harbor a tremendous amount of guilt for not being more diligent in steering Amber away from her newfound attractions in life, because before I knew it she was mixed up with the wrong male and I had lost any power I ever had as her older sister. Through trial and error I was learning how to cover my tracks with stories about safe sleepovers at Danielle's while we were out late finding house parties and tasting new pleasures.

"Yo Dee, where are we going exactly?" We had been walking for twenty minutes and about to head into the projects.

"Kareem is having a party tonight."

"I know, but where?"

"It's at his house on Hobbs Street."

Walking the streets that made up the Hill I noticed the lack of privacy in the area as most of the doors were propped open and a large quantity of windows were either bare or barely covered with a pinned-up piece of fabric like a pillowcase or a torn sheet. There were no screens in the windows or on any of the storm doors. I have always valued my privacy, so this community of openness was extremely foreign to me.

We walked between the buildings housing four two-floor apartments horizontally in each. There was an overhang above the concrete steps at the front door. On one side of each entryway was a privacy screen of vertical siding plywood, though nothing was private in this densely packed complex of five hundred units. Overall they looked so similar I was surprised Danielle could distinguish them even with the numbers on the front.

"I don't really know people out here, and if something goes down and my parents find out I was in the Hill I will live the rest of my days stuck in my bedroom like Casey."

"Chill out. Kareem's parents are home."

"His parents let him throw parties?"

"I guess so. Actually I think it's just him and his dad. Ain't that so cool? I wish my parents did."

"Shit girl, your parents let you do just about anything you ask. I bet if you asked to throw a party they would let you."

"You're right, but they wouldn't let anyone drink alcohol."

"Well, they are lenient, Dee, not fucking stupid!"

"So what does that say about Kareem's dad?"

"I will believe the parent of a fourteen-year-old will allow his kid and his friends to drink when I see it."

"Well, get ready to believe 'cause here we are."

"You mean that dark house with all those people around? Ay, what am I doing here?" I mumbled.

We walked through a crowd of older kids up to the door. I noticed some school kids through the front window.

"What's up, girls? Welcome to my crib." Kareem invited us in.

"Hey Kareem! Thanks for inviting us," I said, following him through the apartment.

"Look, there's a table over there on the side with rum and coke, ice and plastic cups. Help yourself."

"For real?" I asked as Danielle had already thanked him and started towards the table.

"Kareem, I thought your dad was gonna be here."

"Yeah, he's around here somewhere." He said looking over people's heads for him.

"He let's you drink?"

"Girl, I am the man. I can do what I want. Just don't go getting stupid on me and it will be all good."

"Nah, I ain't like that."

"I know that's why you're here. But I had to say it anyway. I'll check you later. My cousin is coming through with Tom and them." Kareem walked back to the front door to meet his new guests.

I met up with Danielle, who was trying to mix a drink. She was pouring a little bit of the rum and then a little bit of Coke and repeating the process again and again, studying the contents.

"How do you know how to make it?" I asked.

"Girl, does it look like I know what the fuck I am doing?"

"Um yeah?"

"Hello, young ladies. Looks like you could use a little assistance. Here let me see that." A large black man stood behind us and grabbed Danielle's cup. He sniffed the light-colored contents and made an awful face. "Oh yeah, you need help alright."

The older man gulped the drink and started from scratch with two cups. "Pay attention now. I can't be here all night, ya hear? I don't want to incriminate myself. Do it right and you will be alright." He started with a couple cubes of ice in two cups and then poured the rum, counting three seconds as he poured. Then he filled the cups with Coke. He gave one drink to me and the other to Danielle.

"Thanks," we said, taking the cups and sipping them right away.

"Yo K, I am going up now. Keep this shit tight and there won't be no problems," the man called to Kareem.

"I know, Pop. It's all good." Kareem yelled back to his dad who then retreated up the staircase.

"So, believe yet?" Danielle whispered.

"Not really! Could you imagine?" I took another sip of my drink. "How does yours taste?"

"Pretty nasty! But I will drink it anyway."

"I hear that. It makes it taste like flat soda, doesn't it?"

"Something like that!" We stood back up against the wall watching the crowd. Mostly everybody in the house was black or some shade of it. It didn't bother me. Some of the girls made a dance floor in the center of the living room. I was comfortable on the side.

"Hey Reba, do you see that kid over there with the light skin next to Kareem?"

"Yeah, what's his name, Tom?"

"I think so. Ain't he cute?"

"He's alright."

"C'mon let's go talk to Kareem and see if we can talk with him too." She grabbed my arm and walked through the dancing girls.

"Danielle, what are we gonna say? We don't even know him."

We pleasantly said hello to a couple of girls that we knew from school as we squeezed through. Her focus was on the boys standing by the front door in a circle. "I dunno; I am sure you'll think of something."

"ME?"

We were right by Kareem's side and I couldn't think of anything to say. Then a tall dark skinned kid said, "Hey Casper!"

The boys laughed and Danielle did too.

"Real original!" I replied.

"I'm playing, girl. You're not just the only white girl up in here, but you are *white*!"

"I'm Irish," I said, unaffected.

"No shit, me too!" he continued.

"Are you?" I asked as everyone laughed.

"Do I look fucking Irish to you?"

"No mutha fucka, but she's Irish too and she don't look it either."

"Is that so?" Tom asked.

"Yeah, I'm Cape Verdean mostly, but I got some Irish in me." Danielle said.

"Well, give it up to the Irish then, 'cause they make some pretty girls!" Kareem declared.

"Well, I am gonna go check out the black chicks over there getting their groove on." Kareem's cousin left the circle and another large kid followed him.

"Sorry about that," Tom excused his friend.

"Sorry for what?" Kareem asked. "He's my cousin and I don't make excuses for his ignorant ass. Sides, Reba handled herself just fine."

"It don't bother me. I know how white I am. What difference does it make? I ain't looking at his ass anyway!"

"You're better off keeping it that way!" Kareem exclaimed. "Now me, on the other hand. I ain't ignorant like him. I know how to make you smile!" He stood closer to me and put his arm around my shoulder.

I smiled meekly, and then took a step back to face him and discreetly gain some distance, "I just can't get over the fact that your dad allows you to drink like this with all these people too." I used my hands when I spoke to keep him at arms length.

"Yeah, he's alright. If something goes wrong, it's my ass, make no mistake. How's the rum?"

"It's alright."

"Go get another one then." He nudged us towards the table.

We went the long way around the group of dancers as we made our way to the liquor table. Tom went the opposite way, mingling with some of the guys in the house.

"Well, what do you think?" I asked, referring to Tom.

"I think I like!"

"He seems real nice. I wasn't expecting that." I put some ice in my cup. "So are you gonna try again or should I make the drinks this time?"

"I am gonna try to make my own and you try making yours. We'll see whose is better."

"Okay."

We were in no rush making the drinks. I wondered why I was there. Though I knew a lot of the people at the house none of them were really my friends. And it didn't bother me that I was one of the few white people and the only white girl, but I wondered how it affected others.

We finished mixing the drinks and sipped from our own cups. I was swaying to the music.

"How's it taste?" Tom asked over my shoulder.

"Hey, we meet again," I said, still grooving.

"It's really not that good," Danielle admitted.

"Then why are you drinking it?" Tom asked.

"Why? You want it?" I interrupted.

"Nah, I don't drink that shit, it's bad for you," he said seriously. "Why aren't you girls dancing?"

"I don't dance," Danielle said.

"I know you do," Tom said, looking at me. "I seen you on stage at school. You know you're good, so why ain't you dancing?"

"I'm all set over here. There's no need to get all in the mix of things. There's really no room out there anyway. I don't mind dancing up along the side."

"Alright, let me holla at your girl," he said as he moved past me and next to her.

"Go on, holla. I'll be around."

A while passed as Danielle and Tom appeared to be silently enjoying one another's company. I danced with some school friends and kept my eye on Danielle and Tom. Occasionally one of their mouths would open but not for long. Again I wondered why we were there.

Eventually a fight broke out in the dance section in the center of the room. Kareem's dad came bolting downstairs, demanding that everyone leave immediately.

"I told you, boy, no incidents or it's your ass," he said to Kareem.

"Damn you stupid mutha… Get the fuck out!" Kareem yelled to the guys who were involved in the altercation.

"GET OUT OF MY HOUSE! And forget where you came from because if I got trouble after this I will hunt you down. AND YOU DON'T WANT ME TO HUNT YOU DOWN!" The place was cleared.

It was too late for Danielle or me to go back home. The crowd dispersed into the dull night and Danielle and I felt stranded.

"If we go to my house it will be the last time I see you for a long time." I said.

"Well, I guess we can go to mine but that means we will be up all night listening to my parents ream us out," Danielle suggested.

"I guess that's better."

We started walking back towards town, and we saw Shonnie behind one of the housing units with a few girls from school in the same predicament as Danielle and me. We overheard their dilemma and I said, "Oh, you too, huh? We got the same problem."

"Alright look," Shonnie had motherly tendencies. "I can take you all into my house but you have to be real quiet. I can explain everything to my mom in the morning, but if we're loud enough to get her up tonight she will be pissed and might send you all home. Then you're all on your own."

"Shonnie, I ain't trying to get you in a bunch of shit with your mom," I said.

"Nah mommy, she won't care that you're all here. She won't even care if she hears us come in. I don't have curfew so I won't get in trouble. But if you all start acting like fools and then she gets up, I can't really do nothing for you. And believe me chicas, you do not want to piss mi madre off! Keep in mind, we're gonna be cramped."

"I call the bed!" I yelled.

"I don't care, Shonnie. I just need a blanket and I am all good," someone else said.

We walked a ways over to Shonnie's and quietly crept through the door. In her tiny room some girls found a spot on the floor and Shonnie shared the bed with me. Danielle slept on the fluffy chair. And when there was conceivably no more room for bodies the last two girls slept on boxes in her closet.

Chapter Two

"Suppression — Ignorance is Not Bliss"

I wasn't overly intrigued by the mischievousness of visiting the Hill and it didn't hold any more excitement than the streets nearer to my home. I would rather have been loitering on Broadway taking note of the latest derogatory comments from the passengers of the bass-bumping vehicles passing by. It was never shocking to hear what a young man had to say knowing he would never be held accountable for his words. The remarks that got under my skin were the ones from nasty old truckers.

My parents were beer drinkers, so I already learned that I didn't like the taste of a malt beverage. I'd heard it was an acquired taste like coffee, but I was not inclined to take the time to acquire a taste for either. Hard liquor was much more appealing, especially if it could be mixed with a beverage I was already used to drinking, like juice or lemonade.

Soon enough I became the occasional drinker, although keeping my rendezvous within my curfew as not to irritate my parents. They never asked where I was or what I was doing, and I certainly volunteered no information. The projects were considered to be dangerous and supposed to be off limits to me. I didn't like to be dishonest, so I learned to keep my mouth shut for fear of incriminating myself.

I made an effort to stay unnoticed, until one day in my own neighborhood when someone caught my eye. Then I wanted to be noticed, but I wasn't sure how to get his attention.

One look was all it took. I had just turned fifteen when I first saw him. By then it was May. People were coming out of their winter shells. Flower buds were blooming. The city's blood was thawed out and returning to its natural flow.

Danielle and Casey were walking with me when a juvenile delinquent ran by with the devil gleaming on his shoulder. He and a few others had pulled a prank on an innocent and unsuspecting pedestrian. As they ran past us on the opposite side of the street, that juvenile delinquent's eyes met mine. My heart began racing.

He was an agile young man, swift and giddy. With his Caucasian complexion and dark features he was remarkable even from a distance. I made no expression, but then his lips parted in a vivacious smile and I was immediately captivated. Suddenly I felt my bright red perfect heart-shaped organ inflate with each pump. It was pushing through my shirt.

"Oh Lord, what are they up to now?" Casey exclaimed.

"Who was that? John Brown?" I asked.

"Yeah," Casey replied.

"Who was he with?" I needed to know who that young man was, and how often that devil proudly perched upon his shoulder.

"His name is Josh. He lives a few houses down from Casey. She thinks he's cute. Well, I think he's cute too, but he's not my type."

"He is cute," Casey admitted, "but he's such a clown, and always getting into trouble. Besides he don't get with white girls anyways."

"What? How do you know he don't date white girls? Ain't he white?"

"Yeah, he's white. But I think he only gets with black girls."

"That's because he thinks he's black," Danielle added.

"Thinks he's black, huh? Hmmm," I mumbled. He wasn't too far out of my reach because my friends knew him, but unfortunately there were other obstacles in my path. Instantly my heart returned to normal.

I was intrigued with his bad-boy attitude. Although I knew so little about him, he managed to occupy so many of my thoughts.

Sensations had come over me that I never felt before, and I hoped the girls didn't notice.

About a week later I was able to meet him. Danielle and I were in Casey's front yard trying to think of an escape plan for her because she was on punishment.

Josh walked by with Brown, Tom, and Tyler while we were trying to sneak Casey out.

"What are you clowns going to do," Casey hollered, "or should I say, who are you going to terrorize today?"

"Nah, man, we ain't like that," Tom said defensively, looking toward Danielle.

"We're going to the Rec to play some ball. Wanna come?" Josh looked at me for the second time. I would've felt like an idiot as I involuntarily smiled at him, but luckily the smile was returned. Instantly, I heard my heart beat again. Then I felt it pushing through my chest and next my shirt. I didn't know how to contain it.

"Me and Reba have to help Casey get out of the house. It might take a while," Danielle explained.

"Well, we're in no hurry," Tom quickly stated.

"Yeah, I'm good!" Josh agreed.

Tyler and Brown interjected, "Well, you and Josh can get your groove on, but we wanna play some ball. You down or not?"

While Danielle and Tom were overtly flirting with each other, Tyler grew impatient and started down the street bouncing the basketball. Brown followed.

"We'll see you later then," Josh said before he joined his friends.

Tom brushed Danielle's arm, grinning before he turned away.

Finally, the pumping organ retreated back into my chest. Since no one seemed to notice I didn't obsess about this strange occurrence, but I needed to learn how to control it before it got in the way.

That was about as formal an introduction as you could get from a bunch of young teenagers. We had similar sporadic encounters like that over the next few months. It wasn't until the following school year when Danielle and Tom became serious that Josh and I really got to know one another. Danielle and I were beginning our sophomore year of high school. Tom and Josh were a year ahead of us. As it went, the four of us were together all the time.

Casey's description of Josh couldn't have been more accurate. Josh acted like a clown. Most of the time it was all in good fun, but he would do whatever it took for people to notice him, even if it meant doing something wrong.

Tom was a good influence on Josh. He was on the starting lineup for the basketball team. The Vikings were on a winning streak that year and we ended up in the championships. Josh didn't get involved in any extracurricular activities but often joined in supporting Tom and the rest of the Vikings from the bleachers. Danielle and I didn't miss a game.

Tom Planter was a sixteen-year-old with broad shoulders, coffee-colored skin, and chocolate brown eyes. He was slightly above average in build and height for his age. His long, curled eyelashes had every female envious, and with his pleasant disposition he was a joy to spend time with.

Tom and Josh had drivers' licenses, but only Tom owned his own car. It wasn't much, a little shit-box bronze Chevette, but it had wheels. He was the most responsible driver I had ever seen.

He was preparing Danielle for her unsupervised trips trailing the bus to the travel games behind the wheel of his car. Josh and I went along in the back seat.

"Look, look at that guy. Look at the way he is walking. Woah, what is he on? He's walking like a half cocked giraffe!" He started laughing hysterically at himself.

"You're ridiculous!" Tom laughed.

"Where are we going?" Danielle asked.

"Turn here."

"Which way? Turn where?"

"Relax, girl. Turn wherever you want. You can't flip out and panic when you are driving. Slow down a little."

"Why? You think I am driving too fast?"

"You're doing alright, but if you're gonna freak like that over a turn maybe you should drive a little slower."

"Oh, you think I am doing good?"

"Yeah. You're doing real good!"

"Oh man! What the hell is that? Yo, is that a girl or a fucking warthog? What is this, night at the zoo?" Josh tugged at my arm again, poking viciously at his window at the unsuspecting pedestrian.

"Wow, Josh, I think you got it right with that one," Danielle agreed.

"Danielle, you have got to keep your eyes on the road. Do not listen to his silly ass."

"What's up with you, Shorty? Cat got your tongue?"

"I ain't real good with dogging people like you!"

"Oh you think I am a bad person or something?"

"Well, I wouldn't say you're a bad person just because you're getting your kicks off making fun of people passing by. You seem to be good at it anyway!"

"Oh yeah? You think I am funny?"

"Don't encourage him, Reba!" Tom advised from in front of me.

"Hey, can we go to the store so you can buy me a drink?" Danielle asked.

"Alright, go to Cumby's right up here."

"Whoa, Speedy Gonzales. Slow turning, alright? She's gonna get us killed doing fifty on two wheels just to get the front parking space." Josh tumbled himself onto my lap.

Everyone in the car was laughing. Josh hurriedly beat everyone to the door. He pulled it open a bit into the tip of his sneaker, falling back and holding his head, spinning in circles and screaming, "Ouch! Oh my head. That's it—I'm suing. I'm suing for all you got. But right now I want a free Twix!"

"I hear that!" I said, walking past him into the store with my friends.

I followed Danielle to the cooler and pulled out a Diet Coke. I brought it up to the register while Danielle took her time choosing her beverage.

Josh came up behind me and put two Twix on the counter next to my drink. "I got this."

"Thanks."

"Here, this one's for you!" He handed me one of his Twix after paying the cashier.

"Ooo, I love Twix!"

"Shit Danielle, pick a drink already. The store is gonna close before you make up your mind! Do you want the dark drink with the bubbles, or the see-through drink with the bubbles?" Josh yelled to the other side of the store.

"I'm coming. I got it."

"Oh, I see. You had to get all-fancy on us and get the red drink with the bubbles. And I was for sure you would get the see-through one because the bubbles look pretty!"

"My God, are you always like this?" I asked.

"YES!" replied Tom.

"Ooo, how about some chips too?" Danielle asked Tom.

"You can't eat chips and drive at the same time."

"Shit, she can't even talk and drive at the same time. Besides, we don't have another half an hour waiting for you to pick out which chip has the best crunch. Let's go, man."

"What's your rush anyway?" Danielle asked.

"Who said I am in a rush? I just don't like spending an hour picking out a drink."

"Ya know what, Josh? You should probably shut your mouth before I crash your side into something."

"Man, you can't crash on my side 'cause I am sitting behind you, and you definitely can't maneuver that one without hurting yourself."

"I probably could," Tom said.

"Chill, I'm just playing with her, fool."

"I know," Danielle replied.

"So am I, fool. Like your ass is worth my ride," Tom said.

On the ride home Danielle was brave enough to continue with her lesson despite Josh's remarks. "Reba, do you want me to drop you home?"

"No. I still got time. Just go to your house and I can walk home from there."

As we rapidly approached the car in front of us, Tom calmly stated, "When the car in front of you has his brake lights on you should brake too."

"Oh, right!" Danielle slammed on the brakes.

"Damn girl. I was just playing. You're a *grrreat* driver. Just get me home, okay?"

"Shut up, Josh. Don't make me nervous!"

"Josh don't make her nervous, for real!"

"I'm just saying. I wanna hang with Reba again, alright, so don't kill me."

Tom snickered and Danielle giggled in her bashful way. I snapped my head in marvel toward Josh, who just gave me a dazzling smile. I could hear that thumping against my sternum again. I was glad that Danielle's house wasn't very far.

During weeks of ballgames at the recreational center, Josh used every opportunity he could to brush up against me. The exciting new feeling I experienced in his presence intensified when he guarded me, reaching both arms around me. Then one night Tom walked Danielle home and Josh volunteered to walk me home.

At the corner of my street we stopped to say goodbye when he finally took the initiative to kiss me. He slowly pulled me closer to him and leaned in. My lips felt his for the first time. They were so soft and full I knew what was coming next. My heart started again. As the smoothness of his tongue lightly tasted mine, my heart sounded louder and faster, before pumping up again. I began floating upward. I felt like I was going to burst, but his gentle grasp of my hand kept me grounded with him.

"Good night!" I said before deflating to my doorstep.

I was happy to gloat to my friends, "I guess he doesn't only date black girls after all."

"Yeah, maybe I should've tried for him." Casey teased.

"Too late!" I said.

"I'm playing, girl. You know I don't have the patience for his ass. Good luck with that one."

Josh Silveira was a couple of inches shorter than Tom. His curly, dark brown hair was trimmed into a high-top fade and his eyebrows were thick and dark. His eyelashes were full enough to conceal his unforeseen emerald green eyes. He had an oval-shaped face with high cheekbones and a nose that protruded outward more than most. Josh's bold attitude and loud personality more than compensated for anything he lacked in height. I was glad he was taller than me—it didn't matter by how little.

His rebellious nature was alluring, and the thrill of breaking the rules was exhilarating. We wound up outside the gymnasium by the track field sharing a pint of Bacardi. His Cheshire smile was gleaming in the moonlight. It was magnificent; he was magnificent. Entranced by him I tripped over my own footing and tumbled down the hill onto the track. All for a laugh Josh came tumbling after.

Upon returning to the end of the game some kids on the bleachers made note of the leaves stuck in my hair. I was immediately embarrassed, discreetly trying to brush them out with my fingers. It bothered me that my schoolmates suspected we were doing something we weren't.

At that point I was feeling the effects of the alcohol. I got the impression that my peers didn't approve of my relationship with Josh. Some thought he was too wild for me, and still others thought I was too white for him. Josh wasn't the only one who thought he was black. Apparently everyone else did too, despite his obvious Portuguese complexion.

"Ah the good old days. I was young, naïve, and hmmm … clueless now that I think about it." I whisper reminiscently. But that was the furthest description of myself at the time. I take a deep breath and realize I have a smile on my face. "Gosh, what a child I was. I really thought I was so mature!"

I was misunderstood like so many teenagers are. I chuckle to myself. I had ambition and goals; I was active and energetic.

Although I lived for fun I have always been responsible. That hasn't changed. What on earth possessed me to trust Josh? I had learned that lesson so long ago. What a fool I was to continue the charade.

Two months of good-hearted fun with Josh was over as carelessly and unplanned as it began. Josh started dealing drugs. He had advanced from selling dime bags of marijuana here and there to selling crack cocaine in foils, which meant he was spending more and more time out in the Hill. That's where the crack heads were, so naturally that's where the crack dealer should be.

Inevitably, the rapport between us began to wane as we left it to dwindle in the wind. Being in the project and selling drugs was more important than hanging out with Danielle, Tom, and me. When he did share his time with us he was shoving liquor down my throat. Then one night I found out why.

Tom had to house sit for his older cousin, Mike, and his wife, Deana, one weekend. I told my mother I was sleeping at Danielle's and vice versa so we could accompany Tom Friday night. I met Mike and Deana briefly before they left for their romantic getaway. Mike was not a bit threatened by a couple of teenagers trashing his house or getting into trouble, because he was a well-built correctional officer at the state penitentiary. He was armed with intimidation and was not afraid to use it.

Being in houses other than my own has always been uncomfortable for me. But those days being at home was no treat either, so I opted to hang out with my friends. I felt awkward not knowing what to do or where to sit. I was the odd man out until Josh arrived soon after the homeowners left.

I was relieved when he pulled a liter of Bacardi and a shot glass from the inside pocket of his coat. Danielle was not an avid drinker, so it didn't surprise me when after a single shot each Danielle and Tom went upstairs. I was occupied playing quarters with Josh in the kitchen. After a while I could no longer sit straight on a chair so the game was continued on the floor. After twelve, I lost count of how many shots I had. That was the night I lost my virginity.

I was fifteen years old and completely inebriated. Any recollection I have is very blurred. I do recall that my loosely fit black knit sweater remained in place after Josh pulled my white jeans down. I was lying on the kitchen floor. There may have been a blanket, a brown and tan comforter, underneath me or next to me to cover us. I remember being confused and asking him what he was doing. In picking my brain, I can't hear his response, if he even had one. The only other thing I remember is that the whole incident didn't last more than a few minutes. Afterwards I wasn't even sure if what had happened was what I thought had happened. I don't recollect seeing Josh afterwards.

I woke up the next morning on the couch in the living room fully dressed and alone in complete oblivion. The brown comforter was around me. A moment later Tom and Danielle came downstairs.

"Josh left early to go to the Hill," Tom informed me.

"Oh, did you see him this morning?"

"Yeah, he left not too long ago."

"Did he say anything?"

"No, just that he'll see us later," Danielle replied. "Are you ready to go?"

"Yeah, let's go."

Since their behavior lacked suspicion I was relieved in concluding it was a bad dream.

Danielle and I walked home together. I barely knew myself what had actually occurred overnight, so I didn't share any of my thoughts. I hoped if I didn't talk about it then maybe it would go away.

The ache in my back and soreness in between my legs revealed the truth, that it wasn't a dream. I felt naked and transparent, as though everybody could see right through me. I was devoured by the impressions of a tramp. I received the scarlet letter, except this one was a big fat "L" for loser held out the window of a passing car. All drivers and passengers following stared at me with bulging bubble-like eyes. I couldn't wait to go home, take a shower, and snuggle up in my bed. I felt so dirty.

The weekend quietly snuck by and Monday morning school commenced. That afternoon Danielle sat with me on the bus. "What is going on with you? I know something is up. Why won't you tell me?"

"Because I don't really know what happened."

"What do you mean?"

"I drank so much damn Bacardi I lost track of the occurrences that night at Mike's."

"Well, what do you think happened?"

"I am pretty sure Josh pulled my pants down."

"What?"

"Reba, how the hell do you not know that?"

"Well, I was sore walking home, so I guess my visions aren't dreams. It's weird. Like what I remember is just bits and pieces. Like images scattered and blurry."

"Josh never said anything to Tom."

"Well, that's good. I hope he keeps it that way."

"I won't tell Tom anything but I will see if I can get any info out of him after school." Danielle never judged me or treated me condescendingly, and I was grateful she didn't start then.

We went to Tom's as usual. Upstairs in his room Josh and Brown were already playing Sega Genesis. I paused, wondering if I should enter or not, but Danielle grabbed my hand and walked me in.

The seemingly average day was shattered once Brown and Josh began making sexual innuendos through tunes of a well-known song: "Laying, laying like a rock."

Josh sang, "That's what it was li-ike. And she was saying 'huh huh huh huh …'"

Brown burst into laughter. Stunned, I shot my head towards Danielle. She took a quick glance at an otherwise unsuspecting Tom. He seemed unaffected. So she gestured for me to blow it off.

I stared hard at Brown, who fell silent when he caught my eye. Then I did the same toward Josh, but he wouldn't look at me, instead he continued to play the video game.

I couldn't tell if the boys were referring to my night in the track field with Josh or about the night in question. It was possible they weren't referring to me at all.

But after a moment Brown squawked "Wahoo," while Josh moaned.

I jumped up gave Josh a wretchedly evil look before storming out of the house without saying a word.

All the feelings of humiliation and vulnerability had returned. I again felt ashamed and dirty. Meanwhile, I could hardly remember what took place. I hurried home with my arms tightly hugging my body. The heavens were looking down on me in scorn. I had to dodge the lightning bolts blasting out of the clear blue sky as I ran home.

Distance remained between Josh and me. I barely even saw him at school. He didn't attend half of the time. I'd heard he was spending a lot of time out in the Hill trying to make some money. I minded my business, went to school and dance practice afterwards, and went to work. Since it was the dead of winter there wasn't much going on around town.

One chilly day after dance practice I was walking home in the rain when a car stopped alongside me just outside the rear parking lot of the school. The driver's side window rolled down, revealing the face of an older gentleman with grey hair. I did not recognize him. I assumed he might have wanted directions so I smiled at him.

"We thought you could use a ride to get out of the rain," the old man said. I took a closer look and saw Josh in the passenger seat. His grandfather had picked him up from detention.

Since his grandfather was kind enough to stop and offer me a ride, I took it. As would be expected, it was an uncomfortably quiet ride home. He dropped us both off in front of Josh's house and drove away. I lived two blocks around the corner.

"Thanks for the ride," I said, without looking in Josh's direction as I began to walk away.

"I thought it was the least I could do after I was mean to you," he said sincerely.

I stopped and turned around to look at him. He smiled a little. "What the hell was that all about?"

"I don't know. I was so drunk that night. I didn't know what happened. I thought you would be mad at me so I started acting stupid. I'm sorry."

"Yeah, you sure did!" I turned back to head for home.

"I'm sorry!" he called after me.

It didn't take much to appease me back then; therefore I accepted that as a satisfactory apology to start over. The incident was so hurtful I didn't want to talk about it. I wanted to pretend the whole thing never happened. So I let it rest.

I should have never talked to him again, but there was something about him I couldn't resist; the way his dimples grew as he smiled, the intensity in his dark eyes, the way his hypnotic voice reached out for me. I tried rationalizing the situation with nonsense to myself. He had me believing that he honestly felt badly for what he had done. We never spoke of the incident again, and that was good enough for me.

He came over to my house several times a week by way of a black Spree moped purchased with drug money. It was unbelievable that my father didn't seem to mind Josh, because he usually didn't approve of any boy my sisters and I brought home.

My mother never said too much about him except, "Nobody can make you laugh like Josh." My parents didn't take our relationship seriously. I'm probably the only one who ever did.

Sometimes Josh and I played video games on my Nintendo in my bedroom. The door was always left wide open.

"So since you're here in my room with me you're not gonna go squawking to your friends about it, are you?"

"No, I don't talk about you like that. Give me some credit."

"Have you matured so much in such a short time? Now you're beyond that?"

"What do you mean? I never talked about you to no one."

"Um, yes you did. We stopped speaking remember?"

"Listen, I *never* talked about *you.*"

I didn't want to further that line of conversation and so remained quiet.

I was able to accept Josh as a confused and misguided young person much like myself. Even though Josh hadn't consumed as much alcohol as I had that dreaded night I knew he was intoxicated well beyond his limit. His judgments were uninhibited just as mine were. I knew in my heart that it wasn't Josh's intention to hurt me. The aftermath was a symptom of his guilt. That is what I had a more difficult time getting over, especially since my memories of intercourse were so minimal.

Shortly after our rekindled friendship our departures ended with a sweet, slow, closed-mouth kiss on the lips. It was the kind that got my heart jumping again, wanting more. But we never ventured further.

By February's end, Josh was involved in a riot that took place out in the Hill. The details of the events evaded me. It was rumored that a lot of people got hurt, but fortunately no one was shot. I was relieved to hear that no guns were involved, although other weapons were used. Many people were arrested, and Josh was one of them. He was charged with assault, resisting arrest, and possession of marijuana.

The judge sent him away to the juvenile detention center, where he served eight months.

We corresponded regularly during his incarceration, but he failed to reveal the true accounts of the riot. He was angry for being sent away since he was only one of three to get sentenced with time to serve. The others arrested who, according to Josh, started the whole affair got away with suspended sentences.

Without warning, Josh started writing me vulgar and cold-hearted letters. Giving him the benefit of the doubt as I always did, I hoped he was just letting off some steam, but they continued. My correspondence ceased because I couldn't deal with his continuous disrespect. When I no longer accepted his phone calls he quit his attempts to contact me.

Chapter Three

"Romance Means Ulterior Motives"

During the final trimester of my sophomore year a senior named Chris Laliberte made giant efforts to grab my attention. He was an extremely good-looking soccer star who attracted all types of girls even though he preferred the meek, conservative types. I often contemplated what attracted him to me. He listened to pop rock; I listened to rap and R&B. He was a recovering alcoholic who drank coffee and smoked Marlboro cigarettes. I was becoming an alcoholic who drank Bacardi and Diet Coke and hated cigarettes and the smell of coffee. My impression was that I was too young, too wild, and too far from his tastes, but he managed to prove me wrong.

Chris was a tall, athletic, attractive young man with floppy, flaxen hair that fell onto his face, sometimes concealing his crystal blue eyes. His wide smile revealed his perfectly aligned teeth in a strong jaw line on his rounded face. His tight rear sat atop his shapely soccer-player legs. And still his sexiest attribute was the way he walked bow-legged.

Moreover Chris displayed old-fashioned chivalry. He opened doors, pulled out chairs, respectfully stood up when a female stood up, refrained from profanity in my presence, kept an even temper and mild manner even when upset, paid for our dates, and more.

He worked weekends at the movie theater and wrote piles of love notes on cinema napkins, complete with animations depicting our last date, and called me on the phone every night to tell me he was thinking about me. On our dates we went to the pond and fed the ducks. We sat on the hood of his car and gazed at the sky. We would go out for coffee and hot chocolate. We'd meet up with his intellectual senior friends at the pizza parlor.

Chris picked me up for dates with a rose in hand every time. I was living a dream. I had no idea guys behaved like Chris in real life, and so I began to care for Chris. He embraced my soft and sensitive side. My life had never been so good.

On the last weekend of every month we attended a local dance held at a naval community center. There was a small fee for admission, which Chris always paid for us both. Our dancing was tastefully seductive, and I especially enjoyed kissing him, all of which made me feel pretty.

One night on the dance floor while dancing to a love song Chris was holding me tightly against him. Then he kissed me.

He stopped abruptly, asking, "You wanna leave?"

Instantly self-conscious I wondered if I had done something wrong, because according to the clock the dance wasn't over for another hour.

"Why do you want to leave so early?" I asked shyly, half afraid to hear his answer.

"I don't know, I thought maybe you would want to go." He was still holding me close to him.

He didn't seem upset. Chris didn't have a history of confusing me. Things with him were very clear and he was always open and straight to the point. I faced the possibility that maybe my fantasy was over. I wasn't prepared for the fairy tale to end yet. Though it wasn't a complete surprise, I never expected it would happen so abruptly.

"Well, I don't wanna go," I finally decided. "Do you?"

"No, I just thought maybe you would want to go, that's all."

"I thought we were having fun?"

"We are. We definitely are. We'll stay then."

I was so relieved that he seemed to be back to himself again. Chris was always in the moment, taking each minute as it came for what it was worth. I admired that about him. We finished out the night at the dance, and he drove me home afterwards like usual.

My mother adored Chris, while my father objected to our courtship. He was suspicious of Chris's smooth finesse, which bewildered me. When the end of the school year came near and Chris had asked me to his senior prom, naturally my father was rather wary of the whole event. He couldn't deny my invitation and wouldn't forbid my acceptance.

My mother and I excitedly went shopping for the perfect dress and accessories, finding a beautiful black halter-top dress fitted with black sequins around my neck and down to the hip where the dress flared out in chiffon down to the knee. I wore black heels and short black satin gloves. We chose to accessorize with a glamorous pair of rhinestone earrings with a black opal teardrop. I felt like a princess.

Chris showed up at my door with a beautiful red rose corsage along with a bouquet of roses for me. My mother wanted the grand entrance, so she had me wait upstairs for him. When I received my cue, I started down the stairs like I normally would. This time I wore a chiffon dress that I normally would *not* have had on. As I descended the staircase my dress flew right up. I stopped abruptly, forcing it back down with my hands. Completely uncouth, I looked around, and my disappointed mother gave me the classic "why can't you act like a lady?" look. I was already so nervous, my face flushed in sheer embarrassment. Frozen for a minute, they urged me to continue with a little more grace. Who was I fooling? I wasn't cut out for the princess routine.

"It's okay," Chris whispered reassuringly when I finally stood beside him.

I managed a slight smile as we posed for pictures in my living room before leaving. I was more than eager to get out of the house. I tried desperately to shake off the inferiority I was feeling. I felt unworthy of the pretty dress and unworthy of the handsome boy at my side. Most of all, I felt unworthy of his kind nature. I was a fraud, not meant for glamour but instead for rags.

To my surprise there was a limousine waiting outside. Excitement took over all other emotions as a huge smile formed on my face. With his usual refinement, Chris gestured for me to proceed toward the chauffeur standing by holding the door open for us.

The prom was delightful. I danced all night, never leaving the dance floor even when Chris did. It was the only place I felt comfortable. I was to be home shortly after, so before taking me home he drove to the hotel where a few of his friends had rented some rooms. Their chitchat bored me. When Chris said his goodbyes I was more than relieved. I was normally uncomfortable around his friends, and that night proved to be no exception.

Chris had the extraordinary ability to make me feel comfortable just being me. It was always a great pleasure to be in his company, with the added bonus that I was attracted to him. In the corridor Chris took my hand and spun me around, pulling me close to him, typical of his debonair style. Then, without notice, the unwanted awkward feeling came again. He gazed into my eyes and told me again how beautiful I was.

"I have something to tell you, but I don't want you to get mad," he said with a straight face. He paused before continuing, "I don't want to make you feel pressured or anything, but I got a room for us upstairs."

I was stunned and temporarily speechless. He had waited until the last minute to tell me. My parents were expecting me home soon. Why would he spring such a huge decision on me like that without giving me any time to think it over first? I was woebegone. Part of me felt almost conned. Whatever negative feelings enveloped me were so uncharacteristic in our relationship that I had to decline, although I apologized for it, thinking I had disappointed him yet not fully realizing how much he had disappointed me. He drove me home, no questions asked.

The following day things seemed as they had been all along. We went out for a lunch date and spent the afternoon in the grass talking and discovering pictures in the clouds. We flirted and made out. The weather was gorgeous. Monday came and began his last few days of high school, in which I didn't see too much of him. He drove me home from school his last day and we hung out on my porch talking. He seemed rather preoccupied.

"What's up?" I asked.

"Reba, I have something to tell you." His voice was solemn.

"Okay," I said, waiting patiently. Despite my nerves I managed a spirited voice.

"Well, I have to tell you because I want you to hear it from me. I don't want you to hear it from anyone at school. I'm sure you soon will." He was taking his time, building up the courage.

"What's the matter?" I had no idea what he was about to disclose to me.

"Ya know that girl, Selena?" he asked.

"No," I spoke too soon. After a second thought I said, "Oh, yeah. Well, I think I know who you're talking about." The only person I could think of was a strange girl with hair in her face. She was new that year, so she kept to herself. I had no clue why my boyfriend would mention her. "What about her?" I presumed he had some tragic gossip to tell me.

"Well, I saw her …" My mind trailed off shortly after he told me he kissed her. It didn't make any sense to me. I stood there dumbfounded. He proceeded to tell me she didn't mean anything to him and had the audacity to demonstrate the kiss on me. I pulled away and saw his eyes well up with tears.

"I understand that you're mad."

"No you don't," I snapped at him.

"Do you think you can forgive me? Do you think we can get past it?" he pleaded.

"I really don't know." I was still in shock. How the hell did that happen? My fantasy was shattered.

"I'll give you your space and let you think things over. I'll understand if you don't want to see me anymore." He was unable to hold back his tears, but his voice stayed strong. He leaned in and kissed me on my cheek before walking away.

We spoke on the phone that night and decided it was over between us. Before the end of my school year I found out he did more than just kiss the girl. He had sex with her. But the seniors were long gone and I didn't see him for years after that. Selena moved out of town before the following school year commenced.

I spent that summer hanging out with my friends when I wasn't working. In August we started practicing for dance again. Dance camp was an expedient yet relentless dance training that didn't leave much time for anything else. Determined that things were going to change for me in my junior year, I came across some personality adjustments. I was prepared to be tougher and promised myself I wouldn't let anyone close to my heart so I wouldn't get hurt.

Just as suddenly as the quarrels between my parents seemed to begin they ceased. My dad switched from second to first shift and they attended the local bar together. Playing pool became one of their favorite pastimes, and they joined a league. I was impressed at the skill my parents displayed in the game, which sparked my interest. It seemed to be the only way I could connect with them at that time, and I found myself down at the bar more and more, learning to play.

Time flew by. The latter part of my high-school career was spent acting as the responsible housekeeper. I was rushing home to cook dinner and feed the dog. I played the role as the parent when I called the bar asking if my parents would be home for dinner. My patience always held out the longest, and my sisters were the first to leave the dinner table. I would clean up before walking down to the bar. I played a few games of pool and received free Diet Cokes until I was ready to ask for use of the car to pick up Danielle and venture out.

Josh finished his time in the juvenile detention center and returned to school with a confusing schedule. Because of the lack of credits he was considered to be half a junior and half a senior. This setback was nothing short of another injustice, according to Josh. He decided he didn't need his diploma after all and quit. But before dropping out there was one more incident in which he had publicly betrayed me. Regrettably, it wasn't the last time I gave him the opportunity.

The first time I saw him in the school corridor he smiled at me. I showed little restraint in smiling back. The next time he smiled and said, "Hello."

I smiled again. I had no willpower in regards to him. During school our interactions remained that way. But my curiosity was building its confounded nest. I broke down one afternoon and called his house.

"Hello?"

My heart stopped, as I was unprepared to hear his voice answer the phone so quickly. "Hello. It's Reba."

"Hey Shorty, what's up?"

"I have been seeing you in school lately and I thought maybe you were on the path to rehabilitation."

I heard his laugh and saw his gleaming smile appear before me. "I'm not bothering you, am I?"

"No way. But um, your new man ain't gonna get mad that you're talking with me?"

"I don't have a man, so how could anyone be mad?"

"Oh, you finally came to your senses and let that punk ass go?"

"No I think he came to his senses and realized I wasn't giving it up."

"Hey Shorty, good for you!"

"Mm hmm!"

"What does that mean?"

"Good for me? Or good for someone else?"

"Good for you."

Trying to hold onto my pride I disclosed the truth, "Well, he cheated on me with some slut before coming to this realization, so ... it wasn't good for me."

He declared, "I knew he was a fucking punk. If he ever comes near you again I will stab his ass!"

"That won't be necessary. He is away at college now anyway and his tramp is long gone too. Just one of those things!"

"Alright then ...well hey, I gotta get going. But I'll be seeing ya real soon."

"Okay, bye!"

"Bye Reba!"

Josh was visiting me at my house in short spurts. Instead of coming in, we sat outside talking. He still made me laugh and he still looked good. I was under the impression he was trying to lay low since his recent bout with the law. I was glad to see he had taken something seriously.

The dance team traditionally did a Christmas concert for the school. I was nervous because Josh was seated in the front with his friends. The seniors had choreographed a dance to a hip-hop song by Nice-N-Smooth. It was a little risqué for my modest nature, and though I was dreading the performance in front of my peers, I was left with little choice. The beat sounded and we began swiveling our hips, pivoting seductively.

The audience cheered; it was a popular song. Suddenly in Josh's row a pack of horny wild animals appeared. They were drooling and howling with their elongated tongues hanging down to the floor. I was so embarrassed. I felt like I was putting on a cheap show. But my pride urged me on. My only alternative was to run off stage like a pathetic coward.

Out of options, I was desperate for a sign. Anything would suffice to get me through this one song. Finally I saw it radiating from above like a lifesaver dangling, but it was just out of reach. The beautifully laced pattern was quite attractive, but it didn't come any closer. It remained suspended before me, teasing me.

A teacher followed the voices of the obnoxious commentators and stood beside Josh's row. There were no more slurs from the pack of wolves before me, but the damage was done, and the image above my reach had vanished. I didn't confront Josh because I wasn't positive their remarks were directed at me in particular. Rather than allow him the knowledge that he had ruffled my emotional feathers I opted to cease all communication with him, again.

By January Josh was no longer in school. I heard through the grapevine that he was making a big name for himself in the drug world. He was collecting a considerable amount of illegal money and deluded himself with big-money dreams.

I was disappointed and thought for sure I'd seen the last of him. Yet despite the trauma he'd put me through, I somehow believed he had a good heart. He was involved in dangerous business and I still prayed for his safety.

Josh found himself a new girlfriend named Tracy, and to no one's surprise she was black. She was a few years older than me and already had her own apartment in the Hill. Word was that he was living with Tracy until the inevitable occurred. Josh was arrested on drug charges and had to serve his time in training school. The specifics of his sentence were unknown to me, but I did know he would have to finish his time out in the adult penitentiary after he turned eighteen.

Chapter Four

"Trust Yourself; Hide Your Pride"

Danielle and I were invited to a Super Bowl party in the Hill. Because I had to work during the day, Danielle arranged for a ride from her cousin, Rodney. He was a clean-cut, young black male who was very particular about his appearance. Rodney escorted Danielle in and then saw an old friend of his, Neil, so he decided to stay.

When Danielle introduced me to her cousin, his immediate interest in me was obvious. "Well, I am glad I came here. I got a good reason to stay now. What's up, little sista?"

"Chillin with my girl. Nothing big. I don't even care for football. This was just somewhere to go, ya know?"

"Now you're hurting me, girl! How can you come to a Super Bowl party and not care for football?"

"I guess the same way you can love football and not plan a Super Bowl party!"

"Ha, alright! You got me there. But you got to understand it's different for me. Being a black man in the projects don't do no justice for me."

"I can imagine, but I gotta say, you don't look like your average black man in the projects. Did you iron your jeans? I mean I ain't never seen jeans that straight before!"

Neil broke out into laughter. "Man, you still iron everything? Some things never change!"

Danielle and Tom were on hiatus since they had a major quarrel over something quite insignificant. She was looking for something new and was a little too eager to latch on to her older cousin's friend. He was a stout white male the same age as Rodney.

During the game Neil and Rodney kept their eyes glued to the television. The commercials were just as appealing to the men. Danielle and I mingled and moseyed about. During halftime Rodney pursued his conversation with me.

"So what are you drinking?"

"Screwdrivers. Are you drinking?"

"Not tonight. When you get to be my age it almost loses its appeal."

"And what age might that be?"

"I'm twenty-two."

"Well hey! So if I need a hook up I know who to go to. 'Cause you know us younglings haven't lost our appeal!"

"I might be able to do a little something for ya."

"I'll hook you girls up." Neil offered, and then sang, "Just call me!"

Danielle was thrilled over Neil's insinuation of future encounters.

After the game was over, Rodney was anxious to leave. "It's getting a bit crazy in here so I'm out. If you need a ride come on."

We followed Rodney out to his Nissan Sentra. Neil jumped onto his sports bike.

"Dude, you gotta take me for a ride sometime!" My only attraction to Neil was as a legal buyer and a motorcycle ride.

"Oh, I almost forgot." He ran in the house and was back out a moment later with a piece of paper. He had written his pager number on it and gave it to Danielle.

"I won't ask for your digits 'cause I don't want your parents questioning me over the phone. Call me."

"I will." She replied.

Rodney drove to Danielle's and parked in front but left the engine on. Then he turned towards me in the back seat, "Do you need me to take you home too?"

"No thanks. I only live right over there."

"No Reba, let him drive you," Danielle insisted.

"For real. I'm all set. Here is fine. Thank you!" I quickly got out. "Bye Rodney. I'll tell my mom and dad you said 'Hi'."

"Bye honey. See you later." He drove away.

"Reba why wouldn't you just let him drive you home? Now you gotta walk in the cold."

"Girl, I only live two blocks away. What's the big deal?"

"'Cause he's into you. You could've exchanged numbers or something."

"I don't think so. Good night! I'll see you tomorrow."

As I headed home Danielle called out, "You can't be hung up on Josh forever!"

"You better chill with that!" I yelled back.

Neil kept his word, and when Danielle paged him after school the next day he showed up at the elementary school further up the street from Danielle's on his motorcycle with an extra helmet ready. He also handed me a pint of Bacardi to pass the time while I waited for my turn. "Don't drink it all now. Save some for your friend."

"Then don't be gone long, 'cause this is my favorite right here!"

Upon their return I could tell Danielle was not happy. Apparently she pitched a fit when Neil attempted a wheelie with her on board.

"Ready Reba? You're not gonna freak out like she did, are you?"

"Hell no, I love that shit!"

We stayed at the school indulging in the pint after the joyride.

"Danielle, why aren't you drinking it?" Neil asked.

"I don't really like it."

"Well, what do you like?"

"I don't know. Is it such a big deal that I don't drink so much?"

"I bet your parents are proud."

"Well, that Bacardi is nasty. Why don't you get something with flavor or something? How the fuck am I supposed to drink it straight like that? You think I am a lush like her?"

"Hey hey, I resemble that remark!" I laughed. "I'm playing. You need to leave me out of this. Anyways," I turned my attention towards Neil, "you from around here?"

"Yeah," they said in unison.

"Oh already in tune like that!"

"We spoke on the phone earlier today. She already got all the questions answered. I work in construction on the condos over on Rhode Island Ave, making decent money. I have my own apartment, but I am not telling you where. Not yet anyway. And I have a car too, not just a motorcycle."

"A purple Probe with black tint," Danielle added.

"Guess there's nothing left to talk about then."

"Actually, I gotta get going. Danielle, page me on Friday." He hopped back on his motorcycle. "See ya, ladies!"

The rest of the week was spent at Rodney's. Danielle was eager for Friday to come. In the meantime Rodney was getting more and more keen on me. At the end of each visit he grew more persistent in asking for a kiss.

"Reba, what is wrong with you? Rodney is awesome and he is so into you. Do you know how many girls would die for a date with him? Just give him a shot; you'll see he's a great guy."

"I know he's nice and everything. There ain't nothing wrong with him, I just don't feel anything for him. I don't know why."

"Is it 'cause he's black?"

"What kind of question is that? Since when is that an issue?"

"I'm just wondering why."

"Nooo, you think if I hook up with Rodney we'll have more chances of bumping into Neil. News flash—Rodney doesn't like to leave the house. He ain't bumping into anyone sitting in his room playing that damn hockey game."

"He's fucking better than Josh. At least he ain't out there running the streets selling drugs and fighting and shit."

"Oh here we go! It has nothing to do with Josh. Why do you keep saying that? He's in jail with a girlfriend. I don't even talk to him anymore. Stop acting like I am hung up on him."

"Look, Josh is cool and everything, and I don't wanna talk bad about him. But Rodney would treat you way better. So he doesn't get out much. Look at it this way, at least you know he won't be cheating on you!"

Many of our days after school were spent waiting on Neil to get off of work. Sometimes we would hang out at Rodney's, and other times we loitered at the elementary school getting to know Neil better while Rodney stayed at home. Neil supplied us with fruit juice to go along with the Bacardi he brought, but Danielle hardly finished one cup.

"Is the juice not good enough for you, princess?" Neil taunted.

"I love fruit punch. I'm drinking it. Why do you get such an attitude about it?"

"I don't have an attitude. I bought it for you. I want you to like it." His voice and manner hardly showed any sincerity.

"I do."

"Good. Then drink it."

"I am."

We planned an evening at the condominium Neil had been working on. It was near completion and no one lived in it yet.

I was pressured into dating Rodney. I was bored with the relationship before it even started. But Danielle was right. I had nothing better to do. I tried to get him out of the house to do more activities, but the most he gave me was a football game in back of his house.

Danielle was ecstatic when we met up with Neil again. He gave us directions to the meeting place and bought us a pint of Peachtree Schnapps each. We were to meet back up after dusk to be less conspicuous, so until then Danielle and I roamed the streets starting on our pints. We walked over to the condos and giddily searched for Neil. He quickly ushered us into the dark condominium. We found a spot on the new carpet by the window where the moonlight shone in. Neil was drinking his Bush beer, which raised a line of inappropriate conversation and jokes. Danielle and I were so drunk we were incapable of hiding it.

Danielle couldn't finish her pint of Schnapps and handed it over to me, so I did without hesitation. I was no longer engaged in their conversation but somewhere between the ceiling and the floor in another dimension, spinning around and around. With Neil's help I managed to get to the bathroom and spent the remainder of my stay at the fancy condo exclusive hung over the tub hurling. A repulsive odor filled the room.

I watched as my stomach contents danced around the tub in circles. It was an entertaining show of sunflower seeds and M&Ms. Danielle interrupted. Even at the level of my intoxication I was able to observe how drunk she was. Danielle was not a tolerant drinker, and I was impressed with how much she drank that evening. There was no sign of Neil, but I was in no condition for company so I didn't bother asking his whereabouts.

On the walk home we displayed no indication that either one of us were in our right minds. We were fortunate the police didn't pick us up. Danielle began to vomit as soon as we began walking, but she remained a trooper and continued on, not giving up. When I heard her sobbing, I only encouraged her to keep moving.

Finally, just before we reached my house, she disclosed her sorrowful secret. Danielle told me that she was coerced to perform fellatio. Her anger with Neil was in her tone as she repeated the mantra, "I didn't want to do it." I was too familiar with the emotions tagging along with being taken advantage of. Danielle stayed at home a lot after that, never receiving the opportunity to confront Neil. My relationship with Rodney continued.

Sex ordinarily happened between couples, and despite my efforts to put it off, I only wanted to be ordinary. I questioned myself if race had something to do with it. I succumbed to Rodney's lame attempts at seduction only after a few rum-and-Cokes. It was a pitiful experience.

The black girls from the Hill detested our relationship. How dare a white girl take one of their available, well-mannered, and handsome black men? The two bitches I could stand the least were Tiesha and Charmaine. They provoked other black females in the school to join their protest. It was the only exciting aspect of my time with him.

I encountered these protestors within the corridors in between classes. They knew nothing of me besides my connection to Rodney, yet they were determined to try to intimidate me. I heard their whispers as I passed by in the hallways, "Look at her. She thinks she's cute ... I don't know who she thinks she is, dating a black man ... What does she think she is, black? ..." I was waiting for one of them, any one, to approach me. It never happened.

The tormenting at school became bolder as one day I was walking by a group of five. A single shoulder hit mine as we walked past one another. I turned around and said, "Do you have a problem?" But the group continued walking away like I wasn't even there.

I wanted to handle the problems at school myself; therefore I made no mention of it to Rodney. Danielle wasn't aware of the true extent of it. We shared none of the same classes due to my parent's insistence on my college preparatory courses.

Josh was locked up in jail and had Tracy, and I was dating Rodney, but none of it stopped Josh from playing a part in my life. To get Tracy jealous he made up a story about cheating on her with me before he got sent away. Word spread through the school first.

During class Charmaine and her friends would walk outside my classroom, yelling threats to jump me. It was embarrassing. My reputation as a good and well-behaved student was just as important to me as my reputation with my peers that I wasn't one to fuck with. Whenever questioned on the matter I denied any correlation between the loudmouths in the corridor and myself, though outside of school I was always on my guard, constantly looking over my shoulder.

One day I asked to use the hall pass. When I reached the corridor Charmaine and her friend were nowhere in sight. The second time I saw the girls steadily walk away from me as I stormed nearer to them without any real plan. I had stood my ground and they went away.

Still in all, nothing could have prepared me for Rodney's reaction to the alleged affair with Josh. When I walked in through the front door his mother was in the kitchen with her boyfriend and his kids. I yelled hello to everyone as I approached, but was told that Rodney was upstairs. I was alarmed when I hadn't received the usual warm welcome.

As I ascended the stairs I tried to step as softly as possible. It was eerily quiet on the second floor. I crept through the hallway and peeked into Rodney's room. He was sitting alone on his bed, cleaning his sneakers with a toothbrush.

"Hey, what's up? What are you doing sitting in here so quiet and lonely?"

"I just got off the phone with Tiesha." He seemed disturbed.

"What the hell does she want?"

He tilted his head and his tone lightened as he asked, "How was school today?"

"Same as any other. What did you have to talk with Tiesha for? Is she trying to persuade you to stick with the black population ... namely her?"

"Do you have something to tell me?"

"No, should I?"

"Well, I think so!"

I was sick of all the bullshit. Why was I wasting my time with him? Despite his age he played games like a school child. Was proving my point to these bitches really worth this agony of boredom? "Do you have a point?" I finally said.

"I heard about you and Josh." His voice was a low grumble.

"What about me and Josh? Why are we discussing Josh when he's been in jail for forever already?"

"I know how you cheated on me with him," he said in the same monotonous tone.

"I didn't cheat on you. What are you talking about?" Up until that time I had been standing. Now that we were getting somewhere and I knew what was on his mind I was a little more relaxed, especially because I knew I had not been unfaithful. I walked closer and sat on the edge of the bed beside him.

Rodney jumped up angrily and yelled, "You didn't cheat on me? C'mon, Tiesha just told me how everyone in school knows. Do I look like a fool to you?" His rage was building with each word.

"Fuck Tiesha, that stupid bitch. You're going to tell me you're taking her word over mine? Them bitches have been fuckin' with me since the day I met you. That rumor has been traveling for a week already. Don't you think Tracy would've approached me by now?"

I was surprised myself that Tracy hadn't confronted me with the allegation, though I was glad. Tracy was a tough girl. She was a no-nonsense chick, so I guessed she was wise to Josh's game plan.

"I don't know why Tracy hasn't gotten to you yet. But you'd better watch your back because you know she'll tear you up." I got the feeling if that day came it would be a happy one for the majority of the black population around the area, including Rodney.

"Well, thank you for the kind words and the load of confidence."

"You don't think you really have a chance with her, do you?" he said as he blatantly chuckled in disbelief.

"Ya know what? I think Tracy knows damn well I wouldn't do something like that. And if she is out to get me, we will just wait and see what happens now, won't we? I'm outta here!" I started to stand.

Rodney was furious. The steam came rushing out from his ears. He pushed me back down on the bed. His eyes glossed over, black and inhuman. I tried to push myself up and he tackled me. He covered my mouth with his strong hands, and I was helpless as they transformed into thick vines gaining length as well as strength. I could hardly breath, let alone speak or yell. The steam from his ears filled up the room, so all I could see was his face inches from mine.

"Are you trying to make a fool outta me? It's not going to work. You think you can play me? You might be able to get away with that shit with the little white boys at school, but you for damn sure ain't here. I ain't your bitch; you are my bitch. You got that?"

I was trying to wiggle my way out of his hold. He was lying directly on top of me. Rodney was five feet eleven inches, one hundred and eighty pounds. I was five feet three inches, one hundred and eighteen pounds. I wasn't going anywhere until he let me.

My left arm was stuck underneath us. His vines were still slithering their way over my body. I started to go numb. I was breathing heavily and not getting enough oxygen.

He got up on his knees, straddling me. My left hand was freed and I fought to get up. During the struggle he flipped me over, pushing all his body weight on top of me. My head was hanging off the edge of the bed, with all the pressure on my neck. I was getting very little oxygen then. I thought I was going to die.

I wondered what he would do with my body. There were people downstairs. Would they assist in the concealment of my lifeless corpse? I wasn't feeling anymore. I wasn't thinking of Josh and his stupid lies or of Tracy, Tiesha, or Charmaine. I wasn't thinking of Danielle and how upset she might be because I didn't like her cousin the way she wanted me to. I was only thinking of Rodney and his overpowering strength. And I couldn't deny my defeat and how it could end in my death.

I stopped struggling and ceased all movement. My breathing was so low it was undetectable. Suddenly the pressure was off. The vines that entrapped me recoiled in haste. In the instant my eyes came back to focus the steam vanished. I slowly began to hear the blood rushing through my veins. I remained still until I finally caught my breath and began gagging and coughing.

Rodney freaked out and rolled me over. "Are you okay?"

Instead of responding, I intentionally stared at the ceiling, just happy to be breathing. Rodney caressed my cheek and embraced my head with his common hands, "Oh my God, were you choking? You scared the shit out of me."

He knew he had violently pressed my throat into the corner of the bed. I never wanted to see his face again, especially with those scary black eyes. But I was worried that my behavior would provoke a further altercation. I was almost paralyzed by fear, and then Rodney sounded as though he was becoming irritated again from my silence.

"I'm fine. Happy?"

"Of course I'm happy. What happened?"

"What do you mean what happened? You were choking me!"

"No I wasn't. You were choking yourself. I didn't do anything but hold you down on the bed. See that's what happens when you provoke me. Now at least you know you won't do that again."

I couldn't believe what I was hearing, but it coincided with his inhuman eyes that had yet to return to normal.

"Let's make up. I'll stick to whooping your ass in hockey rather than in real life." He put his arm around me and led me toward the little couch where we occupied ourselves with the Play Station.

My hands were shaky and I was very quiet. He tried comforting me, but it wasn't working. I was racking my brain on *how* to leave, but a safe exit plan evaded me. I was scared to do the wrong thing, so I resorted to acting like his puppet. When he began kissing my neck and cheek I sat still, unaffected.

"C'mon, let's make up." It led to intercourse on his couch. I refrained from looking at him or kissing him back. When it was over he got up and took a shower as usual. I left without saying a word to anyone.

I decided not to make any mention of the occurrences. I wasn't looking forward to going head to head with Rodney again. I didn't want Tiesha and Charmaine to know they had somehow won the battle. I wanted to prevent Tracy getting word of it so she wouldn't assume the allegation was true. I tried not to seem defeated to anyone. I stayed silent and avoided Rodney's calls for the next week.

When he finally caught me on the phone it was obvious that I wasn't pleased to hear his voice, and I assumed he knew why. Despite my disinterest, he remained very calm and understanding over the phone, so I agreed to see him at his house with his cousin so we could talk.

Upon my arrival, Danielle greeted me. She acknowledged that Rodney and I had gotten into an argument, but I could tell by the way she spoke of it that she hadn't a clue as to what had really taken place. Rodney was in the kitchen with his mom and his mom's boyfriend.

There was another light-skinned woman at the table. Rodney was talking with her as he sat in the chair closest hers. There was a short introduction with our names excluding any explanation of my relationship with Rodney or her relationship with anybody in the house. She was quite attractive in her simple tomboyish way. She smiled a pretty smile after our brief introduction and didn't seem threatened by my arrival.

Danielle invited me upstairs.

"I'll be right up," Rodney said.

We listened to music and gossiped about meaningless topics. A half-hour went by and Danielle went down to summon Rodney. Minutes later I heard footsteps on the stairs. I became paralyzed as

I thought it was he approaching. I was nervous and regretted being there. The footsteps were coming down the hall and I wished I had never gone to that stupid Super Bowl party. The stepping sounded closer and closer. At last I could see a face and end the suspense. I was glad to see Danielle round the doorway.

Danielle apologized for her cousin's rudeness. I tittered to myself, "If she only knew."

Another few minutes went by and I gladly announced, "I'm leaving."

"Please give him a chance."

"I did. What more do you want from me? Are you coming with me or what?"

It was a perfect way to end it. The downfall of our relationship would ultimately be seen as the age difference between us.

I made it a point to stay by myself for a while. Why on earth do girls go crazy over guys? Why did girls publicly stoop to low levels time and time again? I made a vow to myself that I would never be that stupid. I will not submit even to my own feelings. And if I feel weak and powerless I will convince myself that I am not. I will convince myself that the circumstances before me are the circumstances that I have chosen. I was taking control, but I needed a little outside help. Remembering that piece of lace radiating from above the stage, I was determined to get it in my grasp.

I came to excuse Josh since he could not have foreseen how his little lie would affect me. I told myself he didn't do it to hurt me, but was simply toying with Tracy's head. Rodney was fully responsible for his own actions. I was responsible for not letting Rodney go earlier. My tenacity in disproving any myths is what held me through. None of my enemies messed with me after that. I didn't back down, and that was the most important thing.

I was working at the grocery store late one night to get more hours in. Tracy was shopping in the store with one of her friends. It was nearly ten and there were only a few people around.

She came through my express line talking with her friend. I scanned her items as though she was any other customer, listening to their conversation in case either made snide comments about me. They did not.

When I focused on her eyes she did not look at me at all. She placed her money on the counter for her groceries. I picked it up and tendered the register and then placed her change on the counter in the same place. I bagged the few items she had and placed the bag on the counter. Again I looked at her. She did not acknowledge me.

As she picked up her bag my supervisor yelled for me to cash out and go home. I looked at Tracy to see if she heard I was leaving. Alas, she looked at me. I followed my orders and cashed out my drawer.

In exiting the building, my adrenaline was pumping. I looked around to see if she was waiting for me. I saw no one. I walked home that night repeatedly looking over my shoulder, but nobody came near me. Tracy had the perfect opportunity to "get" me if she wanted. I was alone in the dark and out of my territory. She hadn't seized the moment, which wound up being her only chance. It was finally over.

In retrospect I guess the teenage years when I was young and carefree, blissful and naïve, with and without Josh were not as sweet as I remembered. I was determined to convince others that Josh had no place in my heart. Then I was hoping to be able to convince myself. I wonder if I ever will.

Chapter Five

"Always Have a Backup Plan"

I lie back down on my bed dangling my feet while I collect myself. I stare blankly at the ceiling. Some trip down memory lane, I thought. Why is it that human beings insist on learning things the hard way?

I can hear the noise from my neighbors outside my window. The Puerto Ricans across the street have the hose on for the children to cool off. My black neighbors to the left have a slew of the neighborhood kids in two plastic wading pools. I have half a mind to splash in a pool myself. If only I wasn't so embarrassed to show my ugly self out in the real world. I remember what I look like, and reality imbeds itself in the forefront of my brain again.

I attempt to roll over onto my belly. "Ugh!" I immediately roll to my side and curl up in a fetal position. "Not cool. Not cool," I murmur. Just the mere sensation of anything against my belly, makes me nauseous and I may or may not vomit. I rest a minute and wait out the nausea before I loosen up and sprawl out on my bed. "I don't want to throw up again today."

Every morning I begin by brushing my teeth, and then I throw up. Since I haven't eaten anything yet, it's the color of tang and it burns my throat. It is stomach acid.

The taste stays in my mouth even after I force Saltines down in hopes of alleviating the nausea. Two hours later I still feel it, and it is gradually gaining its headache accomplice. If I don't take it slow I will be bombarded with a merciless migraine for an undetermined length of time.

Relaxing myself with a deep breath, I plunge back into my memory bank; quite amazed at all I had forgotten about my years in high school. Now I can see why. I still haven't told anyone about Rodney and the frightful fight. That's what made it easier to repress.

My senior year of high school was simplistically quiet. Josh was in prison. Rodney was a fading memory. I stayed away from romance altogether. My parents were in the midst of a divorce yet still drinking at the bar together. I focused on my schoolwork and my after-school jobs.

I had no intention of attending my senior prom and certainly had no prospective dates in mind. Unfortunately that was just the beginning of many major adjustments to my plans in life. Alas, Casey persuaded a classmate named Greg to ask me strictly as friends and assured him I would accept. Prom wasn't anything spectacular. I must admit, although uneventful, the night ended better than the last prom.

My high-school graduation was a pathetic celebratory moment. I got an extra ticket for Danielle, who had a baby and dropped out of school two months prior. We experienced all of the important milestones and typical teenage bullshit together. She had witnessed fights between my parents. She'd seen my dad passed out drunk on the floor as we snuck out and back in the house. I was there for her pregnancy and the birth of her son, the ups, the downs, and the outs with the baby's father, Tom. I always imagined graduation by each other's side throughout the natural flow of life.

It was tremendously lonely standing before everyone's family and friends. The spotlight was on me alone. I had other friends and, of course, an entire class of two hundred or so young adults surrounding me, but I was miserable.

Instead of being in the row behind me, Danielle sat next to my mother and sisters twenty rows back. The stage lights shone over her head and onto us, the graduating class of '94, a group she was no longer included in. She wasn't invited to the after-party. She had already missed senior banquet and prom. She would never be invited to the class reunions. None of it seemed to bother her as much as it did me. Danielle wanted me to go to the graduation, so I did for her and my parents.

The audience was full of proud relatives. Way up in the nosebleed section of the auditorium stood my father alone. Though my parents still shared an address, their marriage was coming to an end. My father isolated himself. The surrounding seats were empty in the entire section. He stood there in the dark vacant area with his black jeans and black leather coat. Even with his brown hair, complete with a full beard and mustache, standing in the shadows I could see the tears of pride and joy, in turn validating my decision to attend.

Out in the corridor my father stood waiting for me. I jumped out of line and ran up to him. He gave me a great big bear hug and forced a slight smile.

"I just wanted to catch you before your mother and everybody came over to see you. I gotta go, Hun. I wanted to say congratulations and I'm proud of you. You know that." With that he gave me a kiss on my forehead and a pat on the shoulder and he disappeared into the crowd.

In the corridor I searched for the other members of my family. They hugged me and congratulated me, and then started gossiping. Danielle and I inched away.

"How fucking cheesy was that? Casey and me were talking and it was so boring standing there. I can't believe I got all soft like that. What a moron. I'm glad that's over."

"C'mon, you were not the only one who shed a tear!"

"Yeah, I just wished you were there with me, ya know? God, did you see my father standing up top by himself? I thought I was gonna lose it. Whoa, what a dismal sight, man."

"No, but we saw him before we came in and he looked sad."

"Well, maybe my mother didn't see how miserable he looked!" I really don't know why it was so important to me that my mother didn't see how broken he was.

Casey interrupted Danielle from behind. "Hey, hey, hey, what's up girl? How's the babe?"

"He's good." Like me, she's not into small talk.

"Where is Sebastian anyway?" Casey constantly asked Danielle if she could baby-sit. Danielle let her a few times, but she didn't do much with the free time. For Casey it was a treat to play with babies. Casey showcased Sebastian around like he was a porcelain doll. Danielle never had to pay her for that.

"He's at home with my mom right now."

"DEE DEE! What up what up, girl?" Kristina was cool. She was a real party girl and fun to be around no matter where you were. She came running up between Casey and me, wrapping her arms around both of us.

"K Nice!" Danielle and I greeted her simultaneously.

"How are you?" Danielle asked, obviously happy to see her.

"Same old, same old. You know me," she giggled. "Let the partying begin," she roared as she led us straight toward the doors. Reaching back she pinched the sleeve of Danielle's shirt. "Coming Dee?"

"Nah, I can't. I gotta go home with her mother and back to Sebastian. You guys have fun though." She gave me a smile to let me know it was okay that I go along with the girls. As she waved her smile grew bigger.

I smiled back with a wink. "Love you girl!" The look on her face told me that our paths were headed in different directions. That initial hint that our lives were about to change dramatically and at a rapid pace missed my attention, but it wouldn't have made any bit of difference if I noticed.

In June following my graduation I was flabbergasted to receive a letter from Josh. It sat on my bed while I contemplated tossing it. I glanced at it often, but I continued styling my hair. At my vanity I could see it behind me through the mirror. A subtle twinkle reflected in the glass. It brightened as minutes passed, taunting my curiosity.

Almost an hour later the shimmer was as bright as the sun reflecting off a mirror. Finally I picked the letter up.

The Cheshire smile was the culprit of the annoying light imprinted on the width of the envelope. On the back bottom was a stamp in red ink. It stated, "This is a correspondence from the Adult Correctional Institute of Rhode Island. The contents of this package have not been censored." I became aware of my beating heart as I began to open it.

It was a full page long, written on a piece of yellow legal paper. I had barely gotten halfway down the page before I crinkled it up and tossed it across my room.

Instead I picked up a book on Southern Connecticut State University. I flopped down on my twin-size bed and read the same paragraph four times before realizing my mind was elsewhere and it was foolish to try to read. I tried studying the photographs to fantasize about life on campus. I was eager to go away and ready to start a new life. I'd earned it.

Some time passed before I noticed the letter again. I walked across my bedroom, bent down, and picked it up. I tried to smooth it out so I could continue to read it and found the spot where I left off. My heart was noticeable again, and I saw it pump right out of my chest just once.

"I'm just writing to congratulate you on your graduation." A quick flashback of the heart-wrenching ceremony flew across my mind. I was sore that Josh would bring that back into my head. He hadn't a clue what I had endured the past year. All of a sudden he pretended to care. I crumpled it back up and chucked it against the back of my door. This time I began crying.

"Why is he doing this to me? That fucking bastard …" I was cursing him under my breath.

My sister, Amber, entered my room. "What's going on?"

"I got this stupid letter from Josh." I was still sobbing.

"No way. What's he saying this time?"

"Same sorry-ass apology, same sorry-ass excuse, 'I was young and stupid' blasé blah."

"Well, where is it?"

"Behind the door."

Seeing the crumpled-up paper on the floor she began to laugh as she bent down and picked it up. "Can I read it?"

"No, I'll read it to you. I didn't finish it yet anyway." I snatched the yellow ball from her hand. I read it aloud from the beginning. The closing read, "If you want to write me back here's the address. But if not that's okay. I will understand and I won't hold it against you." There was a post office box on the bottom left-hand corner. "That fuckin' bastard!"

"Are you gonna write him back?"

"Hell yeah, I'm gonna give him a peace of my mind. That's for damn sure."

SCSU was the only college I had applied to. We moved to the tiny state of Rhode Island from Brooklyn, New York, when I was just a baby. I figured Connecticut is a happy medium, a good equidistance from each place, a city livelier than the seasonal city I live in but not as big and chaotic as New York. That was the only reason I chose to apply to that college.

About a month later I received the response from the school. I read the SCSU correspondence in the privacy of my own room.

"YES, ha ha ha!" I jumped in the air, bouncing off the ceiling. "I knew I quit my job for a reason. I'm going away to college!"

Bouncing downstairs, I went to tell my parents the great news. By this time they were always in separate rooms of the house. I saw my mother sitting on the couch. I smiled, handing her the acceptance letter. As she read it her eyebrows were scrunched and her lips were tight. I anxiously awaited her proud response of joy. She looked square at me and said, "Why the fuck do you want to go there?" She handed the paper back to me and continued watching television.

Confused and dismayed, I went downstairs to the basement, no longer bouncing, where my father was working on the new PVC pipes he had installed with the help of my sister and me.

"Hey Dad, read this!" I gave him the letter and stood proudly before him.

"Oh ho ho!" he gasped. "Congratulations, girl!" He gave me a hug and after a pause continued, "Now don't you worry, we have the money for this. Give me a second and I'll show you the books." He gave me a reassuring glance and I went upstairs to my room. I had no idea what that was all about but at least he was happy for me.

I called Danielle to give her the news. She was unconditionally ecstatic. Finally the response I was looking for. She in turn yelled to her parents and I heard their excitement through the phone. That lifted my spirits a little.

"Reba, I am so proud of you!"

"Thank you! Do you mind if I come over? These people are acting really weird."

"C'mon over. I'll see you when you get here."

My father knocked on the door; he pushed it open and stood there with the ledger containing all his financial records. As he promised, he pointed out where it was documented that he had twenty-three thousand dollars and some change in the bank. "See, Hun, we have the money for you to go to college."

I smiled at him and kept it simple, "Okay!"

The cloud of uncertainty wasn't lifted, and I never bounced again. Why was my mother angry with me for getting accepted to college? And why on earth was my father showing me his ledger? College after high school was the only plan I had ever heard. Stacy attended college, then it was my turn.

Josh replied to my nasty correspondence by saying he understood why I was so angry but asked if I could find it in my heart to forgive him. He just wanted my friendship. He missed the harmony we shared. I continued to write him, hoping for some sort of explanation for his lie to Tracy. Even after I realized I wasn't going to receive the proper level of apology with a good-enough excuse, we continued a cordial correspondence.

I heard that he and Tracy broke it off while I was still in school. Even though I never asked for any information, someone somewhere felt obligated to tell me. I refrained from speaking her name, as did he.

On August 1, 1994, my parent's divorce was finalized and my father officially moved out. We didn't see him much after that. He spent a lot of time in the bar by himself. There was no further discussion of college. By the end of August I knew I wasn't going. I quit my job at the grocery store for the summer off. I had been so busy with school, dance, and a job for the past three consecutive years I gave myself a well-deserved break.

My mother told me to get a job because I had to start paying two hundred dollars a month to live there on top of the hundred and change I'd been paying for insurance coverage. Since the divorce she couldn't afford the mortgage payment by herself.

Two months after that we had a "family meeting" to discuss our future living arrangements. My mother's financial limitations caused a foreclosure on the house. She was checking into apartments for herself and Amber, who by that time was well into an abusive relationship with her unborn daughter's father. She was in the third trimester of her pregnancy. Stacy decided to move out of state with her boyfriend. I was left to find my own apartment.

I found a housekeeping position at the Doubletree Hotel on the water. I was only making $6.20/hour, which was twenty cents more than the grocery store, plus I received tips. That was far from enough to afford me an apartment in the historic and touristy city in which I lived. The only place I could afford was the very place I had fought with Josh for spending so much time at and the place I was forbidden by my parents to go.

Josh and I sent about one letter a week. Eventually his notes read, "I love you" and "come visit me." Weak with little restraint, I did. Often he sent cards with flowers and corny sappy sayings inside. But I never told him I loved him. Like a foolish child I thought that if I didn't say it then I wouldn't feel it. I believed that if I pretended not to care as much as he did then that would give me the advantage. Even as I grew and matured, I was still so young and blind when it came to him.

During the time Josh spent away, he went through phases, feeling his lack of control while reality would slap him in the face. He had to accept his fate of imprisonment. He lashed out, usually by pulling a stupid test or prank on me. It didn't take much provocation.

I wrote to Josh explaining my family situation and how it led me to get an apartment in the Hill. I wasn't expecting the infuriated response I received. He yelled at me as though it was my fault and I had some sort of choice.

A week later I received a bogus letter from an inmate Josh conjured up. I wrote Josh saying I didn't appreciate him giving my address out to anybody, especially in jail. I knew the letter was a fake. I knew the supposed sender didn't exist. Even as he underestimated my intelligence and disrespected me I decided not to let Josh know I knew how low he had stooped. I shouldn't have cared about sparing him the humiliation, but I was a sucker for him.

Disgusted with myself I get up and go to the bathroom. I splash some water on my face and wipe it dry with my shirt. I don't know why I am wasting my time reliving the past. It's my only day off this week, and I waste it away tripping down memory lane.

I am exhausted from working two jobs. I have a housekeeping job at a four-star hotel downtown, not the Doubletree, the Vanderbilt. I begin work at six every morning and usually stay until four. Between six and nine in the morning I clean the public areas of the hotel. I assign the rooms to the girls for cleaning. Then I clean rooms before inspecting the others. Throughout the day we also have to do the laundry and restock the closets with the linens. Before I leave in the afternoon I assign the turndowns for the night shift. I do it all for a miserable $8.50/hour without the supervisor title.

I have just enough time to go home and take a shower. I try to eat something or I make it to go. Then I am scheduled to be at my night job as a telephone operator no later than six o'clock in the evening. I do billing and answer the phone until midnight. I usually get extremely nauseous at this job, possibly because I sit in front of a computer and phone all night as opposed to running around like a wild woman trying to single-handedly accomplish enough tasks for three people.

I need to keep myself busy. I've replaced the partying with work. Besides, I need all the money I can get. I may as well be productive for a change. I'll go crazy sitting in my house all by myself. Right now I remember why I work so hard. Oh, what I wouldn't do for a drink this minute.

"I can't think about my bullshit life in the present. It's too depressing!" I sigh to myself.

After that fiasco with the bogus letter from the phony inmate I stopped speaking and corresponding with Josh. At that point it was becoming second nature to love him one day and despise him the next. It was becoming much easier for me to let him go knowing that Josh would come around again, apologizing again, and would be a part of my life again. Of that I was certain, and so I released concern over the details of how or when.

I was working for a living cleaning up other people's shit-stained toilets and changing someone else's cum-stained sheets. It was not an admirable position in life. My mother told me the world was my oyster. What the hell did that mean? I felt more like an oyster getting thrown around the waves of muddy water.

I was a bitter and angry person. Living in the ghetto was hardly a choice, just like being uneducated. And still I wasn't spared the disrespect that comes along with cleaning up after the rich. I suddenly became a peon, and the very idea of it disgusted me.

My friends are what kept me sane. They knew all along that college wasn't in their reach. I don't know if they even wanted it. Their aspirations didn't go beyond creating a family. They searched for a good guy to settle down and have children with. Some of them wanted it so badly they rushed things and started a family without insuring they had the man.

They were looking for love. I was looking for respect. Power came from being hard, and so I worked hard, I walked hard, and I played hard with a hard expression permanently glued to my face. I was beginning to forget what a smile was.

My friend Shonnie and I were walking on Hillside Ave, which is the main street running through the Hill, hence the nickname. Since Amber set aside all her connections when she fell under the control of her kid's father, we built a stronger friendship. To my utter amazement she had been dating Rodney for almost a year already and was six months pregnant.

I kept my senses in tune for any sign of maltreatment by her man, but I never found one. In time I concluded that it was just I, maybe because I was white. It wasn't the first scenario in which I observed black men treating women of color with more respect than they do white women.

Shonnie and I share the kind of relationship that no distance or even time could destroy. Although we don't see one another every day and sometimes our paths veer off in slightly different directions, she is never more than a phone call away. She is a God-given true friend.

She and I had just gotten off the bus. As we were walking we saw a sky-blue Dodge Caravan speeding down Hillside Ave. The vehicle slowed down just alongside of us, and Josh popped his head out of the driver's side window.

"Hey, yo!" He yelled just before he made a haphazard turn into the next street.

"Well, I knew he would be out soon, but I didn't know when," I said calmly.

"Ay mommy, now we know."

He parked the caravan in the middle of the road with the tail end on Hillside Ave. Upon getting out, he left the van door wide open in his haste. With a skip in his step, he was approaching us quickly. We hadn't had contact since the phony letter incident, which happened several months prior.

"You stay here; I'll go see what he wants." I was concerned for her safety, not thinking about my own. She stayed behind as I walked quickly towards Josh. He was crossing the street before me with his magnificent smile that failed to completely gain my trust. I was reluctant to believe he was happy to see me.

"What's up?" I asked.

Josh ran all the way up to me and hugged me before speaking. "Hey, girl! I missed you. How have you been?"

"I'm alright. Are you out? Or did you just get a furlough?"

"I'm out! I'm out for good." The Cheshire gleamed.

"When did you get out?" I felt the coast was clear and started back towards Shonnie.

"They let me go at ten o'clock."

"Today?" It was only shortly after two o'clock in the afternoon. I thought he had been out at least a few days. "And already you're out here!"

"Nah, it ain't like that, I was looking for you," he admitted, on the defensive.

"Well, here I am. I was just walking Shonnie home. Then I was going home."

"Hola amiga!"

"Hello, Josh."

"I wanted to see your crib," he said back towards me.

"Well, you can't leave your van like that in the middle of the street! Acting all crazy, rushing up on someone like you're about to take care of some business."

"Nah, I was just happy to see you is all. I'm gonna go to the Rec to see about a job and then I'll come to your place. What number is it again?"

"Fifty-seven, like you don't know!" I was happy to see him again.

My lack of self-worth led me to accept the unpredictable and crazy way of our time together. I should have demanded more respect. I should've demanded more stability. I should've demanded more sanity! But I wanted to be cool and act like I was "down" with whatever. I wanted to be wild and not give a fuck about the way things turned out.

But I did care. It mattered to me how badly he treated me sometimes. I cared about making amends and forgiving and moving on. How was that supposed to be the case if we pretended as though nothing bad happened yesterday or a hundred yesterdays ago?

Certain I would get hurt I felt I could never explain those feelings and thoughts to Josh. He'd failed to earn my trust, and without it there isn't much of a relationship. That much I knew. That's why I took what I could get from him, no questions asked, no looking back.

Chapter Six

"All In Good Fun?"

I remember as a little girl gazing out the back window of the car at the fabulous Newport life when my parents would take visitors from New York for a tour of downtown. It was a fantasy adult world that I couldn't wait to join. The men were well groomed in fashionable button-down shirts and dress slacks holding hands with equally exquisite women adorned in pretty dresses or short skirts with fancy high heels. The latest trends were constantly walking up and down Thames Street, and I was in awe of it all.

In my admiring teenage eyes being twenty-one was all about embellishments, live music, dancing, drinks, and exhilarating people. There were too many clubs downtown to count, and they all had waiting lines outside their doors.

Spring kicked the action into gear. As the seasons heated up so did the events. Newport hosted festivals of all kinds, from art and film to music, folk, and jazz. The Tall Ships festival was our family favorite, and the Black Ships came a close second. The Irish festival is held in late August, and then Oktoberfest is the last grand affair. I couldn't possibly keep track of them all.

During Thanksgiving the nightclubs host holiday parties and advertise specials for the college kids returning home. Christmas in

Newport is a beautiful scene in the small city. New Year's is a big blowout anywhere you go. And suddenly there is silence.

Business dies down for hotels, and the Doubletree was no exception. The employees receive partial unemployment checks and beg for as many hours as possible. So when I called out sick two days in a row during the downtime of business, my supervisors shifted to suspicion.

I feared they would infer that I was a liability if they learned the reason for my absence. I presumed I was in danger of losing my job. Shonnie's aunt was a supervisor in housekeeping, so my secret was kept from her also.

Earlier that week I was cleaning a stay, as we called them when the guest rents the room another night. A middle-aged man was assigned a room on my floor. When I knocked on the door, he answered neatly dressed, appearing as though he was ready to leave.

"Well hello, darling. Come on in."

I was immediately on guard by his suave demeanor. I didn't appreciate the way he so blatantly panned his eyes up and down my body. I noticed the glistening of saliva forming at the corners of his mouth, like a dog sizing up a T-bone steak.

"I can come back later." I told the guest.

"No, no. Don't be silly. I'll be outta here in a few minutes." He assured me.

I took my time propping the door open and emptying the trash. I was normally uncomfortable when a guest remained in the room during the cleaning, but this time was worse. I decided to clean the bathroom first. I could still hear him rustling about in the room and my anxiety was building. Images of getting victimized played on the bathroom tiles as I scrubbed them away with trepidation. My exit plan reformed with each new scenario. I cleaned that bathroom quicker than I have ever cleaned a bathroom in my life.

I tried to be just as expedient in the rest of the room. He lingered about, watching me.

"So what's life like for you in Newport, Rhode Island?"

"It's fine." I answered meekly.

"You must have a boyfriend?"

I finished the dusting quietly and was eager to make the bed, vacuum, and leave. "Where do you want me to put your suitcase while I make the bed?"

"Anywhere is fine." He didn't even attempt to assist. Instead he enjoyed the view from his chair. "So what is the exciting thing to do around here?"

"Oh, I wouldn't know. It's all twenty-one plus out here." My nerves eased up a bit as he sat stationary.

"Well, how old are you then?"

"I'm not twenty one!" I promised myself I wouldn't overreact until he moved toward the door, which remained propped open according to hotel policy.

"Well, that could mean a lot of things. Are you at least le—"?

"Do you mind if I vacuum?" I interrupted.

"Why don't you come back later to vacuum? I need a nap before the evening. Do you have a wake-up call?"

"Yes."

"Then could you give me a call at six?"

Reluctantly I smiled in compliance. But then I saw the bulge in his pelvic region.

"I'll see you then," he said, handing me a twenty-dollar bill.

His protrusion was growing to an enormous size. I snatched the money and hurried away as it was chasing me out of the room. I slammed the door and quickly parked my cart in my closet, then went outside for a cigarette break. I had two rooms left but couldn't conceive of going back up there, so I went to use the pay phone on the other end of the building.

Unfortunately I ran into Rodney, who was working in banquet setup. He was carrying tables into one of the function rooms. We were friendly to one another and I had learned to leave the past in the past. Rodney and Josh had been acquaintances from the streets. Rodney was well known in the area for being a rehabilitated drug dealer without any intervention from the authorities and was highly regarded for that. His reputation contributed to my conclusion that our past misunderstanding was an isolated incident and must have something to do with my faults.

"Hey, what are you doing over here?"

"Oh, I needed to use the phone."

"Something wrong with the phone downstairs?"

"Not that I know of. But you know how it is. I don't need everyone all up in my business. Besides sometimes a change of scenery is nice."

"Ah, need a little privacy. I always knew you and Josh would hook back up."

"There you go again. It's not like that. I gotta hurry up, instead of wasting time talking with you. I got work to do."

"It's your destiny. I ain't mad at ya!"

"Yeah, yeah." I said walking quickly to the pay phone.

I reached in my pocket for a quarter and dialed Amber's number.

"Hello?"

"Amber it's me. I need a wicked huge favor."

"What's up?"

"I need you to call work for me and make up some reason to call me out."

"Oh God, not again. Why this time?"

"Same as last, but don't tell anyone. I just want to come home and forget it."

"Like last time?"

"It worked anyway. Listen I don't want to lose my job over something so stupid."

"Ya know, Reba, maybe you should get a different job if this keeps happening to you."

"Well, this time was more subtle. He's a guest on my floor, but he slipped me a twenty so it was the same proposition. C'mon Amber, please. I can't go back up there today."

"You know I will. Are you coming here?"

"Yeah, I'll come right over for a while. Then I gotta go home and get dressed 'cause Josh will probably be over early since he has to work tonight."

I rushed back up to my closet on the sixth floor where I hid, tidying up my cart and stocking it high with amenities. I organized the sheets on the shelf, trying to be patient until my dismissal. Finally it came.

One of my grandparents passed away again. I was used to expressing the look of drop-dead shock over my loss. Before leaving I stopped at the front desk to put in a wake-up call for the guest. I had no idea how long the man was staying, so I called out for my final days that week.

The only one at the hotel I trusted my strange encounters with was the old security guard. I was confident he would keep it to himself like before, and continue to keep a special eye on me. Unfortunately, these types of encounters never occurred on his shifts.

Josh was working as a short-order cook for the recreational center in town. He was programmed for the fast-paced environment and appreciated the opportunity to make some honest money. The people at the Rec treated Josh well. He was good company for his co-workers, keeping up morale. Before his shift ended he'd call me to ask what I wanted to eat. Then he personally delivered it.

Any dependence on others was held in contempt in my mind. Needing assistance was never an option, therefore I never asked for help, least of all from Josh. He was living with his mother and stepfather, so he spent the majority of his time at my house. In exchange for my hospitality, he offered me use of his Caravan. Sometimes I'd go clubbing while he stayed in the peace and quiet of my home. When I returned Josh would be doing household chores or cooking. It was confusing how he could be so thoughtful and helpful yet other times he could be a complete ass and so cruel.

This day he kept his van and only stayed at my house a short time before leaving for work.

"Hey I got this bootleg video for you to watch."

"Another one?"

"I got *Scream*. The picture is better than the last movie, but the audience is a little louder. It was good so I got it for you to watch."

"You want me to watch it by myself?"

"Course not, Shorty. Can we watch it now?"

"Go on. Throw it in."

Aside from his occasional chuckle as he grabbed my arm urging me to laugh with him, we sat in silence side by side on the couch. The plot was finally unraveling, and the killer was soon to be discovered.

But Josh's leisure time was over and he had to leave for work. I ignored him, engrossed in the video, as he stood up to leave.

"Well, I am gonna go. You can finish the movie and I will be back later."

"Uh huh." My eyes remained glued to the television.

"I gotta go to work."

"Yup."

"Are you at least gonna say good-bye?"

"BYE!"

He walked in front of the television. "That's it. That's all I get? I just let you watch a movie for free."

"Then let me watch it. Or at least let me pause it 'til you go."

"Damn, girl, you're rough."

"What do you want from me? A fucking Joshua cheer? You get up right when they reveal the killer. Why can't I just watch the end?"

"Oh you wanna know the end so bad? It's him, their friend, and that guy helps him." Josh was pointing to the actors on the screen. "There! Now I can leave and you can watch it."

I had nothing to say. I stared blankly at him and watched him leave somewhat satisfied.

Nobody else in Josh's life gave him the amount of attention I did nor did anyone show him that they cared as much as I did. When he didn't feel my love he did odd things.

Josh had Attention-Deficit/Hyperactive Disorder, with emphasis on the HYPER. On an average night he only slept about five hours and was constantly on the go during the day. He tried to keep a low profile; not spending his time with the same group of drug dealers that he did before he was sent away. I was proud of him for that. His efforts made me hopeful for the chance of a normal life.

We spent a considerable amount of time in apartment sixty directly across the street from mine. Shonnie and Rodney rented it. It was great because we could get smashed and walk fifty paces home. We played card games like Rummy and Spades. Shonnie and Josh smoked Philly blunts gutted and replaced with marijuana. I had never smoked weed before. Shonnie pressured me into smoking for the first time. Josh gave his "permission."

I never had the urge to try it before. I was petrified to do drugs. My parents had taught me their effects and the negative impact they had on people's entire lives. I listened well, and when the times presented themselves I steered away with no problem. I had also seen some ugly creatures doped up, or coming down desperate for more in my neighborhood. I never wanted to look like that.

I had been left out of a smoke circle often enough that it didn't bother me. I had caught a contact high before. Initially I felt lighter on my feet, accompanied by a bit of giddiness followed by a slight tingling sensation all over my body. After I disclosed that information to my friends, Shonnie turned on the pressure for me to get a direct high.

Shonnie had this whiny way about her that could make the men in her life give her anything she wanted. That tone usually didn't work with me, but I let it get to me.

"Reba, please smoke with us tonight. I know you'll like it. You're my friend and I've always wanted you to smoke with me. It's more fun when you can smoke with someone. Please, Mommy. You live right across the street, so if you get sick or don't like it you can go right home to bed. Josh will take care of you and I won't let anything happen to you. Please. You have to! C'mon."

I looked at Josh, who was studying my face. He knew me well enough to predict my next response. His lips turned up and I anticipated the gorgeous Cheshire.

"You can do it," he said before I opened my mouth.

"Yeah?" I said, "maybe just one hit."

"Yeah, just start off with one hit and then you can see how it feels and see if you want another when it comes back around." It was the little girl in her that incessantly whined and pushed for more.

Josh and Shonnie were so excited to teach me how to smoke a blunt. I found their elation over the concept amusing.

"Hold it at the very end, but don't cover it. I hold it with my nails, but don't squeeze it so hard you don't get anything. And don't inhale it like it's a cigarette. Just take a little hit for your first time." Shonnie continued getting into too much detail. I was getting worrisome just listening to her. By then I wished I were more intoxicated so if I did it wrong I wouldn't feel so stupid.

"All right all ready," I yelled, "can I smoke the damn thing or do you want to just do it for me?"

"No Mommy, you smoke it," she whined.

"Then shut the fuck up already, you're making me nervous. It's a fucking blunt!"

"I just want you to like it."

I did everything they told me to. I held it in until they gave me the okay to exhale a few seconds later. I felt the high immediately. It was basically the same as a contact just much stronger. One hit was all I could handle, being an amateur smoker. The taste of the blunt was less than palatable, so I continuously spat in an effort to get the taste off of my lips. The potheads around me found that hilarious.

"Funny, huh?" I said. "Ugh, the taste from the blunt is gross."

Shonnie laughed, "You get used to it."

Josh admitted, "I like it."

Rodney agreed with Josh.

"I don't really think I want to get used to it," I said in between spits.

"Well, you can smoke a joint next time or we can use one of Rodney's pipes." Shonnie didn't want her new protégé to slip away.

It was usually past midnight when we parted. My relationship with Josh remained strictly platonic. He spent the night at my apartment in the spare room, and I was relieved that he never showed any sign of wanting more. Building pleasant memories and being his friend was most important to me. Whenever we leapt toward intimacy our relationship turned ugly in no time.

Yet for reasons beyond my control, I continued falling for him. The intellectual voice in my head was a perpetual reminder of the catastrophe that waited ahead. I had to blanket either the voice or the brewing affection. I was eager to find something up for the task. I wished it was as simple as blanketing with a sheet, but all that was available was alcohol.

A new phase ensued through my conscious effort to already be under the influence when he showed up at my house after work. As he realized this he became frustrated.

"Why are you always drunk lately?" Josh interrogated.

"What are you talking about?" I was feeling tingly and warm from the booze.

"When we drink with Shonnie and Rodney you drink way more than everyone else."

"Not true. Shonnie's never more than a drink behind me."

"You're delusional!"

"You're just jealous because I can hold more liquor than you." I was being smug, but Josh was sober and in no mood.

"It is not a competition, Reba!"

"Whatever, man, there's nothing to talk about. Have a beer already!" I bailed out of the conversation by walking across the street.

I didn't see Josh for a few days. I wouldn't dare question where he was or whom he had chosen to spend his time with. Although he called me every day we'd speak for a half-hour at most with no discussion on meeting up with one another. I had a tendency to worry about him getting into trouble, but conceded that it was his life.

When he migrated back to the scene with Shonnie, Rodney, and me, he would ridicule a particular girl in the neighborhood. This was his roundabout way of getting our opinion of her before discreetly disclosing to Rodney that he had slept with her. The female he spoke of was always a black girl.

I knew how Josh operated. He most likely associated with her the first or second day of our separation then needed extra days to cleanse as much guilt as he could before facing me again. In reality he needn't feel guilty, because we had no romantic ties. He had just spent quite some time behind bars and I wasn't giving him any sex, so it didn't surprise me that he was getting it elsewhere on sporadic occasions.

It was difficult, though not impossible, to hide my maladjustment. Though he was getting the occasional thrill in bed, I wasn't. I had resolved to take precautions with the opposite sex. No man really had a chance.

Josh had the key to my apartment. Nothing was ever official with us. He troubled his mother, and so she was constantly on his case. As justified as her concerns were, he needed a safe haven. I allowed my home to be just that for him.

After work one day I took the bus home as usual. I used my key to unlock my front door. When I walked in the lights were off and the apartment was dark. I owned heavy drapes, which were kept drawn in hopes of deterring a possible thief.

The main entrance is through the kitchen. The forest green shade was permanently drawn, with a sunflower valance above it. The only counter space available was just big enough for a small microwave. The cabinets hung above the counter and sink, which were beside the refrigerator and miniature stove.

Against the opposite wall were a glass hexagon table and four black padded chairs. Two black sunflower placemats and a matching vase containing small, fabricated sunflowers adorned the table. The lone occupant on the wall above the table was a sunflower clock.

In the living room a grey plush couch and matching fluffy chair were accompanied by black end tables with a brass strip around the edge and a matching coffee table. The twenty-inch TV with cable box and VCR was on the opposite wall from the couch. The small stereo system I'd had for years was placed next to the TV. Behind it was the open staircase leading to the second floor.

The picture on the television screen was visible from the kitchen, and I couldn't resist a smile. Instead of hanging my keys on the nail in the four-inch space of wall between the door and the window like I always do, I dropped my keys on the table so he could hear them hit the glass. I proceeded to the living room, where I saw Josh enjoying the solitude of my home. There was the faint scent of marijuana in the air mixed with his Drakaar cologne. The only stipulation I had to his smoking weed in my house was that he did so with minimal guests. He respected my apartment and the rules in it.

The football game was on and the volume was so low I couldn't imagine he could hear the commentaries. At first sight of him on my couch my heartbeat raced aloud. His baggy jeans hung low, the belt tight around his hips revealing the top of his boxers. He wore a vertically striped yellow, burgundy, and white button-down, which was left open, revealing his nicely toned chest and abdomen.

The inflation started again. My heart was pumping through my shirt and I feared I would soon float away. Why did he have this effect on me?

Was it his high cheekbones and chiseled jaw line, or the curls in his hair? The high-top fade he used to wear was out of fashion; now it was short around the sides and slightly longer on the top, just enough to see it curl. Very relaxed in the center of my couch he looked up at me. His dimples appeared as his lips parted in a smile. My how I wanted him!

The big balloon filling with each second was obscuring my view. The emotions that arose left me in fear of saying something terribly stupid. I just wanted to jump on top of him, but I didn't have nearly enough nerve for that, so I tried to think of something clever or sexy to say.

"Hello!" I said, disappointing myself. I couldn't believe that was all I could come up with. I would've settled for interesting. I blew my chance with a boring and non-insinuating hello.

"Hey," he said. "I was just watching the game. You don't mind, do you?"

"Of course not. I just got off of work. I need to take a shower." I pointed upstairs.

"Oh, alright. Well, I gotta go somewhere right now anyway," he said as he got up and buttoned his shirt.

"Okay, whatever you got to do!" I deflated my way upstairs. "Just lock me in, would ya?"

That night I decided to go to Amber's house. By then she had two children eighteen months apart. My niece, Alexandria, was two years old at the time, and my nephew, Jason, was just a baby. Because of the dire circumstances surrounding her home life my visits were restricted, but I refused to give up, unlike most others. When Amber's boyfriend left the house I would visit as long as possible. That night her perpetrator was working.

Josh called a couple hours later.

"Hey Shorty, what's going on tonight?"

"I am going up the street. What are you doing?"

"Oh, I got something to do in town."

"Cool. So I will just talk to you later then."

"Oh, okay. Maybe I will come up and check you guys out. Are you going to Danielle's or your sister's?"

"Amber's, and I'm not sure if what's his face is going to be there."

"Okay, I'll check you tomorrow then."

"Bye."

I was determined to keep away from him for a while. Especially knowing he was sleeping with other people it was wise we remained only friends. I could've gone crazy brooding the many possibilities of his plans in town, so I released concern and focused on the kids. The important thing was that we were in two different places.

I left Amber's house and went home at quarter past eleven o'clock. Josh was not at my house. I watched the late show before going to sleep, ending the night without hearing from him.

The following night Josh had to work, so Shonnie watched a movie with me. There was a knock on my door. I peered into the peephole through the kitchen door. The outside light was off as usual so people wouldn't misinterpret it as an invitation and to prevent the nosy neighborhood from seeing who was in and out of my apartment.

I saw a tall, thin, but-broad shouldered male figure slightly hunched in the dark. He had on big untied Timberland boots. His oversized pants were tucked into the tongue of the boot. He was wearing all dark colors, including an extra-large sweatshirt with the hood up. It was too dark to see his face, or even what skin tone he had. And although his silhouette looked like most of the people our age in the area, I knew exactly who it was.

It was John Brown, Josh's prison pal. I had spoken to him over the phone when Josh called me from prison. Although he was a very nice guy, he was about as dumb as a bucket of rocks. I almost felt sorry for him. The only sense John had came from his knowledge of hustling the streets. Unfortunately he wasn't going anywhere else in life, but back and forth from these streets to prison.

"Who is it?" Shonnie whispered.

"It's Brown!"

"Uh-oh, What does that mean, he's looking to start up again with Josh?"

"We'll soon find out." I opened the door and smiled. I held my arms out for a hug and welcomed him right away. "What's up, John?"

"What's up, girl? How are you?" he said as he squeezed me tightly.

"I'm good. Come in." I stepped aside, and shut the door behind him. "When did you get out?"

"I got out this morning. Is Josh around?"

"No," I said slowly. "How would you know to find Josh here?"

"He told me to check him out here when I got out. I didn't mean to bother you."

"Nah, it ain't that. I thought you couldn't have contact with each other when you were inside and he was out, or vice versa." I explained my confusion.

"I haven't spoken to him since before he got out. He told me right before he left to check him out here."

"Really?" I snuck a look of suspicion toward Shonnie. "So what are you doing now?"

"I'm staying at my sister's up the street."

"And?"

"And what?" Brown didn't know where I was going with this so I just came straight out and said my peace.

"And, you gotta stay off the streets, man. Or you know they'll send your ass right back up. You gotta do something with yourself. Get a job. You gonna get a job?"

"Of course. Damn, girl, you sound like my mom and shit!"

"I'm just looking out for you, man. You know how it is. I would hate to see you live in jail for the rest of your life. You're too good for that. You know that, right?" Brown knew he didn't have much potential in the real world. People didn't have any qualms with telling him how stupid he was. I figured the least I could do was give him a compliment once in a while.

"Yeah, so, um, Josh ain't here?"

"No, he's at work. I don't want him getting into any shit either."

"He won't." He opened the door. "All right then. I'm out!" He leaned in and gave me a hug.

I whispered in his ear, "Take care of yourself, okay?"

After shutting the door and habitually locking it I walked back over to receive Shonnie's reaction. She was sitting patiently on the couch with her fingers in her mouth, a terrible childhood habit she still clung on to. I could see her smile form on the corners of her mouth.

"Oh, man!" I said as I backtracked a few steps to grab a beer out of the fridge.

"What does that mean?" she asked.

"I don't know. But I hope he don't get involved with him again. I care about John and all, but he ain't got a chance. Josh does." I sat down and gulped my beer. I lit a cigarette and took a deep drag, leaning back in my "princess chair." "Oh well, let's watch the movie."

When I finally spoke to Josh again it seemed like an eternity had gone by. I asked him about telling Brown to come to my house to see him when he got out. He said, "Our paths always cross." That was the same truth that kept me going. I wanted to talk about the situation at hand, but he kept skirting around the issue. I knew what he was thinking anyway; he felt he couldn't turn away from Brown.

They shared a street bond. It's like following a code of ethics for the street. The consequences of disloyalty can be tragic. Even if not mortally fatal, the results can be mentally devastating, and the reputation that took years to build could be devoured by one word of infidelity. Someone was bound to make you pay for such lack of respect.

Josh was in no position to make any rash decisions. The way his head was so scrambled, I knew whatever he said was subject to change when the time or John Brown presented himself.

All of the "what ifs" were beating heavily into my skull. I could only imagine they were doing the same in Josh's head. What if he runs into Brown and what if Brown wants him to join the old scheme of things? Even if Josh can refrain from dealing again, what if Brown gets into some shit and needs Josh's help? What if, what if, what if … I reckoned Josh and I should rent a movie to distract our minds.

I had some business to take care of before I could relax so Josh went to pick one out at Blockbuster. All of my business mail was set-aside in a wicker flower basket. The process of evaluating my current financial situation started with sorting through the basket of bills every Friday. Before arriving home on payday I stopped at the bank and cashed my check. At home I set aside the money I needed to pay my bills up to date and then immediately stuffed it into one of the envelopes for the next time I went to the convenient store to purchase money orders.

I didn't trust the bank enough to own a checking account and I didn't mind spending the thirty cents for each money order. With a money order the bill was mailed and paid for. Money orders come with a receipt that I attached to each billing invoice I kept filed away in a simple multi-file folder.

A small stash from my check was set aside for a week's worth of cigarettes, liquor, and groceries. I also left myself ten dollars or so extra to rent movies through the week. Then I saw how much money was left and how much I could spend on nightlife. I usually didn't save any money unless I had a specific short-term goal in mind. I couldn't save for my inconceivable future.

When Josh returned from Blockbuster he couldn't hide his excitement. He started rambling on about bumping into his old high-school friends Tyler and Jay, who were looking for another roommate to rent a three-bedroom apartment with. It was a spacious first-floor apartment with hardwood floors throughout and a deck leading out to the side yard. It was located in the center of town away from the projects. There was a six-car driveway of pea stone and a small fenced-in back yard.

The lease was a year-round lease, which was rare in our tourist town. Anything in the city doubled and tripled from May through October. They were lucky to find this place, but they needed another person to live there and split the rent. Tyler explained it all to Josh, hoping he would want in. He told Tyler he had to check with me and see how much he had saved but he was definitely interested.

"And oh, by the way, Tyler said hello!" he managed to fit in. He had his number ready to call and confirm.

I was truly happy for Josh. If he moved in with Tyler and Jay half the risk of getting caught up in the bullshit of the projects would be eliminated. I almost felt guilty for living in the Hill myself and being the cause of his presence in the tempting environment.

In the past few months he'd been out and working he had given me most of his earnings to put aside in hopes we could get an apartment together. He searched for a one-bedroom, but I was trying to be realistic. I was highly skeptical about leaving my home to share one with someone else, rendering myself dependent on the other person's half of the rent. The whole reason I lived in the Hill was because I couldn't afford anywhere else on my own. Josh wasn't exactly a reliable person.

Aside from party and gas money, he only spent his wages on some groceries for my house. Every so often he'd slip me a twenty or so as spending cash. Because Josh was determined to get me out of the Hill he was reluctant to leave me behind.

"I can take care of myself."

"Believe me, NO ONE disputes that."

"Besides I would be spending so much time at your house it would be just like taking me out of here."

"Yeah, yeah. Exactly! Instead of me coming here every day, you can just come to my crib. You're right."

With the funds in order Josh was ready to move in the next day. He called Tyler with the good news. Josh only needed to furnish his room. The ball was rolling smoothly. Things had never been so in order before in his life. It seemed things should've really settled in for us as well.

Josh bought some cigars for the celebration with Shonnie and Rodney. He bought four of them, one for each of us. Aside from the usual choices of Heinekens for the men and Bacardi and juice for the girls, Josh bought a bottle of champagne.

As he passed out the cigars I declined. "The taste of the blunt I had last time was repulsive; there's no way I'm gonna smoke a whole cigar."

"But it's a celebration," Josh insisted.

"I got my cigarettes. I'll pretend. Besides, we have champagne."

Shonnie joined in and took a few puffs, trying her best to hang tough. "Dios mio, I can't smoke this, Josh. It's too nasty. Sorry!"

"Oh, you're a sucker." Josh taunted.

Disappointed in herself she put the cigar out and picked up a cigarette instead.

Josh and Rodney were entertaining each other smoking their cigars like some old professors. They were talking with a poor rendition of an Old English accent sitting upright in their chairs.

"Well, I must say, Sir Rodney, that these are the finest cigars I have had the pleasure of yet." Josh started.

"Yes, Sir Josh, I must concur, the finest yet. And where, pray tell, did you find these superb stogies?"

Shonnie interrupted, "UM, sirs, you shouldn't be inhaling it like that."

"Did you hear something?" Rodney asked.

"Afraid not. As we were saying … Surely, you mustn't tell a soul. For it is a most precious secret." Josh failed as he tried to exhale smoke circles.

After a brief period of silence, Rodney resumed, "You still didn't tell me, sir."

"AND you still are inhaling, dummies!"

"If you are not of English-speaking descent then we please ask that you refrain from this conversation," Rodney requested.

Shonnie began slurring one Spanish derogative after another, maintaining focus on the card game we were playing. She ended with, "Good, I hope you get sick."

The men continued, "Well, I dare say that I am a wee bit hungry now. How about a bowl of scrumptious Cocoa Crispies?"

"Wonderful idea, laddy."

"Indeed." Josh got up and searched the cabinets for bowls as Rodney grabbed the milk from the fridge and the cereal from the cabinet.

"Don't go ransacking my kitchen!" Shonnie yelled at Josh. "Over to the left. Yeah, that one."

"Lo siento, senorita," Josh apologized.

"Take spoons from the strainer," she said.

"Gracias."

"Gracias," she mocked him.

"Mmm, excellent choice," Josh said back in the professor role as he took his first sloppy spoonful of the cereal.

Josh immediately decided to smoke the next cigar.

"Oh I don't know if I can handle another one," Rodney admitted.

"Well, it's quite a nasty combination of milk, beer, champagne, cigars, and cereal!" I said.

Josh forced his smile, "C'mon man, don't be a sucker!"

"Don't do it if you know you're gonna get sick," Shonnie advised, putting her arm around her man.

"You gonna let her tell you what to do? Are you the man or what?" Josh taunted.

"Why you talking like that in my house?" Shonnie asked.

"I'm just playing. But for real, let the man decide if he's man enough."

"Man enough?" Rodney interrupted.

"Only men of the finest caliber will be told the secret of the stogie!" Josh continued in character.

"Whatever, man. Give me the fucking cigar and shut up!"

"Don't do it, Poppy, I'm trying to tell you!"

They lit the cigars and I watched as they held back the nausea trying to impress Shonnie and me.

Rodney wasn't done with the second cigar before he suddenly got up and mumbled, "Ugh, I don't feel too good. I think I'm going to throw up."

Shonnie stood up, "Uh-oh! I see it coming!" Twisted as she was at times she was delightfully anticipating her boyfriend's puke.

Just then Rodney turned around to the kitchen trash barrel behind him and began vomiting.

"Oh man, take that shit upstairs to the toilet!" Josh exclaimed. "You're gonna make me sick!"

As Shonnie practically dragged Rodney upstairs to the bathroom I called out, "We're out of here, girl, I'll check you out tomorrow."

"Okay," she hollered back.

Back at my house I went straight upstairs to my room and shut the door. I changed into my nightclothes. I figured Josh was doing the same, until I heard him heaving in the bathroom. I opened my door and saw Josh leaning over the toilet. I couldn't help but chuckle to myself as I ran downstairs to the phone, excited to exploit his moment of weakness.

"Hello?" she answered.

"Guess what Josh is doing?" I said into the cordless phone as I walked back upstairs.

"Oh, no! Not him too!"

"Oh yeah! He is hugging the porcelain god."

"Listen, listen, can you hear Rodney? He's still going at it. I tried to tell him he shouldn't have inhaled the smoke." Addressing Rodney she said, "But you didn't want to listen. Did ya?"

After we got in a triumphant laugh I regained my composure and said, "Okay. Let me go so I can help him. I'll talk to you tomorrow."

I ran back downstairs to hang the phone up and went to the kitchen for a glass of ice water to bring upstairs to my handsome hurling guest. I had to step over him to rest at the edge of the tub.

"Where do you want me to put this?" I asked as I held the glass up.

"Right here is fine." He motioned toward the floor. I stood over him and rubbed his back. When he took his head out of the toilet and sat back against the wall, I wet a washcloth and placed it on his forehead.

"You okay?" I asked.

"Yeah, I think I'm good now. Thank you."

"Be glad I cleaned the toilet today after work."

"You're the best."

"Well, if you don't need me I'm gonna go to bed now."

Chapter Seven

"Inferiority Complex Over Rules"

The city in which I live has such a motley crew of residents. The more financially stable people live near the high school. On the other end of Newport is the low-income housing section. This area is located near the border of Newport's only abutting neighbor, Middletown. There are five different apartment complexes that are subsidized rentals. The Hill was the most dangerous, had the most drug traffic, and sheltered the youngest mothers, the poorest people, and the most thuggish young men on Aquidneck Island. The population was predominantly black in the Hill, with Caucasians holding the second-largest percentage and a rapidly growing Spanish-speaking population.

In between the two sections of Newport are the average middle-class Joes and Janes. There was a time in our adolescence when Josh and I were a part of that population. His mother and stepfather were renting an apartment in a three-family house. He was about to once again be a part of the working middle-class men of the city, and I was proud of him for that.

There is only one high school in Newport. Growing up in the midst of such diversity was greatly beneficial. As youngsters we chose our friends based on how well we got along with each other trusting in our hearts, as only children know how.

Josh and Tyler became good friends in junior high school. Josh fell victim to feelings of inferiority during his high-school years due to the lack of attention he was getting at home. Once Josh's mother remarried, he was pushed aside. There is only so much a child can endure after being abandoned by one parent. Josh's father had left him and his mother so many years ago.

Now he had the opportunity to find himself again. He needed to let go of the low self-esteem issues and focus on being the best he could be. I had faith in him.

Mirror

Look in the glass
Reflection of flesh
Shows reality
Of which I hate
Look at my hand
Clench a fist
Smash the looking glass
Broken pieces
Reflect from the floor
I see the flesh
Nothing's changed
Reality remains

Josh and I were hanging with quite a different crowd. Tyler and Jay were part of that middle class we went to school with. We were all friends then, and we were about to rekindle that friendship. Collectively we were young adults with the same basic agenda, to find our way in this life God had given us.

Every February I tried applying for financial aid for college and every March I received the same response: denied. It would be years before I was twenty-three and they would discount my parent's income, but all I could do was apply. I was frustrated with feeling cheated. These people who were deciding my fate had no real information about *me*.

I settled for my housekeeping job. It was a fast-paced workout, which kept me afloat, if nothing else. It also allotted me plenty of playtime. Cleaning rooms doesn't take an ounce of brainpower. I could go to work as hung over as I liked and still manage.

Josh was making nearly twice as much money as I was. He had a beautiful apartment that he shared with dependable people working just as hard. Although he was on probation, I felt like he had more freedom than I did. I was so disheartened with not being able to attend college. If I weren't able to gain a degree, who would I become? And what was I to do in the meantime? I had no other view of my life after high school, so my way was completely blinded to me. My life lacked meaning, and I was desperate to find it.

There is no respect in the housekeeping department. The guests sure as hell don't respect you. The employers don't have respect for you, as they do a terrible job in pretending they do. The other departments don't even respect you. The housekeeping department is on the bottom rung of the hotel business ladder, and I was at that bottom of housekeeping. I lived in the dirtiest project in the city. I was all alone and beginning to fall victim to my own inferiority complex unbeknownst to any one around me or even myself.

God was always a positive influence in my life. My family was active in the same Catholic parish since we moved here. I tried to hide the hurt of our family breakup praying for God's help. I prayed for Him to help my father win his struggle with alcohol. I prayed for Him to help my sister get out of her abuse. I prayed for my mother's acceptance. I prayed for others so that they would not be jealous, secretly harboring ill feelings towards me. I felt neglected by Him. I couldn't figure out why He ignored me. I must have deserved it somehow.

If my father had abandoned me and my mother had thrown me to the wolves and my family was no longer a support system I could turn to, then I only had myself to rely on. God was playing an awful joke on me. Not only did I lose my faith but I also didn't trust the God I used to believe in. Either He was capable of evil just as everything else in life, or He really didn't exist. What God would allow innocent children to endure such tragedy well worse than my own, anyway?

Besides, why do we have to thank God for all the good in our lives, but take full responsibility for the wrong? If I have to take the responsibility for the wrong, I am damn sure going to take the credit for the good, as limited as it was. I left it at that for years.

Tyler and Jay didn't seem to mind my frequent visits. On the contrary, they rather enjoyed my company. I was drinking with them the majority of the week. My friend Casey was hanging out at Josh's house, too. She and Jay were new sweethearts.

Casey was a tall, thin blonde with blue eyes. Her hair was kept short above her shoulders. In between 5'8" and 5'9" she had more than five inches on me. She didn't embellish in makeup and wore Gap clothing. I favored Express clothing and liked to use black eyeliner and mascara with espresso lipstick. She had an athletic body and played basketball in high school, a game in which I have absolutely no skill. I could dance all night long and Casey would rather mingle and chat with everyone. Her favorite movie was *Grease* and mine was *The Godfather*. Our taste in men differed tremendously. This was a girl who found Dave Letterman sexy. That, I would never understand!

It didn't take long before the word spread through the small city that Tyler, Jay, and Josh had their new place. It turned into quite the party house. Since the three occupants were respectable people in our peer group, there was not much disorder. It was great to have a place to go to where I could get drunk and not have to worry about getting jumped or plan ahead for the best evacuation route.

Tyler was Josh's closest friend. He was a five-foot-seven black kid with golden brown eyes. Tyler was a metro sexual, very particular about the way he dressed. He was a handsome guy with a complex about his height and spent at least an hour every day at the gym. He hoped what he built in muscle could make up for what he lacked in height.

He was the least judgmental person I knew beside myself. Tyler and Casey were my only confidants. Still, they received selected information. They knew me as well as I would allow one to know me. I was an enigma to the rest of the world.

"So Reba it's great to have you around again. I forgot how fun you were." Tyler put his arm around my shoulder. "Well, if I forgot, then maybe you're not really that fun. Maybe I am just drunk!"

"Very funny. I know how you feel about me. There's no denying it! But your secret is safe with me, I won't tell all your hoes." I took his arm off of me.

"Ah, so how long have you and Josh been together?"

"We're not and he hasn't even been out a year yet."

"Well yeah, but you guys were doing your thing in high school weren't you?" He searched for an answer in my eyes.

I turned my head from him a minute, regretting the situation. I hated feeling so deeply for Josh, but not being able to trust him. It was an odd concept. It was a tough fight to suppress my adoration for him. As far as he was concerned I was on his list of abandoners. And he was on the list of people who had neglected my heart. We desperately wanted each other, but we didn't know how to make it work.

"C'mon, it's me. You guys think you're fooling everybody, but you're only fooling yourselves."

"Nah, we're fooling everyone *including* ourselves, just maybe not you. But whatever with that, what about you? Where's your queen?"

"Who needs a queen to share the throne with? I'd rather have it all to myself."

"Now you're talking!"

"So what's up? Summer's over so where's your color? I thought you said you could get tanned. 'Cause right now it hurts my eyes just looking at you gleaming like that." Tyler makes himself laugh every time with the pale jokes.

"That's not my reflection that's hurting your eyes; it's all that muscle going straight to your head!"

"Touché!" he said as he moseyed over to the group of girls who had just arrived. I stayed at the island with Jay and Casey in the kitchen.

"Damn, there are so many randoms here, man! How can you stand all these people in your house?" I was consuming some mixed drinks Jay was concocting for Casey and me almost faster than he could make them.

"It makes things more interesting. It doesn't really bother me—they're not getting any of these!"

"That's because Reba's drinking them all!" Casey exclaimed.

"Sorry, he keeps making me more. Am I gonna let them go to waste? I don't think so!"

"Besides we just kick everybody out whenever we feel like it. Josh and Ty don't fuck around. When someone wants to chill we all agree the party's over. Why you got a problem with my house?"

"It's not my house. There's no way you'd catch this many randoms in my house."

"You know we don't mind. As long as we're drinking!" Casey added.

"I'm just fuckin with Reba. Everyone knows she don't like all those kids from school."

"Seriously man, look at that hoochie Tyler's kicking it to. What is *that* all about?"

"Now you know Tyler has low standards. He don't care what the bitch acts like. If she looks good enough he'll fuck her." Casey said.

Jay laughed in agreement, spitting a little of his drink.

"I'm gonna have to have a talk with him later."

"Reba don't go cock blockin'. Where's Josh? I'll get him to occupy you."

"I said LATER. Don't you guys care that you could get some nasty disease?"

"That's what condoms are for," Jay replied.

"They make pills for people like Tyler. Why you acting like you don't know what a man-whore he is?" Casey could have cared less about other people's problems.

"I don't know. I think it's nasty."

"So do I, but he ain't my man!"

Jay stopped making the drinks, and I was thirsty for more. He was suddenly more interested in fondling Casey. "What? Are you done making those yummy drinks?"

"Yeah, I can't keep up with you. You got your Molsons, don't you?"

Along the way, I had acquired the taste for beer. The fact that it was a lot more affordable than liquor played a major role in my change of heart. Molson Ice was my choice. It has a higher alcohol content percentage by volume then domestic beers, which I appreciated along with the distinct taste.

"Alright, I guess I'll go join that card table over there. You two look like you're about to get frisky. My virgin eyes can't handle all that affection." The comment made everyone chuckle a bit, and then as I tried to get up off the stool I slipped on someone's jacket, falling flat on my butt. Casey and Jay laughed hysterically, and so did the random walking towards me with his hand out. I thought he was pointing in my face, so I lunged forward, punching him in the gut, which made Casey and Jay laugh even more.

"What did you do that for?" he asked. "I was just trying to help you up."

"Oh, sorry then," I said, lacking sincerity.

I joined in a laughing sigh, leaving my present company. Just as I sat at the table they were starting a new game of Rummy. Josh ran over and sat next to me.

"Hey, where have you been?" he asked.

"Jay was making some mixed drinks for me and Casey. But then they got all entwined so I came here. What were you doing?"

"I was outside with some of the fellas. But then I saw you, so here I am." He beamed at me. "Actually, I came in to take a piss. Can you save my seat for me?"

"Sure!"

I was delighted with his enthusiasm to be near me. During the card session the room began spinning. I noticed that the randoms were finally filtering out. I wanted to be able to chill in a quieter atmosphere with my friends. I tried to control my mind, but it was no use.

Josh carried me to his room and laid me on his bed. The room was spinning so fast I couldn't keep up.

"What can I get you?" he asked.

I just apologized over and over for various things like drinking too much, taking up his bed, and not hanging longer. He was nothing short of kind and sensitive to me. He was caring for me, and I was secretly in need of a caregiver.

I woke up the next morning fully dressed. I turned over, surprised to see Josh sleeping in a sliver of the bed available. Instead of moving me he took whatever amount of room he could get. He could've pushed me to the floor, and in my drunken stupor I would've never known. He could've lied and said that's where I passed out, or that I rolled off myself. He didn't.

He was so still next to me. I was slightly embarrassed at not being able to make it through the night. I was ashamed for getting so drunk and not being in control of myself. I tried to softly and quietly slip off the bed without waking him, but I heard his groggy voice exclaim, "Hey, sleepyhead!"

I turned around to see him propped up on his elbows. He, too, was fully dressed. "I'm sorry I took up your whole bed last night!" I said meekly.

"It's alright," he said with a giggle. "I would say I enjoyed sleeping with you, but with your snoring it was hard for me to fall asleep at first."

I let my chin drop to my chest. Here I stood before Josh again giving him the opportunity to crush me. Why did I put myself in such compromising positions?

"It was cute though. Don't be embarrassed. I snore louder than that, I think! Are you hungry? Let's get something to eat," he said.

I still couldn't find it in myself to speak yet. Was he expressing true sincerity and sensitivity? Josh had the perfect moment to make a fool of me, yet he forfeited. I must still be dreaming.

He got up and walked towards me. "What do you want to eat?" he asked as he opened his bedroom door.

"Uh, I'm not hungry," I managed with a dry, sore throat. "I could go for a tall glass of water." After a quick look around the bedroom I added, "do you to know where my purse is? I need my toothbrush." I carried around a spare toothbrush and a travel-size tube of toothpaste. Consistent oral hygiene was a habit of mine, since I hated that stale taste from smoking cigarettes.

"Oh, yeah. Your girl, Casey, called last night after she left. She said she got it in her car," he said as he handed me my water. "You can use mine if you want." He gave me a quick glance and a smirk. I didn't know if he was serious or not, but I had to pee anyway, so I went to the bathroom. I tried using my finger with their toothpaste but it wasn't successful in getting rid of the grit on my teeth. "How do people do that?"

"Hey, Josh, can I really use yours?" I asked through a crack of the bathroom door.

"Yeah, it's the blue one."

I shut the door again and splashed my face with cold water. I picked up the blue toothbrush and studied it, making sure no food particles were stuck. I washed his toothbrush with soap before brushing then again before returning it to its place. I tried using my fingers to brush through my hair. I did the best I could before I realized there was nothing more I could do for myself.

I went back to the island in the kitchen that separated it from the dining area. They had three tall stools behind the island. I sat on the same one I occupied the previous night drinking my ice-cold water.

"How do you feel?" he asked.

"I'm doing good now that I brushed my teeth and rinsed off my face," I replied.

"Nah ah, why is your head down?" When he was done making his instant coffee, he turned the kitchen light off. "You're hanging hard, huh?"

"Well, of course I'm hung over, but I'm used to that. I can handle it. You got any ibuprofen?" I was more afraid of what he would think of me without my makeup on and hair all mangled.

He shook his head no as he lit a cigarette and handed it to me. "Are these mine or yours?" I asked. We both smoked Newport.

"Mine, I think." He showed me the box.

"Mine must have gotten jacked. Well, I'm gonna go home now. Thank you for the bed and the water and cigarette," I said as I stood up. My keys were still in my pocket. I could feel them digging into my hip upon awakening.

"Hold on, Shorty, I'll give you a ride home. Can I finish my coffee?" he said.

"Yeah, you don't mind? I didn't know if you had to work or not," I excused my abruptness.

"Not 'til eleven." It was nine o'clock in the morning. I assumed Tyler and Jay were already at work. "I work 'til nine tonight. I got a ten-hour shift today."

"Ugh, sucks to be you."

We were finally ready to go. Josh drank his coffee quickly; he did everything quickly. On the way home he pulled into the Cumberland Farms parking lot. We both got out of the van and went inside. He bought two packs of Newport and handed one to me. "I know you'll be needing these today." He smiled.

I adored that Cheshire smile, so sweet and innocent. Maybe it was because he had dimples, or maybe it was because his whole face lit up. He harbored such sorrow behind his eyes that almost seemed to fade when he smiled.

The following night Josh came over to my house for a nice change of pace. I made Blue Whales with rum, Blue Curacao, and pineapple juice. Josh and I sat on my couch together for hours.

As the night progressed I became entranced in his every move. The way he got up abruptly in telling an exciting story, the way he tapped my arm or leg to make sure he had my full and undivided attention, the way he giggled at his own words made me feel as though there was no one else for me. I especially liked it when we were engaged in a serious conversation and he was just as attentive and participating as when he told a tale.

There were no interruptions in our time together. Josh was facing me on the couch and moved closer to grab my hand. Up until then my heart was pumping up against my sternum, making its presence known but undetectable to anyone outside. He studied my hand a moment before gently pulling me towards him. Overwhelmed by my own emotion I dared not look up into his eyes.

Josh and I kissed again for the first time in such a long time. It was like I had never kissed him before. Romance filled the air with dim lights and scented candles. When I reached up to caress his face I noticed my awkward inflating heart once again getting in between us.

As the kissing grew hotter and heavier I knew where it was headed. My apprehension prevented the rising obstacle from lifting me into the air. I didn't know what I wanted or what to expect. Our romantic history was a horror story that filled my head with subtle reminders, but my heart was fervently telling me to go for it. We were two broken souls who deserved a chance, so I agreed to cease the fight, but not without drinking a considerable amount more to take the edge off my jitters.

With a glimmering virtue surrounding his being he led me upstairs confidently. His outstretched hand reached into my core with deepest sensitivity. We began to float harmoniously.

Suspended in midair, I was praying he wouldn't let me down. My twin bed, which once was part of the bunk bed I shared with Amber so many years ago, waited beneath our lusting bodies. His words were as gentle as his touch. He poured his love onto me with silken drops awakening my senses. Kisses gave a proper re-introduction to my femininity. I was wrapped in satiny smooth finesse carefully escorted to a kingdom on cloud nine. With our bodies entwined, floating in a realm where time didn't exist, we made love for the first time.

The last thing he said to me before we fell asleep was those dreamy three words, "I love you." As usual, I held back a response. Fortunately, he was used to that. It didn't spoil the moment. I had sweet dreams that night and for countless nights to follow.

Chapter Eight

"Relates My Haunted Soul"

Halloween was approaching. It was my favorite holiday. The costumes, the secret identity, the suspense were all so intriguing to me. As a child I was petrified of vampires. I slept with a small blanket wrapped around my neck. When my mother decided I was too old for a baby blanket I had to turn to floppy stuffed animals for neck protection while I slept. I had a barricade of stuffed animals along the perimeter of my bed. My mother used to refer to them as the tea party.

One October when I was the age of eight or so, my parents took my sisters and me to a haunted house. Inside the abandoned building was a bunch of rooms decorated in gory and ghastly scenes. Each room had its own theme. A group of ten individuals was escorted by the grim reaper through a dark corridor and a new door to a separate haunting scene. Some of the attractions featured live ghouls and goblins that rehearsed a skit.

After exiting a pitch-black passageway, we were led into a room with a strobe light on a single coffin. The coffin was plain looking and standing upright. There was a pause from the crowd as we patiently awaited the grim reaper's gesture to continue on.

Suddenly out from the coffin jumped Dracula. I was horrified. My parents immediately began to whisper soothing words to me because they knew how I felt about vampires. I tried inching toward the exit, but the group didn't budge. I was left centered in the front row. Dracula pranced around mysteriously through the strobe-lit room. He frightened a few onlookers before running up to me. My tempting blood stopped pumping through my veins. But nonetheless he reached for me and swooped me under his flowing cape. With one swing of his arm he kidnapped me and brought me into the coffin with him. Dracula shut the door to the coffin.

At that point I don't believe I was breathing. I was scared stiff. I suspected I went deaf and blind, too, but maybe that was just the total darkness hindering my sight. I stood there heavily concentrating; listening for a heartbeat, mine in particular. In the movies the audience hears the victim's heartbeat grow louder and louder before the inevitable fatal bite on the neck. I tried to use psychic powers to produce an impenetrable shield to cover my neck.

I listened carefully. Finally I heard something, but it wasn't my heartbeat. It was a man's voice, and it came from behind me. It was almost in a whisper. The sound was so comforting I tuned in to listen to the message.

"Don't be scared. I won't hurt you. This is all a part of the show. If you can wait in here with me for a few minutes we can scare the crowd together. Then we will come out, and I promise your parents will be waiting right there."

The man didn't touch me. Not even so much as a comforting squeeze of the shoulder. But I had watched way too many horror films on vampires to be at ease. Dracula is known to have a hypnotic way about him. The grim reaper must be in on the trick I reckoned, and when the coffin opened the room would be empty. I was wondering what my parents would be doing without me as I was left to fend for myself.

This time Dracula was true to his word. In what seemed like ten minutes but was actually thirty seconds, the coffin door opened. I saw the same crowd I had been traveling with through the maze of haunting rooms. Still untrusting, I didn't dismiss the idea that they were turned into zombies or possibly something worse. It was then that Dracula finally touched my shoulders from behind to urge me on back to my family. My parents gave me a warm welcome with open arms. They were concerned with how I took the whole experience. That was when I knew things were as Dracula had said they'd be.

I turned to look at him one more time. Even as he was still in character he managed a sincere smile, thus the end of my Dracula phobia and the beginning of a vampire infatuation.

Relates My Haunted Soul

Complex silk web on the wall
Spiders feeding never fall
Relates my haunted soul
I, Black Widow, could kill all

Creatures of the night evil hissed
Vagabonds dancing in the midst
Relates my haunted soul
Because the devil has been kissed

Of immortals dreadful sounds
High shrieks of blood hungry hounds
Relates my haunted soul
Exit gate of hell it pounds

A crow in the graveyard cries
Tombstone to tombstone it flies
Relates my haunted soul
Because in time it's told lies

Ebony sky's daemonic cast
Shadows befriending the feared past
Relates my haunted soul
Hoping now it has seen the last

Miles of jack-o-lanterns remind
Flaming fire in the night behind
Relates my haunted soul
That blinding fire was so unkind

A full moon hangs laughing aloud
Thunder rolling over a cloud
Relates my haunted soul
Trying desperately to stand proud

Dry dead leaves blowing in the wind
Cool, crisp air when the door's opened
Relates my haunted soul
Because in this life it has sinned

The fellas were planning an extravagant Halloween bash at their house. They were serving alcoholic Halloween punches and so charged admission. Casey and I helped with the plans and decorating and were therefore exempt from paying. I donated some of my Halloween decorations and music as well. I had fun with the preparation. Casey drove back and forth all day from the grocery store to the liquor store to the party shop. Wherever anybody needed to go she was ready to drive.

Tyler, Josh, and Jay decided to dress as mobsters. Casey dressed as Raggedy Ann. I was a sexy vampire. The vampire teeth I had didn't stay in my mouth for very long. Big Dawg Jake borrowed them from me because he was a vampire also.

Although not very tall, at around five feet nine inches, Big Dawg was a stocky kid, slightly overweight with a raspy voice. He and his brother, Jay, were like night and day. He didn't put too much thought or time into getting dressed. He lacked any skill in sweet-talking a lady, but it wasn't something he aspired to obtain. He had a tough time understanding and therefore connecting with females. Big Dawg was the one who initiated me into their group of men. I became "Skirt Dog." This way I was more like a guy, making his connection with me more logical.

Tyler came up behind me once the house was decorated and people started filing in. "I don't know if it's the dark makeup or what but you are looking awfully pale tonight."

"Actually, Tyler, tonight I will take that as a compliment!"

"You didn't? Did you?" He smeared my cheek with two fingers.

"Don't rub it off Ty!" I moved back.

"Oh my goodness. Why would someone as pale as you even waste your time putting white makeup on?"

"It's just powder, fuck head!"

"Somehow you still look good though. Mm mm! Only you, girl!"

"No, don't try to make up for it now. Go on. Go find some slut with her coochie wide open!" I pushed his muscular arm away from me.

"Girls aren't even supposed to talk like that."

"I'm special."

Tyler was walking away from me and said, "I'll give you that," pointing at me.

Just then, my mobster came to my side. He had a drink in one hand and my waist in his other.

"Hey, sexy!" His touch sent chills all over my body. My black attire faded to red as I was in lust city.

"Hey, sexy, yourself! Is that a piece in your pocket or are you just happy to see me?"

"Both, Shorty! Dance with me?"

There was an unbelievable amount of people at the house. Josh and I designated the dance floor. Others quickly joined us.

"What was Tyler bothering you about?" His nonchalance didn't fool me.

"Oh nothing. He thinks it's funny to crack jokes on how white I am."

Josh laughed in relief, "Well, you are pretty white."

"Yeah, yeah."

"I'm just playing. Why don't you let me see what you're working with underneath that cape?"

"Well I would, but you know someone will jack it in an instant. You're just gonna have to use your imagination for now!"

He freed his hand to occupy both of my hips. His gaze was fixed on my figure and I made it worth his while to keep watching. He sucked his bottom lip and I knew I had him where I wanted him. Like a magnet his pelvis was attracted to mine. The physical connection was seductive as our bodies swayed to the same rhythm of our hearts pounding through our chests. But the love connection was too overwhelming.

I broke away from him to circle him seductively, reaching for something to get me through this heated moment. Magically it came to me, thin and flowing. I was uncertain if it was enough for the confidence to face him again. Big Dawg intervened.

"Hey, Skirt Dog, can I get a stogie?"

"Sure, what do I get in return?"

"What?"

"Show me your moves!"

"You're crazy—I don't dance!"

"C'mon, I can teach you a little something, something!"

"Sure can, Shorty, but I don't think he's so willing." Josh said.

"Yeah man, save that shit for your lover boy here. Hook me up!"

"First my teeth, now my cigarettes …" I gave Big Dawg a cigarette from my gargoyle purse strapped across my torso.

"You want your teeth back?" He took them out of his mouth and sucked off the spit.

"Ill, no thanks! Besides, they fit you better. I can't drink or smoke with them in."

"Sweet!" Big Dawg put them back in and lit the cigarette with ease. "See ya!"

I intentionally lost my partner in the crowd. There was an abundance of beer and liquor at the party. The upstairs neighbors were informed of the party and allowed to attend for free. They spent most of their time on the stairwell out of the mainstream. Although they were exceptionally different from my group of friends, there wasn't a group that didn't fit in with the diversity of the attendants that night.

When Joe showed up he was loud and obnoxious from the beginning. He brought fireworks, unbeknownst to the hosts. When a show of lights caught Tyler's eye through the front window, he ran to Jay and Josh. Together they ventured outside to see what the lights were. Joe was being irresponsible, not watching who might be in the path of the rockets he had.

"Joe man, what the fuck are you doing?" Josh asked.

"This is my contribution to the festivities," Joe said, joyously throwing his hands out to the side.

"I don't think that's really a great idea," Tyler added. "We are trying to keep a low profile here. We don't want the cops to show up."

"Joe, we can't have that shit. I can't have any problems, man, for real. I'm on probation and you're out here acting like you ain't."

"All right man. I'll chill."

Joe's appearance was scary. He was six feet tall and beefy. His belly hung over his pants, but he dressed in big shirts so it wasn't noticeable. His fat stubby fingers were rough like his hands, which he used aggressively. He had light blue eyes covered with thick eyebrows. He had a harsh face with a large nose and a sandy goatee surrounding his small, tight mouth. Just released from prison a few weeks prior, his head was shaved.

Joe was incarcerated for assault charges. He suddenly was up for parole and out six months earlier than he was supposed to. The rest of the crew thought that kind of odd. When they questioned Joe about it he fabricated an explanation of good behavior. Knowing Joe and his temper, most doubted the veracity of his story.

"Did you guys know your boy is passed out on the deck?" I asked.

"Who?" Tyler and Josh said simultaneously.

"I'll give you one good guess."

"I know who," Joe said. "I'll go get him."

"Craig?" Asked Jay.

"You know it."

We followed Joe leading to the side deck. People were talking, laughing, and drinking all around Craig, who had fallen off the lounge chair.

"Help me pick his ass up," Joe said after he was unsuccessful in waking his buddy. "You got a blanket or something? We should just let him sleep it off."

Jay got a blanket and they left him propped in the chair.

Craig was an alcoholic. He was a friendly soft-spoken guy with an extremely mild manner. He was the type of person who was hard to get to really know, showing little emotion and never voicing his opinion. With all the alcohol he drank it never once changed his pleasant, rather quiet disposition. I think most of us secretly felt sorry for him. Craig looked like your average All-American young man, with brown hair parted on one side, brown eyes with a hint of sorrow, an average build, and average height. There wasn't a single thing that stuck out and grabbed your attention about him.

I met up with Casey, who dragged me into Jay's room. Big Dawg and Jay were inside with a few randoms preparing a large bong. I had never seen one so big before. It stood three feet off the floor. The potheads before me were in heaven.

"What are we doing here?" I whispered in her ear.

"I wanna try it. Do you think I should?"

"You know 'me … but, do what you want, if you don't mind looking like a fiend! That fucking thing is HUGE!"

We watched closely as the owner took the first hit. I was impressed at the amount of smoke inhaled. He didn't even choke.

He finally exhaled, gesturing to Jay, "Dude, try it out."

Jay took a deep breath of fresh air before positioning himself in front of the bong. He took a smaller hit than the other kid but didn't choke either. The next guy who took a hit, choked, and coughed out a lot of smoke. For that he was not only humiliated but also scolded for wasting it. After watching a few more someone asked me, "Are you gonna try?"

"Oh, no thanks. I am all set." I looked at Casey standing next to me with a grin on her face. "You going for it?"

"Okay!"

Casey took a hit bigger than she could handle. She choked and coughed also but did not receive a scorned reaction from the crowd. Instead they showed concern and invited her to try again. She declined, thanking them all the same.

As soon as we left the room we noticed some commotion from Tyler and Josh's direction. The expression on their faces revealed that something wasn't right. Casey went back in to summon Jay and I went towards Josh.

A girl had run in screaming about her eye. Tyler tended to the girl as Josh set out to find the source of her pain. Apparently, Joe wasn't done with his fun. A piece of debris from his fireworks had flown into her eye. After hearing the news Josh went outside with Jay and Tyler right behind him.

All heads turned in the direction of Joe, who was seen walking up the street toward the house. Behind him a patrol car drove past along the adjacent street.

"What's up, dude?" Josh called out.

"Nothing, man. I was trying to light some sparks to make the street pretty," Joe said sarcastically.

"Are you trying to get us in trouble? Seriously!" Tyler asked.

"Lighten up, guys. It's a great party. Everyone is having fun. Chill the fuck out. You're the only ones who don't appreciate my contribution."

"What about home girl with that shit stuck in her eye?" Tyler said.

"I told that whiny bitch to stand back. She's the one out here all drunk and stupid. It's just a little piece of paper, man. She's fine."

I interjected, "Joe, please, I don't want any attention brought to the house. I don't want to go to jail. I just want to have fun. Could you just refrain from displaying your fireworks for tonight?"

"Yeah, Reba, I can. I'll stop if you promise to come see them with me tomorrow night." Joe turned to Tyler. "See, you fuck heads. All you had to do was ask nicely!"

"NICELY?" Josh spoke out.

"Sure, just not tonight, not here, okay?" I interrupted, rubbing Josh's back.

Tyler and Jay were mumbling slurs about Joe's behavior as they apprehensively walked away. I just wanted to keep the peace. I went over to Joe and put my arm around his shoulder. "Are you gonna stay?"

"Yeah, of course. These guys don't bother me. Besides I gotta wait for Craig to wake up. I ain't leaving him here like that."

"Alright. Well, let's go play cards or something."

"Who the hell is in there anyway? They got bunch of suckas at this party man. I ain't playing with a bunch of pussies."

"I hear ya! Josh has a separate deck we can use if we don't like the game or the company. But I ain't gonna let none of these fools stop me from playing. Ya feel me?"

"I feel you!"

Joe and I took over the dining room table card game. The girl who had gotten the paper in her eye walked by.

"Are you alright, sweetheart?" Joe asked.

"Yeah, I'm fine. It was just a little piece but I freaked 'cause I thought it was still lit."

"I told you you'd be fine. You almost got me into trouble!"

"I almost got you in trouble?" She grew agitated.

"No, nobody's in trouble. We're just happy you're okay. Right Joe?"

"Yeah, whatever she says."

The girl stood there staring at us.

"Go on girl, have fun. It's all good!" I ushered her off.

Soon after we saw Craig walking through the slider from the deck.

"There you are!" I greeted.

"Back from the dead or looking for a more comfortable bed?" Joe asked.

"Sorry, 'bout that. Nah, I'm good now. I just puked off the side. Got any beers?"

Joe whispered to Craig where he had hidden his stash, and minutes later Craig was back with his Natty Lights ready to join in the card game.

There was no particular end to the party. People left at their will, and some didn't. Some were still partying at six in the morning. Others were comatose on lounge chairs on the front porch and side deck. Some had passed out at various locations.

There were no noise complaints and there was plenty of liquor and great music, the costumes were impressive, and overall it was a huge success. With the many, many attendants it was amazing that there was neither a fight nor a serious altercation. That Halloween party would go down in history as the best party in town.

Naturally, there were a few people who claimed the couches as their bed for the night. Joe was among that group. He had woken up the same time Josh and I did.

Tyler went downstairs to the basement. He called us down to wake up and embarrass the group of people passed out on the cold basement floor. Big Dawg was closest to the stairs, so I was a bit hesitant to make them feel completely foolish.

He woke up first. "What the hell are all you assholes staring at?"

"What happened to you?" Tyler asked.

Big Dawg took a gander at his surroundings to jump-start his memory. "I bumped my head. What does it look like?"

"It looks like you passed out on the basement floor to me, man!" Josh said.

"Are you all just gonna stand there or is someone gonna help me up?"

Tyler and Josh assisted him to a standing position. Big Dawg was unstable, and he leaned up against the wall to gain his bearings.

"Damn that's one big egg on your head!"

"I fucking told you I hit my head when I was trying to run upstairs. What time is it anyway?"

"Like eight, or something," I said. "I'll get you some ice."

The commotion awoke the others. One by one they said their thanks and goodbyes before filing out the door. Then Josh, Joe, and Tyler helped Big Dawg up to the kitchen. I handed him a glass of water, a bag of ice, and some ibuprofen I always had in my purse.

"Thanks, Reba."

"So how does that explain the pink underpants by your head?" Someone asked, instigating the ridicule. Laughter rang out, waking Jay and Casey.

But Big Dawg had no rebuttal. His eyes were as unsteady as his stance. We concluded that it was best for him to get checked out. Casey volunteered to drop him at the ER three blocks away. Jay went with her to help his brother walk. The rest of us discussed our own interpretation of the night over tall glasses of water or beer and some cigarettes. Then we decided there was no time like the present to start cleaning up. Casey and Jay returned just in time for the process. Joe snuck out.

Chapter Nine

"Weakness is Synonymous with Love"

After Halloween, I was surprised to find that the gatherings at Josh's house hadn't simmered down; instead they continued during the week and roared over the weekends. If Tyler, Josh, and Jay weren't hosting the festivities, Craig and Joe were. By nightfall I was at either house, or at Casey's getting ready to go.

When Josh was at work it didn't stop me from going to his house. And even though the fellas shared their male-bonded friendship, I felt comfortable enough going to Joe and Craig's with or without Josh, with or without Casey.

One night I went over to Josh's house midweek. With only a six-pack each we decided to make it a movie night. I supplied the flick.

Jay and Casey were not speaking to one another since their insignificant drunken tiff over the weekend. When Jay saw me he thought it best that he go to Craig and Joe's to avoid running into Casey.

Ten minutes into the movie there was a knock at the front door and Kevin popped his head in. Tyler pushed the stop button on the remote.

Kevin and I were only barely acquaintances from high school, but I was quite attracted to him, even as we got older. Dan followed behind him, and I let out a sigh of disapproval. Josh, Tyler, Big Dawg, and I were watching the movie peacefully until Dan walked in the door. Since it was a laid-back night with no one around I stored my beer in the fridge.

When Kevin and Dan showed up with a couple of six-packs I immediately took notice that neither was holding Molson. At ease, I left my stash in the fridge, but concluded that if anyone else showed up I wouldn't be able to keep track of everybody's hands and would be forced to guard them by my side as usual.

All the males in the room slapped hands with the new arrivals as they made their way around the coffee table to settle in. As Kevin passed me he smiled flirtatiously. Fortunately, Dan struck up a conversation with Josh at the same time so he didn't notice.

"What ya'll doing?" Kevin asked as he plopped down on the couch next to me.

"Watching a movie, chillin'," said Josh.

"Oh yeah? Which movie?"

"*The Crow*," I answered.

"Ain't that the movie that dude died making?" Dan chimed in.

"Yeah, Brandon Lee," I said in monotone. That fact bothered me. Brandon Lee was a young attractive actor. It was a tragedy that he died during the making of the film. His character in *The Crow* intrigued me. The man's love for his fiancée was so magnificent that nothing could kill it. He comes back from the dead in the film to avenge her horrible death. There was nothing weak about that kind of love. I wondered if it really existed that way.

"No way," Kevin said. "How'd that happen?"

"I heard it was a scene when there was a lot of shooting and something about the gun being too close to him. I don't think there was a real bullet, but they didn't know right away. After the shooting was over he didn't get up. They had to finish a few last scenes with a look-alike." Amber told me something about it once. I wished I had paid more attention when she was telling me. "Now be quiet so we can watch it!" I demanded.

"Oh, I didn't know it was still on. My bad! This looks like a Coke commercial to me." Dan was trying to be cool as usual.

"Whatever, man, we put it on hold when you clowns came in."

"Clowns?" Kevin asked.

"Well, not you, Kevin!" I gave an assuring pat on his knee.

"Sorry, girl. Go ahead and watch the movie. Don't let me stop you." Dan was not one of my favorite people. To say he annoyed me immensely was being polite. He was the type who tried to hang with the "in crowd" but couldn't really keep up.

"Well, I would if you would shut the fuck up already!" I said.

"All right, all right, I'm gonna turn it on now. Is everyone done running their mouth?" With that said, Tyler pushed the play button and we continued watching the movie.

For the duration of the movie, Dan was moderately tolerable. When *The Crow* was over we contemplated which scenes were acted by the look-alike. We debated theories of when and how the lead actor died in the film.

When the conversation veered off the subject I wanted to leave. It was still only ten o'clock, but I could no longer deal with Dan.

Moreover I couldn't help but catch Kevin's vibe. He was eyeing me the whole night. I was certainly flattered by his subtleties, but Josh was familiar territory and things were going well between us. The last thing I wanted was to mess that up. Kevin's boldness unnerved me. All understood that I was Josh's girl.

I walked over to the phone and dialed Casey's number.

"Hey, it's Reba," I whispered into the receiver.

"Hey what's up?" she said. "Why are you whispering?"

"Oh, I'm at Josh's and I don't want anyone to hear me talking."

"Who's there?"

"Just Josh, Tyler, Jake, Kevin, and annoying-ass Dan," I answered. I knew why she asked, so I added, "Jay was here, but I think he went to Craig's a while ago."

"I'm headed outta here though. What are you doing?"

"I'm just chillin'. Kristina stopped by. Did you get into a fight with Josh?"

"No, it's not that. I can't be around Dan anymore tonight. That fucking kid kills me!" I said. "Tell K Nice I said what's up. Do you mind if I stop by then?"

After she was through relaying my message to Kristina she told me to come on over. I told her I'd be there soon and hung up. Then I picked up the receiver again and pressed a bunch of numbers in case someone was nosy enough to press redial.

I walked nonchalantly back to the couch and remained standing while I finished drinking my beer. After another minute I announced that I was leaving and put on my coat as I went to the fridge. The remaining two Molsons were placed into each of my coat pockets and I returned to the living room.

"Where are you going?" Tyler asked suspiciously.

"Nowhere. I'm just going out."

"Who was on the phone?" Josh asked.

"I was just checking my messages." I wanted him to feel guilty for not paying more attention to my discomfort with his guests. Dan wasn't even his friend. I hoped Josh made an attempt to keep me from leaving, but he didn't. And I required Josh to know all of this without my having to tell him.

It seemed monumental that the perception of an outsider was that Josh's interest in my life was greater than mine in his. I believed that if others knew how much I cared for him, then I would be viewed as weak and vulnerable. It was detrimental to be fragile, as I truly was.

I walked to Casey's, which gave me a chance to reflect in the cool night air. I was satisfied with my departure.

I drank my final two beers and listened to Kristina tell her latest tale of sorrow. She fell hard for men, a characteristic not to be envied. Men were her greatest downfall. Naturally, the fact that she got played by assholes time and time again proved that she had self-esteem issues. But who doesn't? The difference is in how we manage.

Her mother was very needy and latched on to noncommittal men. K Nice apparently followed her footsteps. When they were through with her it was with little if any warning. If she was distressed and bewildered she had no qualms about tracking a man down and bugging him to get some answers and maybe a sympathetic retry.

"Let's go for a drive!" Casey suggested.

"Hell yeah! K Nice you need some fresh air."

"What do ya say? The Ocean Drive?"

"Alright," Kristina agreed.

To continue in the spirit of sisterhood the three of us sat in the front seat of the car. We listened to the Prince tapes I had made. We sang aloud gleefully, sitting three deep in the front of the vehicle and leaving a large empty back seat. My mind was focused on the present, and Josh was nowhere in my thoughts. I had completely neglected my decree to stay strong and hold up my guard.

I shared a moment with two ladies as confused and lost, beautiful and broken, tired and still trooping along as I was. Being with them reminded me that I was still human. They reminded me that I was a lady. They showed me that life wasn't always about being tough. It was the first time I had ever experienced a connection to the female species as a whole. It was a moment I will never forget.

Skeptic

Some say love
I say why
She wants love
Must be high
Young wish love
But are shy
Some play love
They should fry
You see love
I don't try
He claims love
It's a lie
I see love
I defy
When in love
I deny

He says love
I say bye
I feel love
And I cry
I am love
I hate I

Josh and I were so harmonious our intimacy had reached new heights. As expected, one of us had to knock it back down.

I wasn't the type to keep a hawk eye out on my man. I hung with the fellas, and if Josh wasn't around I didn't worry my head about his whereabouts. But my girls were more possessive.

"Ummmm, Reba, did you see who Josh was talking to?" K Nice asked.

"No, should I?"

"Hell yeah. He is talking with some f-ugly ass girl."

"Then what do I need to see that for?"

"I think it's *the way* he's taking with her?"

"Did you hear him say something?"

"No, but I mean, …" Kristina sighed in her frustration with my aloof behavior. "Will you fucking look at him?"

Reluctantly, I took a glance in his direction. He was in the corner with a black girl obviously engaged in conversation.

"Okay. So what do you want me to do?"

"You don't care?"

"About what? That he's talking to some girl? No. You said she was ugly anyway." The actual sight of him with another female's full attention certainly unnerved me, but realistically it was just a conversation. How bad could the damage be?

"Alright man, I'll let you win your card game. I just wanted to let you know."

I was relieved when she left. Only Tyler heard parts of the conversation. I continued to sneak peeks in Josh's direction. They never looked like anything more than two people talking. But I had that empty feeling in the pit of my stomach.

A few nights later she was back. This time Casey accompanied K Nice with the warning.

"She's baaack!" K Nice started.

"Yeah, I saw her. She is beyond busted."

"No doubt, but why does your man keep showing her so much attention?"

"Chill with that. He's not my man. And that fucking thing has nothing over me." The girls glared at me in silence. "Why is she acting all innocent like, though? I don't get it. They look like they just talk."

"Do you recognize her?" Casey asked. She knew everyone.

"Not really. I mean I guess I've seen her at school."

"Yeah, Reba. She's like two years behind us. I think she's a junior now. Fucking hoochies need to go do their homework or somethin'."

"Damn, younglings, why are they here then?"

"To get your man." Kristina instigated.

"That girl is dumb. She's real dippy. You can tell by looking at her," Casey added.

"Ugh, I'd rather not. If the bitch is so dumb, and obviously butt-fucking ugly, then why do I need to worry?" I was not only trying to convince the girls she was no threat but also myself.

"Don't sweat it then. She looks like a pug with her face all squished up. She don't even have a nice shape."

"Some would say a pug is cute. Nobody could possibly think *that thing* is cute. Did you see her teeth? It's like she still has her baby teeth. It's weird!" Casey said.

"Okay, she looks like her face got run over by a truck!" K Nice exclaimed.

"Nice!" Casey said. "With no fashion sense whatsoever."

"She's a fucking troll, a dumb-ass, under-the-bridge-dwelling, sluttish, nasty troll," I finalized.

The girls laughed boisterously, but my stomach felt no better. They showed their disapproval more than I ever did. I didn't want to be the cause of any drama. I left the troll alone. I certainly didn't want the fellas getting mad at me for acting like a jealous schoolgirl.

So when K Nice approached me a few parties later with the news of her provocation, I was less than thrilled.

"Okay Reba, I had to say something. I mean the troll looked right at me when I asked her to move out of the way."

"What are you talking about?" I had to walk away from Joe, who was trying to impress me with his cherry stem tongue-tying tricks.

"Well, I was trying to come back in from the deck and she was standing right at the slider. I told her to move her ugly ass but she just looked at me. Josh got a little annoyed and told me to chill."

"Oh God," I grumbled.

"So I told her to get the fuck off Josh because he was taken."

"And you're telling me this so I will know why Josh starts screaming at me?"

"Josh was not happy with me. But you didn't do anything, so why would he flip on you?"

"Man, I told you that troll ain't no fucking threat. I don't like drama, K Nice, I'm not you!"

I rushed away back to Joe, anxious to drink tons more anticipating an unwanted scene. I was in desperate need of assistance. How could I prepare to be utterly humiliated, yelled at like a jealous lover and put in my place, which was not in his heart, for all to see? Suddenly I saw my answer appear right above Joe's head. Silky smoothness was flowing ever so subtly before me. It was a beautiful pattern exuding love and lust, strength and power. I snatched it up discreetly and immediately felt a calming take over. Still, I avoided Josh the remainder of the night and made it a point to keep my distance from Kristina, trying to disassociate myself with her actions.

I made it through the night with no altercations.

As time passed Josh finally gave me some clarification on the matter, sort of. In a soothing manner he took hold of my hand and escorted me to his bedroom. The troll had been undetected all night, and I was disheartened that he chose the time of her absence to be with me.

"Hey, I've missed you." He shut his bedroom door behind him.

"Well, I have been here, ya know? You've just been doing your own thing, I guess."

"That's why I wanted to talk to you. I know how you get and I don't want you to be mad at me, so I wrote you a letter."

"Oh, we're back to that?"

Josh giggled bashfully as he handed the folded piece of paper to me.

"What's this all about?"

"Just read it, please." He stood there waiting.

I sat on the bed and unfolded the paper. The introduction stated how much he cared about me. Then it read, "I hadn't planned any of this and I fell in love with you but I am trying to kick it to someone else." I read that part a few times before skipping down to the end. "I still want to chill like we do. Love, Josh."

"That's it?"

"Yeah."

"Oh. Well. I already got word of that. In case you haven't noticed, Casey and K Nice have been watching. I tried to tell them to let it be. That if you had something to say you would. But I think K Nice took it upon herself to say something to the girl. I want you to know I had nothing to do with it."

"I know you better than that. I knew that when you did say something it wouldn't have been meaningless. That is why I wanted to tell you first."

I glanced at the paper, which was by now burning the skin on my hand, and saw the gleaming Cheshire. I interpreted the smile this time as negative. It was a small figure sneering at me. I tried to put my finger on it but it rapidly scooted across the page away from my touch. I tried again but it shot up to the top of the page. Frustrated, I crumbled the paper.

"Okay, so basically everything is the same except now when I come here you're gonna be all hooked up with some tr … um, girl?"

"Nah, it ain't like that. I am just talking to her. But I didn't want you to see me and get all pissed off at me. It ain't a big deal."

"If you say so."

I left the room in haste and veered away from him the remainder of the night.

"The regulars" included the tenants of the party house, Casey, me, and Craig and Joe, whose apartment became the backup party spot. I steered away during daylight hours unless I had spent the night. But even that was a rare occasion.

Casey and I were disappointed to find party central under lock down. Neither of us had received word from anyone, so we set off to the backup spot. Sure enough it was on at Craig and Joe's. Although I appreciated a change of scenery and the extra place to hang out and drink, I really detested the college girls who flocked to Craig. This annoyed K Nice especially, because she was sweet on him as well. Craig was one of the men who had ditched her in the past, but he was special because he had taken her back a few times, though only to ditch her again and again.

Their apartment was much more maze-like than party central. It was a series of small rooms as opposed to the former, which has an eat-in kitchen, small dining room, and living room all open to one another. There was a lot of separation and, if intended, segregation at Joe and Craig's.

Josh was out on the balcony off of the living room with something that resembled a troll, so I dared not venture that way. Joe was in his typical solemn mood, playing quarters at the kitchen table with Kevin and a few other usuals. He perked right up when I sat in and joined their game. Most saw Joe as rather frightening, including Kevin, who refrained from flirting with me in his presence.

As the night progressed the college girls drank themselves the courage to put on a pathetic display in a competition to win Craig's affection, even if just for one night. They called it dancing, but it didn't resemble anything of the sort to me! Nonetheless the commotion caused us to migrate to the living room. I noticed Josh was nowhere to be seen, nor was the troll.

"Go on, girl, show 'em how it's done!" Joe exclaimed as he nudged me toward the dance floor.

I heard Casey from the other side of the room cheer me on as well. Then K Nice urged me to join her as she stepped out next to the girls. Even though I knew her intention was the same as the college girls', Joe's relentless nudging, "get your fine ass out there," left me little choice.

I took a swig of something. I felt the fire in my chest, and only one more would put the flames to rest for the time being. I danced my way out to the center and felt the beat of the music take me over. Oh how I love to dance!

It didn't take long before the college girls were replaced by my own kind. Some of the guys got up to dance too. Since it was not an ordinary occurrence I took advantage and wore out the floor.

Kevin joined the dance and immediately grabbed my hips from behind, moving with the music. I turned around, happy to see who was so bold. Song after song it appeared to be as innocent as a dance, but when his eyes captured mine it molded into something more.

He offered to drive me home, and I accepted. It was the first time Kevin and I had a one-on-one conversation without all the background noise. I was nervous to be alone with a man other than Josh. But I found Kevin to be warmly inviting. I still guessed his intentions were to knock my name off his list, because that's all I presumed myself to be. It still sparked my interest in learning why.

"So what are you all about anyway, girl?" Kevin asked as he parked in front of my apartment.

"Same as everyone else, I suppose. Just trying to get by, you know!"

"Yeah, I hear you. But where does Josh fit in to that picture?"

I was amazed at his daring inquisition. It wasn't something I was comfortable discussing, because I was so unsure myself. "Josh..." I whispered to myself, "good question."

"What's that?" he asked.

"Nothing."

"Nothing? Well, sometimes it looks like nothing and other times it don't. But I'll take your word for it."

Wow, that was too easy!

We sat in his car listening to Hot 106.3 FM and talking about old school days. Through my own inquisition I learned about his past relationship with his baby's mom and where they stood now. I listened intently; trying to match the expression on his face with the words he spoke all the while secretly questioning if what he said was real or just to lure me in.

When we were out of words for the night he leaned over and kissed me softly on the cheek, then said goodnight. I refrained from looking in his direction and thanked him for the ride.

Kevin's status of "random" suddenly changed to "usual" after that night. His flirting was beyond flattering, bringing out my attraction towards him even more. Josh's relationship with the troll was still a mystery to me, and the distance was surely growing between us.

Chapter Ten

"Veil-Over-View"

Kristina rode her mountain bike to waitress at one of my favorite restaurants in downtown Newport, the Brick Ally Pub. She called me at Josh's house saying she'd be out of work by nine o'clock and wanted to hang.

"Well, just come here then."

"I am not in the mood to be around all those people. I just can't deal with those randoms."

"Me either. Nobody's here."

"Not yet, but you know they are bound to show up."

"It's a chill night, girl, I am telling you. They don't want it big tonight either. They are getting sick of cleaning up after everyone."

"Reba, you're not trying to bail on me are you? Don't diss me for a dick!"

"I'm not. I'm being for real. But if you want we can chill at your place."

"Alright, I'll see you in a little while."

I was already drunk by the time Kristina and I spoke. I had been drinking Bacardi straight out of the bottle. I bought a liter that night. With Josh and his newfound interest in trolls I needed all the self-assurances I could get.

Normally I didn't fare well with females. My "I don't give a fuck" attitude intimidated most. Guys, on the other hand, loved my sassiness. Their flirting flattered me. I needed that to feed my counterfeit confidence.

The fellas were happy to change it up. That night Josh, Tyler, Big Dawg, and Joe were with me. I either hid the effects of the alcohol well or my company was just as intoxicated as I was, because no one seemed to notice how drunk I was.

Tyler locked up behind us all and we piled into Josh's van. When we got to K Nice's house she wasn't there yet. We waited a few minutes outside, but it was frigid. Being a person of my word I couldn't break my plans.

Joe started, "Well, how long are we supposed to wait here for her?"

"She said she'd be here soon. We've only been here a minute—relax."

"It is fucking cold out here, man," Tyler admitted.

"Seriously though, Skirt Dog, we must look like we're up to no good standing here like a bunch of fuckin' dummies freezing our nuts off."

"I'll see if I can see her down the street then. I'll be right back." I walked down to the corner but I saw no sign of her. My nose and hands were chilled to the core. I walked back and rounded the house to the front door.

My brain was dulled by the bitter cold, mixed emotions, and confusion of what was acceptable and expected of me. I wanted to make everyone happy including myself. Double-checking to see if anyone was watching me I searched the flower box on the window and found the emergency key. I remembered to replace it after letting myself in.

I walked through the apartment to the back door and opened it. The guys on the outside were elated to have access to the warmth inside. We waited on her couch for her to come home.

We didn't want to bring any unnecessary attention to ourselves. I turned the radio on low volume. The lights remained off except the one in the hood of the stove that she kept lit at all times. My vision was in single solid colors only.

Josh and I were enthralled with each other on the love seat. Erotic kissing heated the red blood that coursed through my veins. It didn't occur to me that everybody else could see us. I worked my way on top of his lap. Our lips never disconnected. My ballooned heart was hovering above, blending in with our surroundings that appeared to have been dunked into a bucket of scarlet paint. All the excess was dripping down into globs on all surfaces.

Tyler made a sexual comment that caught my attention. The rest of the guys in the room had their elongated tongues hanging out of their faces just like the pack of wolves in the auditorium during our Christmas concert. Though embarrassed, I was hardly willing for our passion to subside. Josh carried me into my friend's bedroom for more privacy. He tried to recline me onto the bed, but I had to put on the brakes. The globs of scarlet paint flushed away, revealing a smoother, softer pink. I couldn't have sex on my friend's bed, especially when she wasn't home. We weren't exactly supposed to be in her house.

Joe snuck a call to his house, telling Casey, Jay, and Craig where we were. When K Nice got in touch with Casey she was informed that we were in her house.

The phone was ringing, but I had no intentions of answering it.

Joe came into the bedroom and announced that Kristina was on the phone. "She wants to speak with you."

"What?" I was angry with Joe for answering her phone. "Why'd you answer it? How … Why is she calling here? We're not supposed to … oh God!"

The romantic soft pink view washed away, splattering on the floor and taking on all the gruesome shades of pea green. Reluctantly I felt my way down the hall to the phone. This couldn't be good.

When I heard Kristina's voice I knew my gut was right. She was enraged. It took her longer to get out of work than she'd planned. She didn't expect me to let everyone in the house.

"I trusted you with my house key for an emergency, Reba!" she yelled through the phone. "Are you fucking Josh in my bed?"

The oily globs of colors were still merging together, yet to find a happy medium. The wall was holding up my limp frame as I squeezed my eyes shut, trying to gain some sense of reality.

"Of course not. I would never do that to you."

"You wouldn't do that to me? You just let those assholes in my house! I'll be home in a minute. I found a ride," she screamed before abruptly hanging up.

The rainbow oil spill was cleared and my view was now a piss color. Kristina came storming through her door minutes later. I was supposed to share a special friendship with her. How could I have invaded her privacy like that?

Her words were muted, though I could tell she was yelling. Each time her mouth opened wide, yellow bubbles floated out. Most of them floated towards Tyler and Big Dawg, who ransacked her kitchen looking for food, but they popped them with a simple poke of their fingers.

I didn't even try to pop the piss bubbles coming my way, and soon enough I was engulfed in them. All that I was aiming to receive by staying with male company disintegrated. I was ashamed of myself. One thing I was always able to pride myself on was being an exceptional friend by putting other's needs before my own. I was an unselfish person no longer. What had become of me? Gigantic yellow foam pushed me out the door.

Being as fair as she was I wasn't the only one who felt her wrath. She didn't speak to Tyler for a good month after he ate her food and drank her juice, and she and Big Dawg never really got along anyway. I deserved more than what she dished out at me and was forgiven quickly, even though I didn't have the capacity to do the same for myself. I was even embarrassed to show my face in front of Casey. I let my own drunken needs interfere with what was right. I had betrayed her trust, and trust is something I never took lightly, and I had done it all for nothing. The following week the troll was spotted at Josh's house.

All of the shame and disgust for myself returned as I recalled that night. "What a drunken loser!" I say aloud. I look at myself in the mirror on my bed. "How could you do such a despicable thing?"

Although I paid K Nice back for the food Tyler and Big Dawg had eaten I never really made peace with myself for my behavior. I wasn't drunk enough to have sex in her bed. I knew that was crossing the line. I knew that letting them in was crossing the line as well. I honestly didn't expect her arrival to take as long as it did. I assumed she'd be home within minutes.

I can't look at myself in the mirror any longer. I want to smoke a cigarette, but I haven't purchased any in weeks. "It was a long time ago, let it go," I try telling myself. "No cigarettes? No beer? No Bacardi? What am I supposed to do now?"

I get up to take a shower. I let the water run extremely hot so I can stand there and wash it all away. I wash my hair, allowing a thick lather to form before rinsing. Then I stand there for another five minutes before proceeding to wash my face and body. I let the steam open my pores and let the ugliness run out of them. I sit a while before shaving my legs.

I take in every breath for what it's worth, and then turn the water off and towel dry. I wrap one towel around my hair and leave it on my head like a turban. I use a second larger towel to wrap around my body. It was a great task before I was pregnant to find something satisfying to wear. I dare not try right now.

Avoiding the mirror on the headboard of my bed, I lie down in the fetal position. Ready to allow myself to sleep I grab the corner of the blanket and pull it over as much of my skin as I can. I don't want to think anymore.

During my futile attempt to take a nap I realize that thoughts are still clamoring in my brain, causing me to get increasingly restless. Will they ever stop? I take a few deep breaths and try ignoring them. I open my eyes and look around the room. It's such a dismal sight I close my eyes again.

I try fantasizing about being rich and living elsewhere. I imagine how wonderful life would be if I had no financial worries. I could work for Save the Bay and it wouldn't matter how much money I made. I need meaning to my life. I could live in a quiet and clean environment. I could keep this pregnancy or not. Oh, that's right, I am pregnant! What am I going to do about that?

I finally obtained my midnight veil. That flowing silken lace suspended before me at times of desperation was in my possession at last. It was similar to the many faces we conceal or reveal at any particular time we deem necessary. My midnight veil was unseen by those around me. A diaphanous midnight black screen shaded my true insecure self. It was my stealthy guise, evading the knowledge of any other.

It served as primary protection over the flawless wall of heavy stones I crafted around my entire being. The best mason in the world could not have built a more magnificent barrier of solid rock with strength and durability.

The wall itself was piled high with somewhat of a conscious effort. These great grey stones were a mirrored reflection of what lies behind. Unbreakable building blocks colored in various degrees of grey were carefully coated with their own armor of diamonds for beauty and strength. Each facet shot off a different color of the rainbow in loosely dense rays, a simple hint of the many emotions and characteristics of the inner being lingering within its walls. Even sparkles of white glimmered all around the structure, reflecting the divinity of the protected, unbeknownst to the creator. She was my love, my life, my body, myself.

My veil was altogether different. I wore my veil as a safeguard on top of my wall. The wall that I built with so much passion over the years had become a part of me. My veil was a separate entity in itself. The more I drank the more secure my veil was. With it on I was vibrant, fun, energetic, strong, and sexy.

I met up with Casey at her apartment. As she got dressed and ready to go out for the night we drank a few beers.

Casey and I shared a few things in common. We were both single young ladies who love to party. We both lived alone in apartment complexes that were considered dangerous. And we both loved to listen to Prince. Other than that we were quite different.

Casey was a good friend. We shared great laughs and built memories. We kept each other's secrets and helped each other in any way. She always had my back, as I had hers. We could depend on one another for support and were there at the drop of a hat. Casey was a true friend indeed. And for that I was grateful.

"So what happened with you and Josh?" Casey yelled from the bathroom.

"Who fuckin knows, man? You know, same shit, same asshole, same shit hole life!" My voice trailed off as I tried to yell back without thinking heavily on our latest development. I lay belly down on the floor kicking my feet back against my butt as I played with the CD player I let her borrow. I skipped to track number three on *The Hits 2* CD by Prince. "I Wanna Be Your Lover" started playing and I raised the volume a little more. That was Casey's favorite Prince song. I lit a cigarette and yelled a little louder, "Shit, girl, you probably know better than me. Did Jay say anything to you about it?"

"You know what your problem is, don't you?" She came into the living room to join me for a cigarette as her hair air-dried for a few minutes. She squatted on the floor next to the CD player.

I was surprised to see how fast she was getting ready that evening. My nerves were more jittery than usual and I was in a hurry to drink them to a simmer. At the rate she was going that night I was afraid I wouldn't be at the height of intoxication as I deemed necessary to face Josh.

"I thought you came to sit here and listen to your song," I slugged my first beer down quickly and anxiously grabbed another. She didn't comment, and there was a long pause. "Oh, are you about to enlighten me?" I finally asked as she smiled back waiting for permission to continue. "Go ahead then!"

"Well, I've been watching the two of you go back and forth for months. You get mad at him but you do the same shit!" she replied matter-of-factly.

"What are you talking about?" I truly had no idea where she was headed.

"You want him to be true to you and reveal his feelings but you don't want to be tied down and you never admit how much you care about him." She took a drag of her cigarette and looked at me to see if I would confirm any of what she had said. I looked completely perplexed. So she continued, "What about Kevin?"

"What about Kevin? Even he knows how I feel about Josh. Everybody knows how I feel about Josh. You're gonna tell me Josh doesn't know? Bullshit! And you're right. I'm not asking for a committed boyfriend-girlfriend relationship. But I don't think it's too much to ask that if he's sleeping with me, could he not fuck anybody else?"

"Don't you think that's asking to have your cake and eat it too?"

"Hello? Having your cake and eating it too would be fuckin him and anybody else I want but he can't. So, no, I don't!" I retorted. "Why the hell are you taking his side anyway?" I was getting tired of being on the defensive.

"I'm not. I'm just looking at it from another way. I don't know what Josh is thinking. Jay doesn't tell me even if they do talk about it."

"He's the one who wants to have his cake and eat it too. It's okay for him to hit on some troll-lookin' chick right in front of my face, but I can't flirt with Kevin? It's the same double standard all men have. He can't handle the fact that I can not only play his game, but I can play it better than him! You know what I'm sayin'?"

"Oh, I know!" She put her hand out. I put my hand on hers and we slid them back to a snap. Then she gasped and blurted out, "Huh, Josh knows about Kevin?"

"Hell no!" I shrieked through a cough as I tried to inhale the smoke at the same time. "Are you crazy? Josh would flip if he found out. Kevin doesn't need that."

"So what *is* goin' on with you and Kevin?"

"Yo, I think dude is really into me. I feel bad," I admitted.

"What do you feel bad about?"

"I don't know. Kev's one of those guys I've always sorta had my eye on in school, ya know. But he had a girl and they had a kid so I never wanted to interfere. Then he was at Craig's house the night Josh was kickin' it with home girl. Kevin had been talkin' to me all night. He wants to hang out, ya know just the two of us but I keep blowing him off."

"I saw you two dancing."

"I know. That was dangerous, huh?"

"So what are you gonna do?"

"I'm just goin' along and seeing what comes next. We'll see how Josh acts tonight. Do you think he'll be all over me tonight or kicking it with under-bridge dwellers?" I asked with a laugh. I don't even know what I wanted her answer to be.

"I don't know, guess it depends on his mood," she laughed back.

"Well, hurry your ass up. The suspense is killing me. I can't sit here any more." I stood up to finish my second beer.

Casey hurried back to the bathroom to finish drying her hair with a blow drier. I rushed to drink another beer before we left. I honestly didn't want Casey to see how much I was drinking before we went out to drink. Anyone could see that I was trying to self-medicate, anticipating the worst. I would have done anything to insure that others would not perceive me as weak.

Casey drove a K-car; a Dodge Aries. The interior was the exact shade of maroon as the exterior. Without bucket seats it was a six-passenger vehicle. It was equipped with a tape deck but not a CD player. Since the radio was busted we made a few tapes of our favorite CDs to play on the road. We popped in Dave Mathews Band as she drove into the center of town to party central.

I evoked curiosity in the minds of all those I came into contact with. Not only did my little charade favor me well, but it was so much fun. One of my greatest achievements in the pathetic life I led was the simple deception I played. My flannel unbuttoned shirt hung loosely, revealing my tight abdomen and the tiny v-neck tee cut just under my perky breasts. I was cool. Baggy blue jeans only touched my skin at my hips and the undeniable curve of my ass. They were completely frayed at the bottom of each leg from dragging on the floor. My thin hair was long, a natural brown, and free flowing, cut in layers to add to my laid-back style. An attractive face featured high cheekbones and green/grey eyes in an almond shape.

I strutted with my head held high and eyes focused ahead. Not aware of the unintentional sway of my hips as I walked, the expression on my face revealed the thought in my head, "I don't give a fuck!" And for this I was envied. For this I was desired. For this I was despised. For this I was Reba!

My veil allowed me to feed others' misperception of me. People wanted to be like me. I laugh at the thought. Tied in a confusing bouquet of knots is a nervously trembling, hateful ball of angry fire waiting to burst if only it had enough sense to. And people wanted to be me? They hadn't a clue.

My body has its own way of dealing with all of the emotional aspects of my life, even though I tried to drink it all away. Every evening almost like clockwork before I went out for the night I began to feel a strange sensation in my chest, just where my bra wrapped around my torso. It was a flittering of sort, a feeling that was not completely foreign to me. I only began to notice it around this time because of its exactness in punctuality on a seemingly daily basis. I drank it away just like I did everything else before it grew to the point of incurable pain.

I had my opened twelve-pack in my left hand. I knocked three times on the door and pushed it open.

"Wuzuuup???"

"Skirt-Dog!" I heard a few of my friends exclaim. I threw out a few hugs around the crowded room.

"Oh yeah, it's on!" I purposely avoided eye contact with Josh, who was sitting across the table in my plain view. I could feel his stare but noticed he wasn't tossing out any greetings. I guessed he was not happy to see me, despite my hopes that he would get over it already, whatever *it* was. My only option was to go with the flow. I told myself to keep cool even though I was upset things were not well between us.

Casey walked in the door a moment later. She was greeted with the same amount of enthusiasm as I was. She worked the room and mingled with all the randoms. I found a seat at the table and saw that the fellas were in the middle of a drinking card game. The game they were playing was called Asshole.

Asshole was usually the game of choice. I was never the asshole aside from coming in the middle of a session. Half the time I was president or VP, so naturally I was always down for a game.

In accordance with our style of play, when a president remains in three consecutive terms then he could make up any silly old rule. The rule that tripped people up the most was the one in which you couldn't use the word "drink." Finding a synonym can be tricky after a lot of beers. And it was quite entertaining watching people get on power trips over a drinking card game!

Being one of the only two females of the regulars I could drink all but two guys under the table. So I gained my respect quickly with the big dogs! They loved to play drinking games with me because I would never back down and I could always handle what they would dish out.

Oracle

Drink the terror away
For fear I do not hold
Give me all you've got
I'll show you one who's bold

Look into these eyes
These eyes so dark as coal
Such depth within them
You'll lose your self-control

Flush the pain right through me
My nerves have then froze
And everything inside
Is something no one knows

Dealing with the present
Future is a mystery
No care for yesterday
Past is now history

Listen to my words
In between the swig
As hard as you may try
My meaning's just too big

I drink my tear away
For you cannot relate
That tear is not just hurt
But of anger so great

Gauge me with your knife
My smile will then grow
'Cause you will never learn
What I already know

My alcohol domain
Where I drink until I'm numb
A soul is kept a secret
So only few will come

"Ay-oh, check out Dan over there trying to kick it to Andrea," whispered Big Dawg Jake to everyone at the table. "The house is crowded tonight, lots of randoms roaming around."

Dan was a usual. He popped up at the party house more often than I fancied because he was the type to bullshit with the fellas about how much action he was getting from the ladies. We saw him get rejected on a regular basis.

He waited until a girl was drunk before he made his move with a weak line like, "Hey, can I t-t-talk to you for a minute? Y-y-you know I've had my e-eye on you. Don't be frontin', girl. You know you're looking g-g-good tonight. Wanna g-go somewhere per-private, s-s-so we can talk?" Lucky for us while Dan was waiting for the females in the area to get uninhibited he got himself tanked. His drunken stupor combined with his excitement and lack of confidence brought out a slight stutter. I knew his routine well because I'd heard it firsthand. Even if I wanted to play the jealousy game with Josh I would never stoop down low enough to entertain Dan's fantasy.

We paused the game for a minute to watch Dan embarrass himself for the umpteenth time. The anticipated rejection was hardly enough for our sinister minds. What came next was the real treat. Holding our cards close to our bodies we sat in silence watching and waiting.

I could read his lips, as he hadn't changed a single syllable, right down to the stutter. It was embedded in his simple mind. Andrea smiled and tried to keep focus as she spoke to Dan, who was sitting on the couch beside her. In no time she did the friendly tap on the knee, got up, and stumbled away.

"There she goes," one of the onlookers noted.

"Yup, and he's scoping out the room to see who saw the disaster," another stated.

Dan caught the eye of a random and began his macho spiel. The random was unaffected and went about his way. Dan resorted to mumbling to himself as he chugged his beer.

"Okay, this is it," Big Dawg said. "Not long now … Skirt Dog, hook me up with a stogie."

"Good idea." I handed one to him and lit one for myself. We smoked and waited.

"… Zonked!" Joe sneered. Dan was down for the count on the couch with the remainder of his twelve-pack on the floor next to him ready for the taking.

"All right," Big Dawg started. "Who's going for it tonight?"

"I don't want him waking' up on me," replied Josh.

A couple of chuckles came from Tyler, the otherwise silent participant.

"He probably drank them all anyway," stated the usually evil-minded Joe.

"Well, I'll go again, but I'm not sharing' any with none of you clowns. Shit, I don't give a fuck if his dumb ass does wake up." Big Dawg pushed back his chair.

"Hey, you shady bitches, I'll do it," I volunteered as I stood up. "It'll be my pleasure."

"And if he wakes up?" Josh asked.

"I'll sing his ass a sweet lullaby!" I walked around my chair and placed my Molson on it, then pushed it in. I stuffed my playing cards in my back pocket. I slunk my way over to the couch and leaned into Dan's face. I could smell the beer on his breath. I turned towards my audience and gave a look as if to say, "It's in the bag!"

Slowly I reached down the side of Dan's leg and carefully felt inside the box. There were many not-so-cold ones left. I smiled to the boys waiting at the table as I sat down on the couch next to Dan and cracked open a brew. With one arm carefully placed on the back of the couch, I held my can up, winked, and started guzzling.

A couple of awes sounded across the room. Then I saw Joe hold up one of my bottles as collateral. I laughed in his victory and took Dan's stash back to the table, then gestured for my Molson back. A can of Bud couldn't compare. I placed my bottle back in my box and counted the rest. Satisfied that the box was just as I left it, I handed out the remaining cans of beer. Lucky for them there was just enough for everyone.

"That's fucked up. You shouldn't have done that to Dan like that," Tyler interjected just seconds before he started drinking his fresh Bud.

"If his dumb ass can't handle all that liquor, he shouldn't try to act so tough and walk in with it," harped Big Dawg.

"Thank you," I exclaimed. "He knows he can't hang with the big dogs, so why try?"

Big Dawg barked a "Woof!" as his fist punched mine.

"Let's resume. Shall we?" I said pulling the cards out of my pocket. "Who's setting it off? Me?"

"Yeah man. You can start it if you hook me up with another stogie, yo," Big Dawg roared back at me.

"Nah man, it wasn't her turn," Josh cut in. "It was …"

"Who man? You? I don't think so Mr. 'I don't want him waking up on me!'" I mimicked him in a girlie voice. The fellas laughed, but Josh shot me the evil eye.

I threw my hands up to form a "W" and lipped "Whatever"! It was a good possibility that I might need a ride from Casey back to my place, so I scoped out the room to find her. Unfortunately for me she was hand in hand with Jay, disappearing down the hallway.

"That's just great," I said under my breath. I always liked to have a backup plan and I just watched that one vanish before my eyes.

Playing cards was entertaining for a long while, although Josh and I didn't speak much to each other even as we spent most of the time side by side due to my VP status and his secretary spot. Around midnight some usuals rolled in.

"Oh, shit!" I whispered to myself when I caught sight of Kevin. I pretended not to notice and kept my focus on the cards. Ignoring Kevin's phone call earlier did not serve me well now.

Kevin and Craig rounded the table, giving daps to everyone including Josh. I smiled, maintaining a cheery disposition as I greeted them both, "What up?" I was relieved when Kevin smiled back, refraining from speaking to me.

"Yo, I'm done," Joe said as he pushed his cards into the dead pile.

"I'm out too." Big Dawg did the same.

Josh got up and went into the kitchen with Craig to discuss the "killer weed" Craig came upon. Since Josh was connoisseur of such, Craig wanted to share it for bragging rights. The rest of the crew followed. I gathered up all the cards without a word and started shuffling at the abandoned table.

As I pulled out a cigarette, a voice asked from behind, "Can I get one of those?"

I hadn't noticed Kevin standing there. I figured he had gone into the kitchen with the rest.

"Wouldn't you rather be smoking that 'killer weed'?" I asked, handing him a cigarette.

"Nah, I already had a taste earlier. I don't really need a cigarette either," he replied. "I called you today."

"Oh yeah?" I had heard his voice on my machine and decided not to answer it. "I must have been at Casey's already. Why'd you call, any reason in particular?"

"Nah just wanted to say what's up. I figured you'd be here."

"Yeah, we got here around nine thirty I guess. She's off with Jay in his room. I don't think I'll be waiting for her tonight."

"What are you doin' after this?"

"I dunno. Nothing planned. Games over, so I'll probably leave shortly. What are you guys doin'?"

"I'm goin' with you," he smiled.

"What about Craig?"

"He ain't blockin'," he said slyly.

I chuckled a little, "Oh really? So you mentioned your intent with me to Craig?"

"Nah girl, I keep my shit tight. I just mean none of my boys would take any disrespect if I left with a girl. They don't need to know anything!"

"Well, there ain't nothing holdin' me here. So where are we goin'?"

"I got a spot! Come on." He grabbed my hand. I took a quick inconspicuous look to make sure Josh wasn't watching. I grabbed my beer and we walked out the door.

It became a game at which I even tested myself. Josh was the ultimate challenge, the never-ending game. The way I allowed him to treat me fueled my need to not only overcome his heart but the heart of many other unsuspecting guys in my life. How close could I get to someone without falling and letting down my guard? How could I get a man to need me and yearn for me yet not do the same for him? Such a game could be easy as pie had I picked any old lad. I decided to really play it well with someone I could actually care about. I needed a challenge.

Chapter Eleven

"What is the Meaning of This?"

Kevin at five feet ten inches was slightly taller and thinner than Josh. He had a pale complexion, yet not as pale as my Irish skin, with light green eyes in an exaggerated almond shape. His straight, light brown hair was kept evenly short. And he possessed a wicked smile, which was no reflection of his personality.

I came to know Kevin as a quiet and caring individual more sentimental than I would've ever guessed. I wasn't as tuned in to his feelings as I could have been. And although he was exactly what I needed, I didn't take full advantage of the spark between us.

Kevin took me to a lighthouse out on the point to sit by the serenity of the ocean as it serenaded us. I finished what was left in my twelve-pack, and Kevin drank his pint of Southern Comfort straight out of the bottle. We talked about life in our tourist-attracting city. Then the conversation swayed towards Josh's house and the motley crew that showed up at party central.

The red flag went up and I quickly caught the warning. Any sign the conversation was leaning towards the relationship between Kevin and me or Josh and me put me in the danger zone. I cunningly redirected the conversation.

"So what about your family? You said you live with your grandmother?"

"Yeah, she's pretty old. She did a lot for me, ya know, practically raised me. So now I try to help her out, pay her back a little. Your grandparents still alive?"

"I never really knew any of my grandfathers. I had three, plus a grandfather figure. But they all passed. Both my grandmothers are in New York."

"Wow, that's far. I don't know what I would do without mine."

"I love it though, ya know. I try to get out there as often as I can. I love the city. Actually, the only reason I am still here is for my niece and nephew."

"Well, I'll have to thank them some time."

He leaned in to rub his nose up and down my cheek. It felt good to be in the company of someone who fought for my attention because he wanted it not *needed* it. His choosing me over his boys flattered me.

I turned towards Kevin, inviting his soft and intimate kiss. Being with someone other than Josh like this was unfamiliar to me. We slowly fell back to the ground. He caressed the contour of my shape. I was tingling with goose bumps, unsure whether to stop him or not. Kevin had feelings for me, but my emotions were always glazed over with alcohol. I had no idea what I truly needed or wanted.

Guilt arose as I thought of Josh. The scent of the green grass damp with the ocean air and the coolness of the ground beneath me reminded me of the time Josh and I went to the high-school basketball game so many years ago, tumbling in the leaves at the track outside of the gym. Throughout the years we remained a major presence in each other's lives. That had to count for something.

But then again, Josh had been flirting with that troll chick. Meanwhile Kevin was getting himself worked up. Although I won myself over and came to the conclusion that I was free to do what I wanted, I wasn't sure if I wanted to be so intimate with Kevin, or anyone other than Josh.

I finally pushed his hands off of me and stopped kissing him. I managed the words, "It's cold out here."

"I'm not keeping you warm enough?"

"No," I replied bluntly.

Kevin rolled over onto his back like a defeated animal. I sat straight up. "Well, I'm all outta brews. So what do ya say?"

Kevin lay still, staring into the night sky. A perplexed look came over his face just before he turned towards me. The last thing I wanted was for him to analyze his time with me. I kissed his ear, whispering, "I'm cold and it's late. Can we go now?"

I had beaten myself up enough for one night. All of the behind-the-scenes drama with Josh made me weary. It was nearing two o'clock in the morning and I was too exhausted, too drunk, and too confused to keep up with my veil charade. I had to go home and sleep it off before I did or said something I'd regret later.

We sat in Kevin's red Honda Civic, but he didn't start the engine. His apprehension made me nervous. I knew what was coming.

"You know the heat doesn't work unless you turn the car on."

Without further ado Kevin turned on the ignition and I quickly turned the volume up on the radio. DMX's voice blasted through his speakers as I inconspicuously watched his every move. His thoughts remained his own.

Suddenly, he pulled the car over to the side of a residential road, just outside of the projects. He shut the lights off but left the car running.

"What's here?" I assumed he had to make a pit stop at one of the nearby houses for a minute. I examined a few close by but didn't recognize any.

"I don't want this night to end yet." He sounded almost whiny. I hate it when people whine.

"It was nice," I tried to be cute in adding, "but all good things must come to an end."

Not acknowledging my cutesy routine he continued, "I need to know if you are with Josh or anyone else."

I wondered why he couldn't just let things be, why we always had to discuss things first. People lie to each other's faces all the time. I tried avoiding intimate conversations because of it. Once the trust is broken it's nearly impossible to get it back.

"I'm with you, ain't I? Sitting here in the car in the middle of nowhere for some reason," I replied evasively.

"You're sure about that?" His intensity boggled me.

"Uh, yeah?" I said silly-like, patting the dash and his leg. Kevin was unlike other men I had come across. During times like these I regretted giving him attention.

He put the car into gear and drove me home. I thanked him for the night and he walked me to my door, a fine attempt at chivalry, but I was already keen on what that meant. The question was what I was going to do about it this time.

I figured I owed it to myself to see what Kevin had to offer. Since Josh had been out of jail, other guys flirted and hit on me but never had enough nerve to take it further. There was no feud or ill feelings between them. His intentions to woo me must have been genuine. And for that he deserved a chance.

I invited him in for a late-night snack, which he graciously accepted. We ate leftover chocolate cake and listened to my favorite Mary J Blige CD. We were very comfortable on my oversized couch. The mood was right, and we began making out. Then my nerves began to get the best of me.

He paused in his advancement a moment but then proceeded to caress me.

"Chill," I said.

"What's the matter?" he asked, his aggression not faltering.

"Nothing's the matter. I'm tired and drunk. We should chill," I suggested, as cool as I could possibly be.

"I just want to be close to you and I keep feeling like something is in my way." His face was inches from mine, looking me straight in the eye. "I knew you were with Josh. That's why you keep stringing me along?"

"I am not with Josh," I said with a slight laugh of relief for the change of pace.

"Then why can't you say it with a straight face?"

Very seriously, with conviction, I heard myself say, "Josh and I are nothing!"

"So that's even worse then. You're not together but you're still hung up on him."

I became very angry with Josh. "Hell no, the fuck I'm not." Did that make any sense? Anyway, no man has that power over me. I can do what I want, when I want.

"Well, I don't believe you," he said.

"Fuck you! I don't give a flying fuck about him, okay?"

"What's the deal then, girl? Why are you afraid to get close to me?"

Had he seen through my façade? He couldn't have. He didn't even know the real me, even if he thought he did. I looked inside myself to make sure my wall was up strong.

"Afraid?" I laughed. "And what the hell do I have to be afraid of?"

"That was going to be my next question."

I exhaled a little laugh and shook my head. Anything would be better than diving into my screwed-up mentality and trying to figure out what I feel and why. I prayed for something else to happen, something to change the subject and get me out of this spotlight.

Kevin moved the rest of his body closer to me and resumed his efforts to seduce me. I allowed myself to react through the alcohol and consented.

Part of me wanted Josh to see that I was not his exclusively. I wanted him to be jealous. I just wanted Josh to realize there was a chance he could lose me. If he came to that realization, I thought he would stop to think about the treasure I truly was.

On Kevin's end I wanted to be in control of the situation. I wanted to be his fantasy girl, so close, yet so far. It fed my ego and gave me a sense of confidence in my sexuality, if nothing else.

Part of the Game

Behind the smile
Treachery lies
Behind the grin
Is quite a surprise
Just all the while

I hold the cries
Loneliness in sin

My lips turned up
And my face aglow
Behind my eyes
Refuse to show
It fills my cup
Because I know
I'm in disguise

When my illusion
Is a success
It's my single goal
In my own interest
And your confusion
Is a building nest
As I gain in control

Now your attitude
A sudden change
Tender is your core
A feeling strange
Your swinging mood
With a wide range
It's my time to score

A cunning defeat
I am the wise
Or am I mistaken
I now realize
A life of deceit
In my demise
My grounds were shaken

I had no idea why it was important to me to tease and manipulate the opposite sex. Didn't I have anything more useful to do with my time? Now that I think about it, the answer is no. That is why I am sitting here with absolutely no value to my life now that I am losing my enticing figure and I don't have the tolerance for light long enough to put makeup on and/or do my hair. If I am no longer the object of men's desire, then what am I?

I ponder the thought of my lack of purpose. Sitting on my bed I take a look around my bare bedroom. "I am of absolutely no use." My voice cracks as I speak the words. I wonder why, out of all the flashbacks and thoughts that have been running through my head the last few hours, I choose those words to say aloud. "Could that actually be a valid statement?" I ask myself aloud, this time with a more solid voice.

Suddenly there's a knock that sounds like it's coming from my front door. I jump off the bed to peek out of the bedroom window but can't see anybody standing below the overhang. Another knock sounds. I run downstairs to answer the door. It's only my second day living in this apartment, so I assume it's somebody I know.

An out-of-shape Caucasian man wearing tattered clothing tight around his potbelly stands on my stoop. His ash blond hair is unkempt and his lost, brown eyes stare blankly at me. He doesn't speak.

"What?" I say impatiently.

"Uh, is Leon here?"

"Nah, man you got the wrong house."

"Leon, uh, Leon lives here right? Thems told me this Leon's place?" The pathetic middle-aged man appears desperate.

"Yo, I just fuckin' told your ass you had the wrong house. So 'thems' is either fuckin' with your sorry ass or they got it wrong. Now back up and be on your way. This is my house and there ain't nobody's Leon here." I have a low tolerance for stupidity.

I slowly shut the door and watch to make sure the crack head is walking away. I lock the door and peek out the kitchen window. I am satisfied he is already slipping in between the buildings towards the next street. "I sure could go for a cigarette right now." I sigh to myself as I peer into the near empty fridge for a beverage of some sort. There is a small jar of mayonnaise, a package of cheese, a loaf of wheat bread, some leftover pieces of pizza, a half-gallon of OJ, and some Poland Spring water bottles. I settle for a water bottle and go back upstairs.

I open the bottled water and take a swig. "Completely tasteless." I stare abhorrently at it, wishing it had some proof or alcohol percentage written on the label. I then curl up next to my pillow and stare at the wall. "Ugh, what am I doing, what am I doing?" I close my eyes and return to memory lane.

Who knows what may have come of our relationship had I taken Kevin more seriously. I could be in a completely different predicament than I am right now. I sigh as I look at my reflection in the mirror on the headboard. I was so caught up in the drama with Josh I didn't stop to take a look around. Maybe if I had I would've realized I had other opportunities.

I couldn't risk losing Josh through my own admission. After all the time I had invested in our crazy relationship, I couldn't let it go with a mere chance of happiness with someone else.

I allowed a couple of days to pass ignoring Kevin's phone calls. I was rarely home, so for him to catch me at the right time was near impossible. I worked all morning into the afternoon. Whenever I was done cleaning all the rooms on my assigned floor at the Doubletree, I was free to leave. Forced to punch out for a lunch break according to Rhode Island law, I went out to the receiving area, the designated smoking area, and smoked a cigarette or two while drinking my Diet Coke.

There were several people outside smoking, including Shonnie.

"How many rooms you got done?" she asked as usual.

"Ten," I answered as I lit my cigarette.

"Damn, girl, you better slow down, or you ain't gonna be getting no hours. How you gonna pay your rent?" Shonnie gave me that speech at least twice a week. She had her daughter to clothe and feed along with Rodney's two older kids from one of his high-school girlfriends.

"I only have my alcohol to pay for other than my rent. I'm all good, girl, don't you worry 'bout me. Where's Rodney?"

"Inside the lunchroom getting my plate for me."

"How many rooms you got left?" I asked.

"Shit, girl, they musta been partying on my floor. I only got six done. Are you gonna stay and get a ride home today?"

"I don't know yet. I'm not feeling too good today."

"Yeah, you're lookin' pretty rough, girl. Were you out all night again?"

"Practically!" I yawned.

"Well, you know it's Sunday. You hate waiting for the bus on Sunday, don't you?"

"Yeah, it only runs every hour instead of every half-hour."

"Come on, Mommy, you're eating lunch today." She grabbed my arm and pulled me toward the door.

"Ay, Shonnie!" I gasped, pulling my arm back and showing her my lit cigarette.

She let go of my arm. "Hurry up and finish your cigarette. I'll get you a plate. Promise you'll come in and eat with us. You gotta take better care of yourself, Mommy." I don't know why the Spanish-speaking population chooses to call each other mommy and poppy as a term of endearment, but I liked it. It showed me that she cared.

"Si, senorita."

"When you finish you come meet me on my floor. If I'm not there, Mommy, come to the conference room. You know Rodney's always the last one to be done."

I felt my energy level rapidly decreasing. The night before was finally catching up with me. Breaking for too long allowed the booze draining out of my system to wear me out more.

After my rooms were completely clean and my linen closet stocked for the following day I went to meet up with Shonnie. By the time we finally finished with everything and punched out it was already half past six.

"Do you want to hang out and have a few drinks with us tonight?" Shonnie asked.

"Sure. Let me take a shower and I'll be over. What you got to drink?"

"Well, I got my Bud," she said, "but I still got your favorite in the cabinet."

"Oh, yeah? Do you have any juice for it?" I asked, "or should I bring some?"

"Could you bring some, Mommy?"

"Of course," I said, crossing the street. "Be back in half an hour." It was dusk and there were groups of people hanging out here and there on stoops. Most of them were smoking something or other. Laughter, beat boxing, and free styling was the usual sound. There was nothing out of the ordinary on the street that dusky night.

The phone rang as I got out of the shower. I answered it. "Yeah?"

"Hey, what's up?" It was Kevin on the other end.

"How are you?" I was happy to hear his voice.

"I was just calling to see what you were doin' tonight."

"I'm taking it easy tonight. I just got off of work and I'm headed up the Hill to hang with my chick from work. Nuttin' big, ya know?"

"So I ain't gonna see you tonight?"

"Nah, I need to chill tonight. I drank too much last night or something. I was hurting at work. Two days in a row would kill me. 'Sides, she's waiting for me now. She gives me a ride sometimes. I can't diss her like that."

"Alright, then. I'll talk to you later."

"Bye!" I cut it short before he tried to ask questions about when he might see me again.

I didn't necessarily enjoy letting him down. I knew that the more I did it lessened the length of time he'd allow me to string him along. I needed space to let the previous night soak in or fade away; whichever one happened didn't make much difference to me.

At Shonnie's we sat in her kitchen and drank a few drinks. We laughed and played with the kids. Josh had paged me while I was visiting, so I used Shonnie's phone to call him back.

"What's going on?" I asked when he answered.

"I was just seeing how you were doing. I haven't seen you in a while."

"I'm across the street with my girl right now. Just chillin'."

"What about tonight?"

"I'm not staying here too long. I am going home in a while."

"Alright. I'll call your house later then."

"Yup, bye!"

I was back home shortly before midnight in time for Josh's call. I'm sure he wanted to see if I would be true to my word. I was as usual. We conversed over the phone for quite some time. I believe it was close to two in the morning when we hung up. Josh and I often had great conversations about our dreams and our goals. He had visions of his grown-up world and I shared mine. Sometimes our stories would include each other and other times they didn't.

Lying in my bed whispering into the phone into the wee hours of the morning in response to his masculine voice spilling the dreams from his heart and oozing the ideas from his mind was by far one of the happiest memories in my life. Josh and I had these conversations often. Once again we were on our separate paths, which were eventually leading us back to each other.

I made it through the beginning of the week without speaking to Kevin. One of those days during my afternoon nap, I was rudely awakened by the sound of my pager. I checked the number but didn't recognize it and noticed the time read ten minutes after six. During my slumber Kevin had called me. I listened to the message he'd left on my machine. He sounded disappointed that I wasn't able to speak with him in person. Instead he was subjected to the unpleasant attitude in my dismal voice on the machine saying, "This is Reba. Leave a message or page me."

Kevin does page me but it's rarely ever from the same number. It was most likely he who had awoken me with the page. When I don't call, I use the excuse that the number was unfamiliar. That night I didn't answer his page or return his call.

Josh paged me several times, all of which received an answer. The constant pages made me feel special. They let me know he was thinking about me as much as I thought about him (but would never admit to).

I spent most of the time at Amber's. Her street was much quieter than mine. The children are so pure and so innocent. They gave me the only sense of hope that life is not always all bad. They had the ability to replenish some of my own natural youthful highs.

Josh came to Amber's house once a day for a quick visit. His knowledge and interest in my familial situations also made me feel more connected with him. He and my sister got along well together.

"You ready yet? I am waiting for the word. You say it and his ass is mine!" Josh never failed to offer a beat-down on her abuser.

"I'm fine," she assured him every time.

In the Hill he never stayed at any location too long. His visits at my sister's place didn't last more than three-quarters of an hour, yet they were always eventful. Josh made us laugh as he entertained us with ridiculous stories of his dealings with crack heads, life in jail, and some other guy's struggle with the ladies. It was the same at Danielle's or Shonnie's.

Josh called me at home in the early evening. He was well aware of my crazy schedule and knew what time would be good to catch me awake at home.

"Alright, are you gonna come back and chill or do I really have to keep chasing your ass down in the Hill? I thought we agreed my place was to give you somewhere to go outside the Hill. You've been spending a lot of time out there. Are you ever coming home?"

"Yeah, I'll be there tonight. Let me call Casey and see what she's doing."

"Okay, but even if she doesn't come you are!"

"I know."

Casey picked me up and we went to the party house. I was so excited to see him. I couldn't help anticipating the times we were more than friends.

Although being a bitch was a very natural defense mechanism, it was much more enjoyable to be less on guard. Dolores Claiborne said it best, "Sometimes, being a bitch is all a woman has to hold on to." And when times were rough on me emotionally, I held on with a death grip!

Josh had purchased a twenty-five-gallon fish tank for fresh-water fish. He came up behind me and put his arms around my shoulders. He whispered in my ear, "Do you wanna come see my new fish?"

"Oh yeah, I heard Tyler talking about it to someone before," I replied with great anticipation.

He spun me around and I followed him into his bedroom. There it was directly ahead of us. "Wow," I exclaimed. "They're awesome."

"This big grey and white one over here is a Convict. I named him Josh Junior. You can call him Junior for short. Then I have two Oscars. This one," he said pointing to the smaller of the two beige colored fish, "is named Pearl, and that guy is her boyfriend named Earl. Then I have the snakehead fish. I don't know what to call him yet."

"He's my favorite. That thing's cool looking," I said.

"Then you can name him."

"He's big!"

"Yeah baby!" He was being a smart ass with a deep voice. "Too bad the name Josh is already taken!"

I laughed and rolled my eyes. "Well, you could call him Josh Senior, then."

"But they're not even the same."

"Then you name him. It's a fuckin fish. Why does he even need a name?" I took his statement as an insult. He didn't respond, so I broke the uncomfortable silence. "What are those other fish?"

"Those are the algae eaters. I think they're called Pleco or something," Josh answered kindly, despite my lingering attitude.

"So what are their names?"

"I didn't think they should have names. They actually serve a purpose as opposed to the others that just look cool."

"So they don't deserve names but the other guys do? That's a little prejudiced don't ya think?" I don't know why I had to always be such a wise guy.

"It doesn't matter."

We sat in silence on his bed, admiring the beautiful fish. The light from the tank illuminated the bedroom. It was almost romantic sitting there. I didn't want to say anything for fear of ruining the moment even more, but at the same time I felt I should say something before the moment passed us by.

I looked away from the tank and turned toward Josh, pleasantly surprised to see he was already looking at me. A shy smile instantly formed on my face. Despite my efforts to push him away he still wanted me. His adoring expression stayed the same.

And then I heard it again. The annoying beating of my heart rang out. I hoped the inflation didn't start back up. In my bumbling state I said without any sign of affection, "What's up?"

He let out a soft giggle at my childlike reaction to the vibe before responding, "I'm really glad you're here. I couldn't wait to show you." I couldn't muster up the will to look away and break the spell he had me under. I stared back into his eyes.

"Yeah, it's um, good to be friends again." I managed to speak a complete sensible sentence. I finally turned away.

Josh stood up and came directly in front of me. I leaned back on both hands and tittered as I looked up at him. He slowly bent down, put his hands on either side of me on the bed and leaned toward my face. His eyes revealed one who really cared for me.

He started kissing me softly. I felt the thumping in my chest break through my sternum once again. I hadn't drunk enough alcohol to be able to handle this. My wall might've crumbled on his bed. It had to stop, immediately. I turned my head and said, "Whoa, where'd that come from?"

"What do you mean, 'where'd that come from?' The same place it always comes from. You know how we do it. It's all good between us now, right?" he said, surprised I had stopped the passion from brewing.

"I know." I tried to remain cool and collected, "You got people in your house right now. You know how these assholes are. Somebody will walk right in here, and I don't feel like putting on a show for them fools! I'm just saying we should chill for now."

Just then there was a quick knock at Josh's bedroom door. Big Dawg walked in and stood at the threshold without waiting for a response to his knock. Josh was still leaning into me. "Yo man, there's some beef that might be kicking up right now. Thought you might wanna step outside. I didn't mean to interrupt. Sorry, man."

"What beef?" I asked. Josh stood up and I followed.

Big Dawg directed his response to Josh. "Brown's outside with some dude who says he burnt him." Big Dawg double-tapped the side of the doorframe and headed out.

"I can't be having this shit at my house man, I'm on probation."

"I got this then. I just wanted to let you know."

I stopped in the kitchen and grabbed a Molson before walking out onto the front porch to see what was going on. Out in the street I saw a crowd dispersing. Brown was mumbling to his friends as they got into a Mazda 626, but I was glad there was no further altercation. I was proud of Josh for responding in the mature way he did. Sometimes I wondered if he cared at all about the probation hanging over his head. That night proved his concerns were there.

When we were back inside the house there was a small meeting between Big Dawg, Josh, Tyler, Jay, Casey, and me in the kitchen. Josh was concerned that something else might happen that night. Tyler was convinced the heat was gone. Big Dawg suggested we move the party over to Craig's house. It was a unanimous decision. Big Dawg used the phone in Tyler's room to call Craig and run the plan by him.

Tyler made the announcement to the rest of the guests. "Yo, yo, yo, the party's over kids. Grab your shit 'cause we are officially closing up shop."

Craig was expected over at Josh and Tyler's, but there were uninvited guests at his house who had detained him. It worked in our favor. We were able to bring the party over to Craig and Joe's place.

K Nice was already there. Casey and I were happy to see her.

"Hey, hey, hey!" I yelled. "What is up? I'm so glad you came. We were getting nervous we hadn't seen you in a while."

"I told Casey I was coming to Craig's. Didn't she tell you?"

"Yeah, like two minutes ago on our way over here. I'm glad we came over then." I noticed Craig, Joe, and K Nice had already started playing quarters, Joe's favorite game, "What'd you guys start without me?"

Craig took it personally, "Well, we would've waited if we knew you were coming."

"Well, maybe you should've called and invited me!" I said with a wink.

"You don't need no damn invitation. You're here now ain't ya? So jump in then and quit ya cryin'!" Joe thundered.

"Grrrrrr!" I growled in Joe's ear. I took the empty seat in the middle and joined in the game.

"We even got your specialty tonight. I got it for you." Joe pointed to the bottle of Bacardi they were playing with. He whispered, "Then later on I have a surprise for you."

Big Dawg stepped into the kitchen after we played a few rounds of quarters. "Craig picked up *Debbie Does Dallas*. We were gonna put it in after we make another trip to the packy."

"Who's goin'?" Joe asked.

"We haven't decided yet. We were thinking you or Tyler were gonna go 'cause you got fake IDs. Tyler doesn't wanna go 'cause he doesn't need anything. But we didn't know who's gonna drive. Casey don't wanna drive and neither does Josh."

"Josh is a pussy. I'll go, if Reba drives me."

"Well, they're all out here trying to figure it out and we only got a half-hour to get our shit together. The store's gonna be closed soon," Big Dawg urged.

"Would you take me?" Joe asked me as we walked into the living room.

"Yeah, I don't mind if Casey will let me use her car."

"She'll let you. See that's why I like you. You don't bullshit around like most of these punks."

Within fifteen minutes we had made our decision on who was going, who was driving what and who was buying what. I drove Casey's car and Joe and Craig came with me. The lights were off at the store when we pulled up in front of it.

Joe rushed out to find the door locked. He started pounding on the glass. The chances of the police driving by were high since the station was only half a block away. I had already been drinking and I didn't want to get in trouble for a DUI.

Craig opened the back door of the car and yelled, "What are you doing man? Is it closed?"

"Nah, man we didn't drive out here for nothing!" Joe acted like it was a long drive, when really it only took us five minutes to get there, five minutes too long it appeared. "There he is!" Joe exclaimed. "Come on, man, hook us up would ya?" he pleaded with the man inside the store.

Two seconds later Joe waved us over to him. The employee was unlocking the store. I guess if I saw Joe persistently pounding on my glass door I would let him in too just to prevent further progression of his temper. Once inside Craig hurriedly got a thirty-pack of Natural Light and a twelve-pack of Coors Light. I was with Joe.

"What do you want?" he asked me after he picked up a twelve-pack of Labatt's Ice for himself.

"I'm all set. I didn't bring any money."

"I didn't ask you if you had any money. I asked you what you wanted."

"I got plenty of Molson Ices at the house. I don't need any more."

"I didn't ask you what you had already either. You and your Molson Ices, why don't you try something else for a change? Stop being so boring." Joe was rude even when he was being nice.

"I don't even like beer. Molson Ice is the only beer I can drink, besides watered-down Natty Lights."

"That's 'cause you never had real beer." Joe put his arm around me. "I'm gonna take you under my wing, young one." The attendant in the store was kind enough to let us in. We were underage and overstaying our welcome. I became uncomfortable as Joe took his sweet time inspecting the contents of each cooler. He bent down in the cooler and picked up a six-pack of Killian's Red. "This one's for you. You'll like it! I'm starting you off slow."

I was in no position to argue with him. Being that Joe was rough around the edges I was privileged by his attraction towards my style. I took all the admiration I could get.

At the counter he asked for a bottle of Jagermeister. He paid for everything while Craig waited patiently. The man behind the counter was glad to see us go. I thanked him as we walked out, since Joe didn't.

Back at their house I sat in the single-person chair beside the couch. Joe came over and sat on the arm of the chair. He handed me an opened Killian's bottle and waited for me to drink it. I took a sip and rested it on my lap.

"Nah, you gotta take a real swig if you want to taste it," Joe insisted as he lifted up my arm.

I took a good long swig to make him happy.

"Good, huh?" He shook his head yes, answering for me.

"Actually it is."

"See? I'll take care of you girl!"

"What you got over there?" Josh asked from his spot on the floor across the room.

Joe answered, "Killian's Red" as I held up the bottle. "I'm gonna teach your girl how to drink the good shit."

Josh looked at me with only half of his captivating smile. He didn't overtly show jealousy over Joe. But I noticed his discomfort in seeing me across the room with another man. Joe slid to the floor in front of my chair. It was difficult for Josh to pay attention to the porno as he kept looking in our direction. It was a riot watching those idiots on the screen, and we laughed collectively throughout, so much so that my jaw hurt afterward.

Shortly after the ridiculous porno film was over a crowd rolled in. A group of young girls including Andrea, the girl Dan was rejected by last, came giggling in. They showed up on the weekends because they were still in high school.

Sure enough Dummy Dan was next through the door with Kevin two steps behind. By that time, luckily for me the house was crowded. That night I wanted to stand clear of Kevin. At the same time it wasn't wise to be next to Josh, so I chose to stick with Joe instead. Kevin wouldn't come near me if I were with Joe all night. Joe was hardly approachable even by his friends. And neither Josh nor Kevin would accuse me of having an affair with Joe. Next to him I was safe from the soap opera drama.

Kevin didn't stay very long. Their only intention was to get weed from Craig. They went into Craig's room with Josh and a few others to smoke out of a bong. Craig wanted to test it out every chance he got because it was a new purchase from the Smoke Shop in town.

Joe and I went into the kitchen to get in on the card games. I decided to hide out there because it was out of the way from Craig's room to the front door. My scheme worked and I missed witnessing Kevin's departure. I spent the remainder of the night like countless others in the kitchen getting wasted playing cards.

Chapter Twelve

"Alcoholism Is a Process that Only One Can Stop"

On the days that I wasn't scheduled to work I went to Craig and Joe's to watch soap operas with them. Craig liked the same shows I did. It gave me a good place to hide out from Kevin during the day. There was no real reason I kept Kevin around except to horde all of my toys like a child. His body lit my fire and made me feel things I had only felt with Josh. His mind thus far had proved to be a real match for my own, yet I couldn't bring myself away from Josh to fully focus on him.

I had written the poem "Oracle" for Craig and Joe. I believed we shared a connection through our relationship with alcohol. I knew they could see it as clearly in me as I could in them. We were the same, unbeknownst to our circle of friends. Craig appreciated the poem I had written and dedicated to him. He seemed touched by my acknowledgment and acceptance of his "problem." It was a problem none of us were willing to fix at that point in our lives. Joe, on the other hand, raved over the poem like it was an admission into some secret club. In his twisted mind the club was the best thing to be a part of, and I had just passed the initiation.

My mother lent me her car one week. She went away on a vacation and wanted me to watch it for her. When I was tipsy I felt compelled to leave my company. This made Joe upset.

"Why are you leaving?"

I was extremely cautious not to play the intriguing "lust me if you dare game" with him. There were rumors that he had raped a girl once, and I didn't want to find out firsthand if he was capable of such atrocities. Therefore, I was always open and honest with him, as much as I was capable of at the time.

"I got my mother's car. I can't be getting shit-faced and risk crashing her shit."

"So where are you going? Let me go with you."

"I am just gonna go home and take a nap. I'll be back later."

"When later?"

"Well, I gotta eat and take a shower and shit. I'll be back tonight at around the usual time."

"Alright, but I am gonna have something waiting for you so you better come back."

But when the usual time approached I went over Josh's to see what the plans were. Since he was working I was free to do whatever. I assumed Joe and Craig would arrive so I started drinking with Tyler, Jay, Casey, and Big Dawg.

There was a mellow atmosphere with no sign of things livening up. There wasn't much beer and no one had liquor. Only Joe and Craig could drink a large quantity of alcoholic beverages consistently throughout the week like me.

Because I was growing increasingly uncomfortable in small groups as my alcoholism progressed, I announced, "Well, I already told Joe I was gonna go over there. So I will see you all tomorrow."

"I'm going with you," Tyler invited himself.

In the car we got into our normal line of conversation.

"So how's Sammy the slut?"

"Man, you are so rough!"

"Well, I know this one is really into you. What are you doing to that girl?"

"Reba, I keep trying to let her down easy, but I can't get it across to her."

"Don't be frontin', Ty. When you stick your dick in her and let her sleep over on a regular basis she thinks it's more than a hook. You can't keep a girl strictly for sex and allow her to sleep in your bed. Then she will feel a connection with you. You can fuck anyone, but sharing your bed for the night is a little more intimate. Don't you have the whole awkward morning after?"

"Yeah, but how do you say 'okay, thanks for the hook now go'?"

"You can't. You gotta say it beforehand. How do you tell her to leave in the morning? Make up an excuse if you have to. But let her know that she ain't sleeping over."

"So is that why your face is always the last one I see at night, but then never see in the morning?"

"Listen, I don't get the boot. I boot myself."

"Oh I know all about that already. You don't have to tell me."

"What are you talking about? Did Josh say something?"

"Nah, I can't really say. But let me put it to you this way. It's a big deal when we see you in his bed the next morning."

"Oh, so that's why sometimes I hear you guys peeking in the door?"

Tyler laughs. "You can hear us?"

"Not really. I wake up to the ruckus. Lucky for me I sleep on my stomach."

His laugh grows louder, "Not for us!"

At Joe's I was pleased to find Kevin but disappointed at the lack of alcohol. They were eager to get out of the house and so they volunteered me to drive them around the Ocean Drive to smoke a bone. Craig was particularly quiet that night and refrained from joining us.

Tyler insisted on sitting in the back to be less conspicuous, as did Joe, who owned a notorious reputation. Kevin by order of circumstance sat with me in the front.

He had his usual pint of Southern Comfort that he was very generous in sharing. Joe was getting prepared to roll the joint. They waited until they were actually en route to the popular drive before smoking. It was more secluded out there along the ocean shoreline. There was little traffic at night on the long stretch of winding road, with no intersections, lights, or stop signs; perfect conditions.

Suddenly there were flashing lights behind me. "Oh shit, guys, we got company. There's a fucking pig behind me and I think he's pulling me over."

There was a rush of "fuck" and "shit" in the back seat as they fumbled to clear the drugs and paraphernalia. "What did you do?" Tyler asked from the back seat.

"I didn't do anything. I don't know why he's pulling me over."

"Fuck," Tyler exclaimed, "he's gonna search us. What do I do with this bottle? I don't want to get in trouble again, man."

"Throw it under the seat," Joe said.

"Fuck you, so I can get in trouble? Don't leave that shit in my mother's car, Ty. There's no fucking way I am going to take the wrap for you guys." I slowed the car to a stop and turned off the ignition.

Kevin kept telling his friends to relax and calm down.

"Reba, please help me," Tyler pleaded.

"This is my mother's car. I am not letting you leave your shit in here so the fucking thing gets towed."

"Well ... well," he said thinking aloud. "Well, will you put it in your shirt? The guy cops can't search the girls. Please?"

"How the fuck am I supposed to get it now? He's already coming over here."

"Dude, just lean down a little and let her grab it behind you. Too late, man, hide that shit," Joe said.

Just then the police officer was at my window. I rolled it down and readily handed him my license, registration, and proof of insurance before he could even ask for it. "Did I do something wrong?" I asked politely.

"Well, I saw who you have with you in your back seat there." He pointed to Joe. "Do you know Mr. Fisher well?"

"I know him from friends."

He asked what we were doing around the drive. I told him we were just going for a ride before I dropped them off at home. I had already been drinking and feared that I might incriminate myself if I spoke too much.

"Get out of the car, Joe." Then he looked at me, "This guy has been into a lot of trouble lately. I just wanted to check up on him."

The overweight officer took Joe to the back of the car. He continued to speak with him candidly. Tyler was sweating profusely; worrying about Joe's fate and his own if he was caught with the bottle.

"Here comes Skinny," I warned.

A second officer came to the passenger-side window. He was much thinner than the first. "Are there any illegal drugs in the car?"

"No," I replied. Joe hid the marijuana and the blunt in a hole in his coat. To my knowledge it wasn't uncovered.

"Whose car is it?"

"My mother's."

"You," he pointed to Kevin, "Step outside here." He repeated the questions to him.

His answers mirrored mine. The officer walked Kevin to the front of the car and searched him. I watched through my rear-view mirror to see the fat officer still talking with Joe.

"Alright, Tyler, this is your chance. Fatty is still occupied with Joe. Keep your eye on Skinny," I said, urging him to make his move. He cautiously leaned forward and tried to slip the bottle of Southern Comfort to me. I couldn't quite reach it, and Skinny was walking towards us with Kevin. Tyler panicked and let go of the bottle before I had a chance to grab it.

"Shit, it's under the seat!"

Kevin was escorted past Tyler and me to the rear. I looked in my mirror again and saw the fat cop handcuff Joe, lead him into the police car, and then sit in the front.

Kevin was left alone as Skinny approached the back door and asked Tyler to get out of the car. He leaned forward and asked if I had anything in the car.

"No," I answered.

"Well, we are going to have to search it, so tell me now if there is."

"There's nothing."

Tyler was frisked in front of the car. They were in my clear view. Kevin was patiently waiting as he was told. Fatty was sitting, checking everyone's name through the computer while keeping an eye on Kevin.

This was my final chance to retrieve the bottle and get it out of sight. I leaned sideways, trying to be as inconspicuous as possible, and reached my hand under the seat. I had to fumble around for a minute before I felt the chilled glass. By then the officer had left Tyler alone in the front of the parade and was coming towards me again. I had the bottle in my right hand inside the car. I reached behind my back and tried to stuff the bottle in the top of my pants under my jacket. But the bottle wasn't secure yet when the officer opened my door and asked me out of the car. As I used my left hand to help myself out of the vehicle I concentrated on securing the bottle with my more hidden right hand and covering it well with my coat. It was a success.

We all got off. There were no existing warrants for any of the guys in the group. My mother's car was clean. And the boys were right—I wasn't frisked. The purpose of asking me outside the vehicle was so they could search it more efficiently.

When we drove away Tyler said to Joe, "Hey, was that your boyfriend or something?"

Joe's voice roared from the back seat, "What the hell are you saying?"

Tyler remained calm as usual. "Well, he just seemed to be real friendly with you. What's that all about?"

"You know these pigs are always on my case, c'mon."

"I know that they threw a lot of threats at me. You two looked like you were having a more personal conversation."

"I was in handcuffs man, were you?"

"Alright, alright, lower the testosterone boys. Can we just get back in town without another incident, please?"

Tyler had a point. I was very attentive to the officers' actions and my friends' reactions while trying to recover the bottle. Joe certainly didn't seem unnerved like Kevin and Tyler. But I kept my thoughts on the subject to myself. Joe wasn't one I was willing to piss off.

I announced that nobody was smoking in my car that night and drove everyone home. Kevin came to my house with me.

Josh was keeping his distance, so I chose to spend more time with Kevin. Our relationship was progressing and I was unprepared. Tyler noticed and mentioned it during one of our private conversations.

"What's up with your boy, man?" I asked Tyler.

"Which one?" he said with a smirk.

"What do you mean, 'which one'? Josh of course."

"Oh well, I didn't know if you were talking about Kevin." His eyes dared to stare into mine for the answer in case my words didn't disclose any information.

"Listen, man, you know how your boy is! He fucking flip-flops. Am I really supposed to sit around here waiting to see which way he'll go today?"

"You do, though!"

"No, I don't. Why do you say that?"

"C'mon Reba, be real. It's me you're talking to."

"So you know I care about Josh. So what? You just asked what was going on with Kevin, so how could you say I do nothing but wait around for him?" I was very defensive, fearing Tyler's intuition.

"Okay, I'll give you that!" he said, relieving my anxiety on the subject.

"Kevin's cool, ya know? It ain't no big thing!" That was good enough to satisfy Tyler's curiosity. And I was finally off the hook, for the time being.

I needed some time to think with my girls and clear my head of the male gender. I planned a night at my mother's house with Casey and K Nice. It was supposed to be just the three of us. We got completely annihilated. I tripped running up the stairs to go to the bathroom. K Nice vomited in my dog's bowl. Casey spilled the beans and called her lover to come to my mother's house. The gin and juice apparently made her horny.

Because Casey made that call, Josh and Tyler showed up too. K Nice passed out in my sister's old bedroom. Casey, Jay, Josh, Tyler, and I continued drinking and played Outburst.

Josh was flirtatious from the beginning. I couldn't turn him down as he sat snuggling up to me in the chair. The alcohol allowed the most recent events in my life to fade out of significance.

Tyler, Josh, and I were at the kitchen table playing cards. Casey made it to the privacy of the dark living room with Jay. They were getting intimate on the couch when the dog started barking.

Somehow Kevin found out where I was and showed up with Dan. It wasn't obvious to the unsuspecting eye that Kevin and I had a personal relationship and so he was coming specifically to see me.

I dreaded answering the door, but the dog's barking didn't falter. I was left with no choice. Surely they'd seen my mother's car parked along the street. I wanted to prevent Josh's suspicion as to why I was apprehensive to answer.

"I can't have a lot of people bringing attention to my mom's house. You guys aren't even supposed to be here."

Kristina and Tyler have been known to hit it off well in the bedroom when they got drunk enough. Tyler was hoping that would be the case that particular night. Josh, of course came to see me, and Jay was there by Casey's request. It was plain to see we were all matched up inside.

Convincing Kevin that I couldn't have any more people in the house out of respect for my mother was the hard part. I tried explaining it several different ways. I tried hinting that the situation would've been different had he come alone, especially considering I was not a fan of Dan. My efforts were futile. Kevin wasn't buying any of my lies.

He left, humiliated in front of his friends and hurt by my decision to be with Josh over him. No matter how hard I tried, there was no denying that was what it boiled down to.

Needless to say, Kevin was off my radar for years after that. I felt like shit about it. I had no idea what to make of the whole affair. I hated hurting people's feelings. Knowing that I might have done so shaded an ugly cloud over my self-image. The only way I could see through the cloud was to put on my veil. They say two wrongs don't make a right, but it certainly eased guilt.

Flight # Infinity

Do you want to fly?
Invincible;
No fear up front

Don't ever ask why
Hidden answers
Behind the mind

Do you want to fly?
Illuminate
Taste the pleasure

Just gesture how high
And spread your wings
This is no dare

Do you want to fly?
Relax blinded
Sweet sensation

Would you like to try?
Spontaneous
This is the life

Do you want to fly?
Take full control
Rebellious choice

Time will still go by
Release your soul
Explore that realm

Do you want to fly?
Don't close your eyes
This is no dream

I drank with whoever would drink with me. Most of the time that was at Josh's house. Other times it was at Craig's, and others yet were at Casey's or at a club. The season was underway, so life was jumping all over Newport. It wasn't hard to find somewhere to go.

The old security guard at the Doubletree was named Bill. He was the one I confided in about the guests who made me feel violated. Bill was a retired Boston policeman. Sharp as shit that old man was, even at seventy-two years old. He had a very slender body topped off with a full head of grey hair. He was slightly hunched at the shoulders. His bright blue eyes reminded me of my father's, also revealing a soul who'd seen more unpleasant scenes in his life than he cared to remember. Around his solemn eyes were heavy bags, which blended into the remaining creases covering his face. Bill's voice was so raspy the employees throughout the hotel found it difficult to understand him. I could understand him just fine, even when he didn't speak. Bill adored me. Men over fifty usually did for reasons beyond my understanding. I looked forward to talking with the old man on my cigarette breaks.

Bill smoked non-filtered Pall Malls, extra long. "I can't believe you can smoke those things. It can't possibly taste good!" I said, looking at Bill's stogie.

"Well, what the hell do you think you got? Sugar cane?" Bill grunted in return.

"At least my Newport has a mint taste other than plain old dirty smoke."

"Oh yeah, that menthol will make your lungs bleed."

I laughed at his comment. I'd heard it so many times before.

"I'm serious," he said with an expression to prove it. He had a funny way of looking after me sometimes. I wondered if he wished he were my grandfather; still other times maybe he wanted to be my sugar daddy.

"Well, when that happens I'll quit."

"Yeah!" He rolled his eyes after shooting me a look and catching my smile.

Just then one of the bellhops came out for a cigarette. He was an Englishmen named Stewart. "Cheers!?" he greeted us in his extremely strong accent. He lowered his lengthy body onto one of the many scattered empty milk crates flipped upside down. I usually chose to stand, as I did that day. Bill always stood.

"What's up, Stew?" I replied wholeheartedly.

Bill was silent, steadying his gaze at the bay ahead.

"Beautiful day, isn't it?" Stew liked to talk. He was a seemingly happy guy with a knack for lifting my spirits. He was very outgoing and friendly to just about everyone, great characteristics for a bellhop.

Stew asked for the twentieth time since I knew him if I would go to the Station nightclub.

"I told you I have no ID. How am I supposed to get in?" I would've loved to go, and so after a while I got frustrated with his request to meet him and his English friends there.

Bill grew agitated and interrupted with comments about work.

Stew responded with a few "Huhs?" and "Whats?" because he couldn't understand him.

Finally, Bill questioned, "Are you guys done bringing in those guests to the Captains Quarters?"

"No, they're not all here yet," Stew answered.

"Then what are you doing sitting on your ass out here?"

"I just wanted a quick smoke."

"You better hurry up with that cigarette then. You know who this group is, don't you?"

"Yeah, I heard," Stew replied as he got up and walked towards the door.

"You don't want to fuck this up," Bill called after him.

The new arrival group hadn't been brought to my attention yet, so I grew a bit curious to see what the fuss was. I figured I'd find out sooner or later from my supervisors, and if not, my curiosity would only last until quitting time anyway.

"This kid," Bill mumbled as he shook his head and pointed with his thumb back towards the door where Stew had just reentered the building, "bet he heard that though!"

Bill didn't like Stew or anyone else that I knew of beside myself. He was a tough old bastard who didn't put up with anybody's shit. I think he'd lost his faith in the human race a long time ago. I could relate to that. He got on a lot of the employees' cases for things that I don't think even pertained to him or his work.

He struck me as a lonely guy, though I dared not show him any pity. I looked forward to our chats on my smoke breaks, and the appearance of his face around the corner on the sixth floor still gave me some peace of mind. He wouldn't stop to chat, but he wouldn't leave the floor until grabbing my attention with a quick nod hello.

Bill hurriedly finished his smoke and followed after Stew to check on the front lobby. I waited a few minutes before returning to work myself.

Like Shonnie, my supervisors used to advise me to slow down and make some more hours. I was naturally a fast-paced person and was certainly not intent on racing the clock. I did the best cleaning job in the department. The sixth floor had the best-kept rooms in the entire hotel, including the suites, so the supervisors couldn't complain. I was nominated for employee of the month several times, but I never won. It was not something I had aspired to be. That people noticed my efforts made me happy enough.

After work I changed into regular street clothes in the locker room before walking to the bus station. I wouldn't be caught dead in my uniform outside of work. The bus drivers knew me by face but not by name. I smiled and said hello every time I entered the bus and would thank the driver as I departed. They were all very kind to me despite the part of town I lived in.

It was good to be in the sanctuary of my own home. I was secluded from the outside world. I felt no pressure to be cool or tough or politically correct. I could relax in the stillness of my sacred space. People rarely came to my house for a visit. Aside from a few of my close friends no one came inside. While Josh had his own place even he hardly came over.

Once home I immediately turned up the radio in my room so I couldn't hear the phone, or the door, or the outside neighbors. Most importantly I couldn't hear myself think. I stripped my clothes off in my bedroom and then rounded the corner to the bathroom for a shower. I turned the water on nice and hot.

During my showers I was able to relax and breathe fresh air. Stripped of any impurities I relished the warmth and simplicity of it all. The showerhead was a good one, and the water pressure was hard enough to resemble a massage. My routine was the same every day. After twenty minutes or so I'd get out of the shower and towel dry, then throw on a terry-cloth bathrobe and smoke a cigarette with a towel still wrapped in my hair.

I could really feel the migraine then. It lingered about all day, but after I relaxed it really kicked into gear. The cigarette after my shower made me a little dizzy and lightheaded. I'd plop down on the bed and rest my eyes. I would nap until six or so. Not many people shared my backwards schedule.

When I awoke, I threw one of Tina's beef and bean burritos on a cookie sheet next to some curly fries and put it in the oven. While it cooked for fifteen minutes I smoked a cigarette and drank one of the many Molson Ices stocked in my fridge. I ran back upstairs and popped four ibuprofen pills because my head was still pounding. I washed them down with a long swig of my beer and got dressed.

I called Casey to confirm our plans for the night. "Hey, are we still going to Josh and Jay's?"

"Good news, girl. You are going to love me! We're not going to party central tonight. I made alternate plans."

"Like what?"

"There's this guy, Vinnie, I know from my cousin. He works at the Station."

"No way!"

"Yup. I saw him at my job today and he told me to come over tonight."

"Yeah, but what about me?"

"Don't be ridiculous. You're coming."

"Is he gonna pitch a fit?"

"No. I told him I was bringing a friend and he was cool with it."

"Get the fuck out!"

"Do you love me or what?"

"I so love you. I'll be over soon."

I filled my backpack with four Molsons and pocketed thirty bucks. Wearing my black three-inch platform-like boots and my black jacket I was ready to go. Even though I lived in low-income housing where the utilities were included in the rent I made sure I shut off all radios and lights. I double-checked to make sure I had my cigarettes, lighter, and pager in my purse and walked out the door, locking it behind me. Casey lived in the neighboring apartment complex so I walked over to her house.

Vinnie let us in the club without paying the cover charge. Since he was working the door he didn't have the opportunity to fraternize. Casey was free to do whatever she wanted inside.

Something about him annoyed me. I couldn't put my finger on it. I barely had the chance to get to know him, since he completely ignored me. I wasn't used to that. He was about twenty-seven years old, maybe twenty-eight. Casey was only nineteen like me, and that was too old for our taste.

We acted the part like we belonged there. I was there to get my dance on and Casey loved to mingle. The crowd at the downtown club was more of a "preppy" uptight bunch mixed with some tourists rather than drug dealers and alcoholic "tough guys."

Stew was in the club with some of his English friends.

I ran up to him, "Surprise!"

"I thought you said …" He paused.

"Long story. Anyway I am here!"

He introduced everyone briefly over the loud music. They all had visas to work in the states for a few months. Stew left us to order our first round of drinks. Upon returning he handed one to Casey and me saying, "Next one's on you!"

"Thanks," I said before sucking down the cosmopolitan he bought me.

"Holy shit, girl, slow down!"

"I came here to dance!" I said.

"Well, let's go." Stew grabbed my arm and pulled me out to the dance floor. I was never happier than while dancing. Stew noticed my relaxed aura and moved in closer to me. I tried to make small talk to keep the dancing on more of a friendly than flirty level.

When I felt Stew get too close again I put my hand up on his chest as a boundary. "Do you want another drink?"

"No thank you, darling, I still have my other."

"Well, I am gonna get one. I'll be back."

While I waited at the bar for the opportunity to get the bartender's attention, the man sitting on my right tried to hit on me. I quickly turned him down, but he wasn't taking no for an answer.

The bartender, ready for my order, interrupted him, "Is he bothering you?"

"I was just leaving," the man replied.

Casey and our English companions were skirting the edge of the dance floor when I returned.

"What the hell is wrong with men?" I asked. They all looked perplexed at me, so I continued, "Why do they think that a young woman without a man at her side wants them to hit on her?"

The English laughed. But Casey wanted an answer, "For real?"

"Is it just Americans or are you English guys the same way?"

"Well, I haven't hit on you yet, have I?" One asked in his defense.

"Yet!" The other joked and they laughed.

"Nah listen, sometimes a girl just wants to go out and have fun without being hounded by some horn dog."

"You girls love that shit," the first said.

"Well, I can't even order a drink without the nearest asshole calling me 'Beautiful' and asking why I'm alone. Is it really so hard for a guy to realize sometimes we *want* to be alone?" I asked.

"Well, I wouldn't exactly call going to a club with over a hundred people alone."

"I figure if I go to a place where I don't know anyone then I am alone and free to do what I want without someone harassing me."

"You're a beautiful girl. What do you expect?"

"Right, that reminds me. Why does my name suddenly become 'Beautiful'? 'Do you wanna dance, Beautiful' 'What is a beautiful girl like you doing alone?' 'Hey, Beautiful, got a cigarette?'" I sighed in disgust.

"I can't believe you don't take that as a compliment," he said as though I was being a snob.

"A compliment? Are you joking? I had this asshole come up to me asking me, 'Beautiful,' to take a walk with him to the bar. I declined, and he said, 'Have you ever been with someone who was rich before?' So I lied, right," I laughed, "and said 'of course.' So he said confidently, 'Well, let's go then,' and tried to grab my arm. Seriously, who the fuck did that guy think he was?"

Mumbles in agreement had no explanation for me, and the conversation died. I had another drink before returning to the dance floor, making my way towards Stew. He danced a bit funny, to his own rhythm. I didn't mind especially since he was obviously enjoying himself. After a few songs people usually have a drink or a cigarette or take a break. Stew was no different in that respect. I could've danced all night and so stayed on the dance floor. A while later Stew danced his way back to me.

"Hey, Beautiful, mind if I join you?" he said suavely.

"Not funny!" I replied with a smirk.

"Really though, when are we going to hook up?"

"We are hooking up; we're dancing, aren't we?" I said, dreading where this was going.

"Well, what are you doing after?"

"Going home *alone* like I always do."

"Well, that's what I mean then. When are we going to hook up?"

"Stew, I am not going to fuck you. Okay?"

"Why not? I am a nice guy, ain't I?"

"Of course you are and I like talking with you, but I don't want to hook up with you."

"Well, what do I have to do?" he pleaded.

"Ugh," I sighed. I didn't want to hurt his feelings or ruin our decent friendship so I decided it would be best to be honest with him. He had no connection with my routine life outside of work, so I told him the truth. "Look, Stew, to be honest with you I already gave my heart to someone else. He still has it. Until he decides to give it back I just don't think about any other guy that way."

"Oh," he paused. I was glad to see his expression was not what I expected. "Well, I can relate to that," he said, suddenly serious. "Mine gave it back and here I am in the states."

"I am sure you'll find another, but it's not me. Let's go get a drink!" Ah, the cure-all!

The youngest male bartender took a liking to me. Because he was stylishly dressed and relatively young he was the only new face in the building I ever noticed. In reality I wouldn't have given him a second glance outside those walls. His name was Mark, and he flirted with me at every order.

I intentionally refrained from flirting with him. I was careful not to reveal too much information about myself, uncertain of how he would take finding out my true age while he was serving me drinks.

When the night ended Casey had to pay our dues. Vinnie was now free to fraternize, and so I sat around waiting for him to get his fill of flirty taps and giggles from my girl who had to go along with it. She did okay for somebody who was not as devious and manipulative as me. I could tell that Vinnie was not going to play along with the sweet, little, innocent role for long though. He wanted something from Casey that she wasn't willing to give.

We were finally able to leave. Vinnie was walking in the opposite direction than we were. "How'd it go?" I asked Casey as we waited to cross the street.

"Ugh! It was fine at first. He wanted me to make plans with him during the week. But I wouldn't make any definite plans."

"Uh-oh! What does he want to hook up for in the middle of the week?"

"Yeah, does he really think I'm going to just schedule him in for a fuck? Who does that? What am I like his prostitute or something?"

"Wow! Is that what he said?" Men's insatiable horny appetite never ceased to amaze me.

"Basically! I asked him what he wanted to do for 'plans' and he just kept giving me this insinuating smile. Ugh, it was gross. I wanted to throw up!"

"Was he for real?"

"Yeah, I'm pretty sure." She hollered in the middle of the road, "I'm all set!"

"So now what? Our Station days are over?"

"Not quite. I think we can pull a few more off. We'll just have to sneak out before closing next time." We snickered at her scheming idea.

"It's up to you, man!" Then I got a little more serious and said, "I just hope it doesn't come down to me jumping on his back choking the shit outta him so he doesn't rape your ass."

"Nah, he ain't like that!"

"Yeah, well, I don't trust him. So don't get too comfortable around him."

"You don't have to worry about that." We were finally at the car and she drove me home.

We continued meeting Stew and his English friends at the Station. Each time Vinnie grew increasingly jealous over Casey's interaction with the English group despite the fact that it couldn't have been any more innocent. It was a shame Vinnie had to ruin that for us.

Our last endeavor ended rather ugly. I tried telling her I didn't think Vinnie was going to go for it, but we went anyway and he blatantly shut the door in our faces, leaving no room for discussion. We should've expected that. So there we stood in the middle of downtown Newport, under twenty-one, all dolled up and no place to go. It was too late in the night to drive to Providence, a forty-five minute drive.

We walked a half a block down to Christie's restaurant. Jay worked there with a couple of his friends. They did odd jobs from working the parking lot or the door to bar backing and cleaning up. She was hoping they could get us in to the live band upstairs, but it wasn't doable.

We walked aimlessly through the misty air. At least we were in downtown Newport and dressed appropriately enough. We were hoping an opportunity would present itself. As we strolled Thames Street I spotted Stew with his English friends in the window of a tavern. We were more than happy to find him there. Casey tapped on the window, successfully getting his attention, and he came outside.

"What are you doing here?" I asked.

"We met here for a pint before dancing."

"Well, we got the official boot out of the Station," I said.

"No way!" he exclaimed.

"Yeah, we can't get in the Station or Christies so now we're bumming."

"Well, there is a window in the ladies room. I'll ask one of the girls if they will let you in."

"Stew, I don't even want to know how you know that!" I laughed.

His plan worked, and we stayed in the back playing darts and shooting pool.

We thanked Stew and the rest when the tavern was closing. Not only did he get us in but he bought our drinks the entire night, too. We stumbled back down the street to the restaurant where Jay was working. Casey was waiting for him to finish up. I was bored and growing more anxious standing around doing nothing. He said it would be a few minutes, but it seemed to take forever.

Downtown was hectic at that hour because all of the clubs and bars were closing. Traffic was lined up to exit every parking lot. I heard the rumble of a motorcycle engine and snapped my head to find it. It was waiting to leave the same wharf where we were. A young guy was sitting on the bike alone, checking out the passersby. He wasn't wearing a helmet, just a white t-shirt and dark-colored jeans. He had a Greek look about him with short wavy hair and a dark complexion. He saw me from a few hundred feet away and smiled.

I called out, "Hey, can I get a ride?"

Without hesitation he yelled back, "Sure!"

I looked at Casey and said, "I'll be right back."

"Where are you going?" she called after me.

"Nowhere." I jumped on the back and put on the helmet. The stranger drove off, weaving in and out of the cars still waiting to leave the wharf.

"Where do you want to go?" he asked as he drove further away from Christie's in the direction of the Ocean Drive.

Hastily I answered, "I don't care, just for a short ride." I was eager to do something. Aside from climbing through the ladies room window in a dress the night thus far had been rather dull.

He drove to a residential area and told me he wanted to get his roommate's bike for the ride because it was better than his. I had no objections.

We approached a large white stucco house with green shutters and trim. He drove to the backyard through an arch in the arborvitae hedge about fifteen feet high and turned off the engine. We got off of the navy blue and chrome Honda motorcycle, which resembled a small Harley Davidson. The bike he was referring to was parked beside the hedges of the back yard. It was a white and blue Suzuki sports bike.

"I'm going to go upstairs to get the keys. You can come up if you want."

There was a snoozing within my inner ear. The peaceful slumber of another was certainly not to end on my behalf. I followed him up the unlit back stairs, which had a bunch of boxes, mops, brooms, and crap lining them. He unlocked the door and gestured for me to enter before him. Without a single thought, I did.

He gave me the tour of his apartment. It was neat and clean and I was impressed, then even more so when I saw how immaculate his bedroom was. I stood at the doorway when he modeled a few of his treasures that rested on his bureau.

His roommate's bedroom door was locked. I learned that three men lived there, but I only saw two bedrooms so I asked, "Well, where's the third bedroom, or do your roommates share a room?"

"No," he mused and led me towards the third. The door was one of those old kitchen doors split in half. Strange as it was, only the bottom portion of the door opened. "You can go in if you like; he won't mind." Again he gestured for me to proceed through the passageway before him. On any normal day I would have never gone in the house, let alone in this mini-room through half a door with a complete stranger, but my drowning head left me quite tranquil.

Inside there was just enough space for a twin-size mattress on the floor and several milk crates that neatly aligned the opposite wall. Papers and schoolbooks were lying around haphazardly. "Wow, I guess he makes it work, huh?"

Just then his roommate entered the house, sounding out a "Hello?"

The second stranger came into his room and into my view. He wasn't maladjusted that I was in the midst of his personal belongings invading his privacy. I would've been if I had come under those circumstances.

On the contrary, he greeted me with a giddy smile on his face. He was an attractive young college student, Caucasian with brown hair parted on one side. He wore a three-button polo and khakis.

The two men stood between me and the only awkward way out of the room. I couldn't recall either one of their first names. Then the dawn arrived, bringing about the realization that I positioned myself in this tiny space with no clear exit. Furthermore, I didn't pay attention to the exact location of this building. I had a dress on. I was beyond drunk. I was neither a very large nor particularly powerful female in a small room with two men I didn't know a single thing about. The fear caught up with me.

The red flag whacked me in the face, accompanied by an alarming bedlam in my head. The sleepy Zs were now screaming. "Get outta here fast, you stupid drunken idiot!"

Politely I apologized for being in his room and expeditiously excused myself.

They followed me back into the living room. The flag was still bonking me on the head and I knew I had to get out of the apartment as quickly as possible. Although it was a huge relief to be out in open space, I was still in a dangerous position. I was no match for two healthy youthful men. I worried that my presence alone gave the wrong implication.

"I don't mean to intrude. I just wanted to go for a bike ride." I started towards the back stairwell, "It was nice to meet you."

The biker couldn't find his friend's keys, so we left the apartment on his Honda again.

"So where do you wanna go?"

"Just bring me back, please."

"Back? Already?"

"I don't want to miss my friends."

He granted my request. As we waited in traffic again before he could cross Thames Street to the wharf, I saw Casey's car. "There she is!" I exclaimed as I jumped off the bike and handed him his helmet.

"But wait, can you tell me your name?" He asked in a desperate attempt to prolong our encounter.

"Reba." I leaned in and kissed him on the cheek and whispered in his ear, "Thanks for the ride."

I ran up to Casey's car and banged on the window, startling her. Jay was in the front seat with one of his co-workers in the back.

"Where the hell did you go?" she asked as I hopped into the back seat.

"I don't know, man. You don't even want to know what just happened to me. I can't believe it myself. I think I am still in shock. Phew." I took a moment to catch my breath. "I'm just in time, huh?"

"Actually we were already almost home when Gary remembered he left his bike here. We drove back to get it. Tell me what happened."

I told them the story as we drove back to Casey's to drink some more beers. Jay and Gary were sober and eager to catch up to us.

"Not gonna happen," I stated.

The night should have been terminated for me. My luck must have been wearing thin after the lunacy I displayed. I was already past my limit, so my taste buds couldn't tell the difference between domestic and imported beer. I drank whatever was available.

"So Reba, you got a man?"

"No, no, I am all set. I don't have a man for good reason! I don't want one." The intent of that response was to deter anything further on the subject. But young men being young men actually interpreted it as meaning I am free to do what I want with whomever I want. This misunderstanding was not something I was aware of at the time, so I was comfortable talking with him.

Gary was happy to befriend me. I could barely see straight as the exhaustion intensified the symptoms of my intoxication. Casey and Jay retreated to the room, calling it a night. I was content with sleeping on Casey's couch because I barely had any energy left to walk home.

As soon as the happy couple was in the back of the apartment, Gary took the liberty of sharing the couch with me.

"I am ready to pass out," I said bluntly.

"Well, can I share the couch with you?"

"What? I told you, I don't want to be with anyone."

"I am not asking for a relationship or anything. Ya know, just a little company for the night."

"The night is over, dude. Time to go home!" I said, stretching out and kicking his butt off the couch.

"Well damn, girl. You don't gotta be a bitch about it."

"Whatever, man. Just leave!" I mumbled.

"Fuck you, bitch."

"No thanks. I already told you, I'm all set!" I said sarcastically as he walked out the door. I told myself to get up and lock it behind him, but I heard Casey go to the bathroom down the hall and assumed she would come down and lock it. I could never go to sleep in my own house without double-checking the door. The room began spinning the second I closed my eyes. My mind was unable to distract from the nausea that was quickly building, and moments later I found myself at Casey's toilet puking.

After a few good upchucks I felt much better and was able to resume my efforts to sleep. I believed I would've been successful had I not been disturbed. I felt large hands caressing my body, but the alcohol was toying with my head. Was I imagining things? The touch was ever so slight; it was so hard to tell if it was real. Then I felt the cold skin of another contact the skin under my dress. The hands were smoothly traveling up to my breast when my brain finally got the message to my arms to push the culprit off. Sure enough I had hit someone's hand.

"Who the hell?" I grumbled.

When I was able to focus my eyes I saw the silhouette of a male leaving Casey's house. This time I mustered up the stability to walk to the door and lock it before returning to my slumber.

The following day I realized Josh was still talking to the troll, which meant that my adventures out on the town the past few weeks had no effect on him. Her deceitful innocence in flirting had Josh relishing her attention. Hot steam filled every inch within my shell. I drank an entire twelve-pack of Molson Ice that night.

Joe flaunted a pint of grain alcohol. It was 100 proof. I had tried grain once when Neil bought it trying to get Danielle drunk. It appealed to my taste buds. So when Joe showed it off I acted like it was nothing new to me. He took a swig of the bottle then belched, simultaneously flicking a lighter in front of his mouth. The flame blew like a torch in front of him.

"Reba, your turn."

"But I don't know how to make myself burp like that!"

"Sure you can. Just try."

I took a swig of the bottle and tried burping. Joe held the lighter in front of me. The steam came rushing out of my mouth, putting the flame to rest.

"I told you."

"You didn't try hard enough."

I tried it again, receiving the same result. He lit the lighter, belched from down in his gut, and flames flew. "Do it like that."

I took a deep breath and tried the same. I just couldn't get anything other than steam out. "I told you I don't know how to make myself burp like that. I'm not a pig like you."

"You can do it!" He and Craig were encouraging me to try again. Finally I grabbed the bottle of grain and chugged it. Joe laughed as I held it bottoms up. Craig frantically cautioned me to stop before I killed myself. But I noticed the troll interested in my actions. She was amazed at how I could drink the harsh contents of the bottle like it was water.

I watched her image through the bottle. I wanted so badly to drink her away. I kept chugging until half the alcohol was gone. I tried the belch one last time and couldn't do it. I was conscious long enough to know I had impressed everyone in the house despite my failure to light a fire.

"I guess I can only light my fires in privacy." I said insinuatingly.

I woke up the next morning on Josh's bed in my own puke. It was foul. I hurriedly wrapped up all of the sheets to bring them home with me. Josh was sleeping on the couch. I couldn't face him after last night. I had no idea how I got into his bed. My memory failed after swigging the grain. Josh would undoubtedly be angry with me for soiling his sheets, and who knows what other dumb things I might have done. I held my breath and swiftly snuck out the front door.

When I brought back Josh's sheets the following day I apologized immediately.

"Casey and K Nice put you in my bed. I saw you in there and tried to lay with you. You were moaning and squirming so I asked if you were going to throw up. You said no but then leaned over and started hurling on the bed. I wasn't about to stay. I just slept on the couch."

"How could you leave me there to sleep in it? That's pretty messed up."

He shrugged his shoulders.

I began blacking out more often after that night. I wondered if I was being so forgetful because I simply didn't want to remember. I doubted there was anything worth space in my memory bank anyway. Josh was being a jerk to me. Who did he think he was trying to play me?

He had to realize what he was missing out on. I was determined to show him. His friends loved hanging out with me—why didn't he?

I found myself passing out more and more, waking up in strange places. One time I woke up on the couch with my head in Joe's lap. Horrified, I jumped up and went home directly.

Sometimes I was in Josh's bed and couldn't remember if we'd had sex or not. When I heard him get up and dress for work I pretended to still be sleeping. I wanted to wait until the coast was clear before seeing anyone in my attempt to sneak out.

I was becoming a constant embarrassment to myself, which only fed my need to be drunk in front of people in order to face them. I found it odd that no one mentioned my drunkard behavior.

Chapter Thirteen

"If You Can't Control Everything, Can You Control Anything?"

At party central I was drinking up some courage until Josh came home from work. He was disenchanted to find me wasted yet again. Reluctantly he followed me into his bedroom to talk.

"I feel like you have been avoiding me lately. What is going on with you?" I asked.

"Nothing is going on with me. I'm just living my life."

"Why are you so mad at me all the time?"

"What makes you think I am mad?" He seemed miles away.

"C'mon Josh. What is up with your troll anyway?"

"My what?"

"That thing you talk to. Are you fucking her?"

"Ya know, you're the one with the fucking problem. Look at you. You're a fucking mess. I should be asking you what is going on but it's obvious you don't have a clue."

"Why are you changing the subject?" I hadn't managed a word yet without slurring.

"Sleep it off or something. Okay? Go ahead and sleep in my bed. We can talk tomorrow."

I was thrown for a loop. Expecting a fight, I was raring to go. But he was calm, and I mistook his disappointment for disassociation. Sitting on his bed replaying the event in my head so as not to forget in the morning his pillow caught my eye.

I brought it up to my face and sniffed it, allowing the scent to penetrate deep inside my lungs. I heard my heart beat loudly then gradually quiet as it became harder against my chest. Suddenly I could no longer hear it beat or feel it pump. It had been replaced with a black diamond lodged in my sternum.

I cried for the first time in a long time. My teardrops were black ice crystals crashing onto his pillow and then melting before my view. I was in mourning. I awoke the next morning fully clothed in his bed. Josh was motionless next to me, but I knew he wasn't sleeping because he wasn't snoring. I left without interference.

I soon favored Craig's over Josh's. I didn't want to face him anymore. If he had fallen off the face of the earth I could have picked myself up and moved on. But with his presence in my world I couldn't keep it together.

Casey became livid when she found out that one of the promiscuous college girls began pursuing Jay. She was instigating drama lately, and I always had her back. Joe's demeanor was that of disappointment and disgust. Although it was unlike him to disapprove of chaos, I assumed that was the cause of this newfound tension between us.

Dan came solo to Craig's, since Kevin no longer joined him. He'd found out that I was the one who took his beer the last time he zonked out. It made no difference to me that he wasn't happy with me.

Alas, Big Dawg barged into the kitchen to confront me no-holds-barred for all to hear, "Did you have sex with Dan?"

"What?" I said in a complete quandary.

"Yo, man, Dan told Andrea you sucked his dick." He paused for my reaction before continuing, "I saw her today at work and she told me." Jake knew Dan was a loser and didn't believe I would hook up with him.

"Whoa, whoa, wait a minute." I hesitated. "Dan is telling people I fucked him?" I had to get the story straight before I could react.

"Nah, he actually said you sucked his dick. I don't know if he said you fucked him."

I shrieked, "Gross!"

"Well, you better tell his ass something then." Big Dawg loved to instigate. "I just saw him come in here."

At first I was horrified by the thought. Then when I saw Dan, all of my resentment toward him multiplied tenfold. Previously I just thought he was a "wanna be." Now he was spreading nasty rumors about me. He was going to regret this challenge.

"Ay-yo, you got some news to tell everyone about me?" I yelled to Dan in the foyer. I was purposely loud so I could clear my name to all in one shot. I didn't want this lie lingering about.

"Nah, what do you mean?" He was truly dumbfounded.

"You wanna tell Andrea I did some nasty favors for you? You son of a bitch!" All of my pent-up anger was vaporizing through my skin and visibly rising off my body.

"I didn't tell her nothing. She got jealous when your name came up and started making accusations. I didn't say nothing." He took a step back towards the open front door.

"I'll kick your fucking ass. You lying-ass mother fucker!" I lunged at him. Big Dawg was standing beside me dodging the hot air steaming from my ears and grabbed my arm.

Joe came up behind me and whispered, "You better get his ass."

"Don't you ever talk about me again! Do you understand me, you fucking pig? Not even in your wildest dreams would you have a chance with me."

I pushed Dan towards the door. When I caught his stupid expression I could contain the pressure-building steam no longer. "You fucking pig!" It propelled me toward him and my clenched fist collided with his jaw. "Don't ever talk about me again!"

Big Dawg stepped in front of me and held me back from Dan, who was now on the landing in the hallway at the top of the stairs. Big Dawg didn't want Dan and me to go tumbling down. He quickly slammed the door. He and Joe walked me back to the kitchen table. Joe poured me a drink while I simmered down. Tyler came over to get the scoop on what happened.

That fiasco made it an accomplished evening. Letting go of some pent-up steam released some of the tension I felt towards Josh. I was satisfied with going home earlier than usual.

It rained on my only day off for the week. I went for a walk, allowing Mother Nature to cleanse my spirit. Rainy days were my favorite. Most people didn't like to go out, which brought about much of its appeal. In addition, the heavy clouds prevented the sun from radiating into my eyes.

On my way back home Mark, the bartender from the Station, drove alongside me.

"Hey, pretty lady, do you need a ride?"

"Hey, I know you!" I said.

"Wow, you are soaked. Come on in!"

"Thanks, that's nice of you to stop, but really I was just going for a walk."

"Then maybe we can just go for a ride? I'm Mark."

"I know." I got into the car.

"Do you think I can get your name now? Or do I have to keep calling you pretty lady?"

"As long as it's not 'Beautiful' I'm fine with it! But my real name is Reba."

"Ah! I knew that too, but I didn't want you to think I was a stalker. I haven't seen you lately. Where have you been?"

"Honestly?"

"Of course."

"Vince was letting us in, but he didn't get what he wanted out of the deal so he literally shut the door in our face. We're only nineteen. That's why I tried not to talk to anyone there. Sorry if I was rude to you."

"No problem, you weren't rude, just a little antisocial. I was jealous of the English blokes though."

"Oh they're great, aren't they? I work with one of them. He was asking me for weeks to go but I told him my dilemma. He was delighted to see me those few times. We had fun. Do they still go?"

"Yeah, I still see them."

"Well, be nice to him. He's just here to have some good old-fashioned fun for a few months before going back."

"Yeah, I know how they work. Every year there is a new group."

We were coming up to Craig and Joe's street. I had no idea where he was headed and I figured it was a good idea not to let him drop me off at home, so I asked him to pull over.

"Is this where you live?"

"No, a friend of mine lives here. I told him I would stop by."

"Friend?"

"Yes, friend."

"So he wouldn't mind if I asked for your number?"

"He might, actually! I'd rather not right now though, maybe next time, if our paths cross again. Thanks!" I got out and raced up the street to the apartment.

I didn't knock on the door; instead I hid in the hallway downstairs counting the minutes until I presumed it safe to hit the streets. Mark was kind to offer me a ride, but he wasn't what I was looking for. I felt nothing next to him.

I was shocked weeks later when I ran into him again at a party Joe took me to in Middletown. It was a random spur-of-the-moment decision for a change of pace. I liked to go unnoticed sometimes. That was one great aspect of going to the Station. During my usual rendezvous the pressure was high to be sassy and rambunctious even when I didn't feel as such. It got exhausting.

In Middletown the houseguests were eerily different from our friends. Half were hippies and half were heavy metal heads. There was a bong or two in use at every scene. Every time I entered a room Joe appeared to be engaged in some sort of secret conversation. I felt really out of place until I saw Mark.

"Now what are the chances?" I said.

"There really is a God! I was praying I would run into you again so I could get your number."

"You know these people?"

"Some of them."

"Did you come with anyone?"

"Nope."

"This is some unusual shit for me, I gotta say," I admitted.

"Why? What's wrong?"

"I just feel extremely out of place here. Look at these guys. I feel like no one even sees me. They're all high."

"What's wrong with that?"

"It's not really my place to say. Not now anyway!"

I lost track of Joe's whereabouts. It didn't take me long to get intoxicated; my tolerance wasn't what it used to be. As we strolled through the house someone actually acknowledged my existence. A hippie was sitting on a built-in shelf above the landing of the staircase with an acoustic guitar.

"I'm taking requests," he said as I walked past.

"I don't know what you can play."

"I can play anything."

"Okay, play … anything!"

He strummed at the guitar and started singing about the earth. I remained attentive with a polite smile as long as I could. The lyrics were juvenile and disconnected, though the music was pleasing. But the entire situation was too eccentric for me. I had enough. Still smiling, we slowly crept away.

Mark offered to drive me home in his Jeep. We explored the house in search of Joe, but he was nowhere to be found, so I regretfully accepted Mark's offer. I just wanted to get out of there. The place was freaking me out.

On the way home he stopped at the Burger King drive thru. He asked if I wanted anything to eat, but I graciously declined. He only bought a soda and some fries. We sat in the parking lot and continued a strange line of conversation. We discussed drugs and druggies, bar drinks and club goers. Mark ate his food and drank his soda while I sipped out of his cup and smoked cigarettes.

The corner of the parking lot he chose to occupy was an unlit, quiet, and isolated area. At that hour there were only two cars parked outside, most likely belonging to the employees. The drive thru was slow.

He had finished his food and I was looking forward to going home. The conversation was running thin. Mark seemed to think so too, but he had further plans for us and he leaned in for the kiss. I grudgingly kissed him back. I planned only for a simple kiss, but he must have enjoyed it because he continued building his curiosity rather than satisfying it.

I wished it to end. His tongue was thick and fat and the kissing was nothing to boast about. Before I knew it he was reaching down my pants. I pushed back, but he turned up the volume on the radio and leaned into me. Suddenly I noticed his tongue growing in my mouth, and the more I tried to move back the bigger his hands swelled. His mouth was pressed against mine and I couldn't speak. The thrusting of his tongue into my mouth became more revolting.

He was causing pain to my lower abdomen in the process of forcing his hands down my pants. My attempt to speak sounded like a moan, and he became even more aroused, making his own moans. Still I was struggling diligently to move in any direction away from his weight and his disgusting mouth.

His head began to double in size. Then it tripled. I wondered if we inhaled something toxic in that strange house. These extraordinary occurrences got my adrenaline flowing but did not benefit my helpless position.

By that time I was pushed up against the door. He took his enlarged hand out of my pants only to reach over my body and release the seat. I unexpectedly reclined back, unsure if I was shrinking or his figure was expanding.

I tried to say "no," but my mouth was full. The next thing I knew my pants were halfway down and I felt his erect penis in between my thighs. Flailing my arm around the inside of the door I hoped to open it. Finally I found the handle and mercilessly yanked on it over and over, but the lock must have been pressed down during the commotion.

My eyes widened in disapproval, but his eyes were closed. In my horror, my efforts to push his body away and the shaking of my head had zero effect. I made a last attempt to say, "Stop!" but it was muffled through his mouth as it covered mine. He moaned again, living some sick fantasy that had occupied his thoughts for several months. In his thrill he grabbed a bunch of my hair and pressed my head closer to his, I feared he was going to swallow me whole.

My mouth was in pain, my stomach felt bruised between the hips, and now my scalp was screaming. His penis penetrated me as one of my hands was stuck powerless in between our chests. His chubby hand enveloped my other. His head was persistently squished up to mine. I pushed against the floor with my feet to position his destination further away from his only working head. I was breathing heavily from the struggle.

Mark only thrust his penis inside me a few times before he ejaculated in his boxers. Thank God for that at least! He rested his enormous body on me, breathing heavily in my face from his excitement. His tongue finally retreated back into his own mouth. His hands were brawny, his body was heavy, and his persistence was relentless. I was exhausted, inebriated, and violated.

"Sorry," he said aloud, "I should've lasted longer."

A ringing deafened me in my state of shock. Were my ears deceiving me or did he just apologize for not prolonging the horrid affair? Did that just happen because he thought I wanted it to? I know I didn't want it to. He didn't give me a chance to really say no. Maybe he didn't understand the way I was pushing back away from him. Maybe he didn't understand the shaking of my head no. Maybe he didn't understand when I kept taking his hands off of me.

Did I not try hard enough? I should've tried to throw him off of me. I should've kneed him in the groin. I should've tried screaming. My resistance should've been tougher all around. Then he would've known I didn't consent.

"Can you get off of me now? You're hurting me."

He did, as he pulled off his messy boxers. He put his pants back on and started the ignition. On the way home he continued apologizing for various things like the size of his penis, climaxing so quickly, or "doing it" in his Jeep. With each act of contrition he diminished in size. But he never apologized for forcing his penis inside of me when I didn't want him to. By the time we reached the Hill, Mark was as small as a Chihuahua.

"Stop here," I requested a few streets away from mine.

"Here?" he asked as he stopped the car.

I said nothing as I jumped out. He called after me but I was steadfast and ignored him as I slipped through the complex units and ran home. I had never been gladder to be in the projects in my life. Who would've guessed I'd be safer in the Hill than anywhere else?

I immediately took a shower, sobbed and scrubbed and sobbed and scrubbed again before going to sleep. I failed myself, and I only had myself to rely on.

Instead of getting angry with all the men in my life who have behaved in ways that suggested they had ownership over me or the right to give my physique the attention they sought fit, I drank. Instead of feeling anger and guilt over every guy who said or did something that reflected sexual harassment, I drank. I had my veil now, and that was consoling in its own way. I vowed to never allow the incident with Mark to surface again.

A few days later Josh paged me like any ordinary day wanting to chat. I was anxious to get back to the way things were. No matter how badly things went with Josh, it was better than the experiences without him.

After the blissful unspoken "let's get back together" period, which lasted two weeks or so, our relationship was noticeably unhealthy and dysfunctional. I was still unsure if he was exclusively with me. I never completely scrubbed all the guilt away when I strayed from him, which inevitably led me to Mark, who victimized me.

Mark left me weakened and more uncertain of myself than ever. I was angry with myself now more than ever. All of the insecurities in my relationship with Josh were still there, unresolved. I was upset with Josh for not being able to see how damaged I had become. I found some indirect way to be angry with him for the incident with Mark. It wasn't long before I made the worst mistake of my life.

Chapter Fourteen

"Careful What You Wish For"

Rampage

The beat of the music hits the soul
Raise the volume to make it whole

Dreams and memories racing through
Hear the yelling screaming at you

Feel the bass pounding in your gut
All else but anger off it's shut

Sweeping the tables tops with one swift arm
Memories crashing all the harm

Tightened fists rapidly strike the wall
Bloody knuckles destruction won't stall

Burning letters and pictures torn
Lower limbs stomping for this scorn

Psycho state of mind it's called
Back to the floor your body's sprawled

Revenge in thought, it will commence
Venomous anger, keeping body tense

Music then fading during this stage
But subsiding not is this rampage

I woke up naked in Josh's bed. He was sleeping beside me. I wasn't drunk enough to forget the pleasurable companionship of my resting lover. Since he was still sleeping I didn't want to disturb him, nor did I want my happiness to end. I fell back asleep.

An hour later, Josh was whispering in my ear. He was saying good morning to me and apologizing because he had to go. "Okay," I said without question. I was upset that he was leaving because I was beginning to feel lost without him. Alas, I fought back negative feelings.

"Stay here and sleep," he told me, "I'll be back in a little while."

He left the room, and as I began to doze back off I heard him talking softly with someone in the living room. Immediately feeling vulnerable in the nude I quickly got up and dressed. After I heard the front door shut I peeked my head out of the bedroom. No one was in sight. I was expecting to see Tyler or Jay. I crept over to the front window and saw Josh walking down the street with a female. I was mortified.

The pain in my chest returned as the black diamond took shape in place of the once soft tissue of my beating heart. Once again I was overcome by my own bewilderment. "Didn't he just tell me to stay here?" I said to myself. I hadn't recognized his female companion. "What the fuck is this all about?"

I grabbed my belongings and walked home. I hadn't a clue what was real any more. Something inside caved in and I didn't care. Life was shit.

Casey wasn't happy with Jay. They were just about enemies at that point. They also had tortured each other enough. Casey was hanging around other friends, but we didn't care for each other. I spent little time with Casey after that point.

Josh left a message on my answering machine. He sounded concerned with why I hadn't been in touch with him. I believed he was genuinely baffled because he had no idea I saw him walking away from me with another female. I couldn't stomach seeing him after that.

I answered my phone without screening the call and heard Josh's voice on the other end. I was trapped.

"What's up, Reba? Where have you been? You don't answer my pages anymore?"

"I've been busy."

There was a pause, "Oh," followed by another bout of silence. "Uh, are you okay?" he continued.

"Fine."

"Well, will you come over then? I can come get you right now if you want."

"Not now. Maybe later."

"Well, Casey and Jay are in the middle of a huge fight right now so I don't think she'll be coming back later. What time do you want me to come get you?"

"I don't need a ride. I'll be there when I get there."

"Well, if you're not here by nine I'll come get you. In the meantime you need to cheer up."

"See ya."

During the course of the night Tyler, Joe, and Big Dawg were downstairs weight lifting. I used it as a getaway from Josh, but I was so bored. I kept going back and forth from the uneventful party to the basement. I wanted to leave so badly but couldn't allow Josh to know how tormented I was.

The third time I nonchalantly ventured to the basement I found Tyler alone. Finally I felt a sense of relief because he usually put me in high spirits. He never took things too seriously.

"Where'd everybody go?"

"I think they went upstairs." He sat up on the bench.

"What are you doing down here?"

"Wandering."

"That bad huh?"

"I'm just bored."

"Wanna try?" He pointed to the weights.

"No, not in front of you, so you can dog me for how much I can't lift."

"You're a girl. I don't expect you to be able to lift as much as me. Even if you were a guy you couldn't lift as much as me."

"Right, Tyler the almighty."

"Ooo, you know it's true. It's tough being me, so good looking and strong, and I even dress good too!" He was cleaning up the area.

"Here we go. All right. I'll give you that, you do dress nicely!"

"Well, I gotta give you props too. You're a hot chick. We got our advantages, but it's work."

"TYLER!" He could go on and on about attractive people, especially himself. I had to end it. "Who are all those people upstairs?"

"I don't know half of them. They work with Jay. That's why we were down here." All the weights were back neatly along the concrete wall. The bench was sprayed and wiped down.

"Ugh," I sighed. "There's nothing to do tonight."

"Yeah well, I know how to cure that." He came towards me.

I laughed as I headed towards the stairs. I turned to see if he was coming and he was directly behind me. He reached past me and turned out the light.

"Well now, I can't see the stairs!" I felt around with my foot. "Damn, it's dark down here."

"Who needs to see? If you want to go up them, then go."

"Tyler, I can't see a thing. This was only the second time I've been down here. I don't know where everything is. You go first." I fumbled in the dark, finding his waist. I grabbed his shirt and urged him to go forward. He blindly led me to the stairs, which I tripped on and fell into his back.

"Damn, girl!" I felt him turn to face me.

"Well, you could've warned me."

The next thing I knew his lips were pressed up against mine. "Um, Tyler, I think you're facing the wrong way."

"No, I like this way better." He kissed me again.

"Have you gone mad?"

"What are you talking about? You're hot. I'm hot. It makes sense."

"What about your boy?"

"What about him? We're two attractive people attracted to each other. Are you two in a serious relationship?"

"No but …"

Tyler was my friend. He entertained thoughts of being more, which flattered me. But he and Josh were so close this was well beyond fantasizing. I cautiously felt my way up the curved staircase. I figured that once he realized there was a chance of Josh catching us he would cease pursuing me. At the top of the stairs the frosted glass door was closed. It sounded quiet on the other side.

Tyler, now semi-visible at the translucent door, made his final advance and kissed me again. The thrill of getting caught set me ablaze. I was intrigued by the fact that Tyler found me enticing enough to risk this potential drama, which he wasn't a fan of under normal circumstances.

But I put an end to the ordeal and opened the basement door. Inside the party was over.

"Well, where the hell did everyone go?"

"Home, I guess. It's pretty late."

"When did that happen?"

"Probably while we were downstairs."

"But I still have a beer left!"

"I'll have one with you. C'mon." He ushered me into his room at the end of the hallway. As we passed Josh's room I noticed the door was closed. I wondered who was on the other side. I couldn't hear anything. We went into Tyler's room and he shut the door behind me. I sat on his bed and opened my last Molson.

"Here, check out my sketch book." He placed it gently on my lap.

Tyler had been sketching since I'd known him. He'd shown others including me a selected few. Access to his entire compilation was a privilege. Sketched in his book were fantastic gargoyles and haunting demons. The artwork depicted possession and protection. Many of the drawings were dark and cryptic, but a few others were of a beautiful angelic creature. My general interpretation was that of our similar views of love. The demonic creatures on guard were in reality us getting in our own way of true happiness in love.

"Wow, that's really something."

"You like it?"

"It's fucking awesome, dude. Thank you for showing me."

"Oh, did you see this guy? He's my favorite." He was kneeling behind me looking over my shoulder. He flipped through to the most majestic demon.

"Yeah, I saw him. That's so good."

"He's cool, right?"

"Yeah, he reminds me of you."

Tyler's response wasn't in words. He commenced kissing my neck and stroking my back.

"What's this all about?" Paranoia got the best of me.

"I'm a good-looking guy, you're a good-looking girl … I'm attracted to you … didn't we already go through this downstairs?" There was no guilt in his voice, or any doubt in his mind that we were entitled to act on our desire. Although Tyler was in fact a good-looking guy and I adored his friendship, there was a major factor missing from this romance. There was absolutely no spark between us. I certainly didn't feel one and couldn't imagine he did.

He leaned over, turning off the light, guiding me down on the bed, and then he climbed on top of me. It was the best revenge I could get on Josh. His best friend wanted me and I was going to make his fantasy come true.

In the dark all I could smell was the scent of a man. I felt the masculinity in his strong back. The muscles were busting through his arms. His eyes, a glowing fluorescent yellow, illuminated the skeletal structure of his head. Each temple stretched up to the ceiling, creating the shape of the gargoyle in his drawing. His razor-sharp teeth teased my neck and I became his tigress.

The black crystals formed at the corners of my eyes as I felt this transformation come over me, my appetite amplified by the scent of a man's unyielding lust. Roaring in pain as the diamond substance of my heart shot through my fingertips like gigantic claws, I unleashed my pain onto the chest and back of the creature with which I shared this adulteration.

The four walls of the room opened up, revealing a world of darkened mystery. Similar creatures were heard as they joined our howling into the night of the rogue. As the cries grew louder and the desires ran free the fires ignited, burning the wilderness in a massive inferno, until nothing was left but ash.

Returning to the vulnerable girl I was, I was struck with questions over the affair. Needing to absolve the guilt that only I had, I discreetly went into Josh's room before leaving the house.

"Hi," I whispered, surprised he was alone. "I just needed to know that we are just friends, right?"

"Yeah," he murmured.

"Okay, good night." I kissed him on his forehead and left the house content that I had not been unfaithful.

The next morning I woke up like any other day and went to work like any other day. Afterwards I rode the bus home like any other day and showered for the second time like any other day. It was plainly ordinary until I received a phone call around 7:00 P.M.

"Hello?"

"Hey, tell me something." It was Casey. She had a sense of urgency in her voice. "Did you sleep with Tyler?"

"What? Why do you ask?" I was reluctant in answering her question. This was my chance to run away from what I had done.

"Tyler and Craig were talking about it. Did you?"

I wasn't going to win any cool points by admitting to my actions. But I was compelled to be honest, "Um, yeah."

"Gross! Why? When?" She paused for a split second before adding, "And what about Josh?"

"Oh no, what about Josh? He doesn't know, does he?" For the first time it occurred to me the magnitude of the fling with Tyler may have been too much. My perception of the trifling plan I devised was quite different sober.

"Yeah, he knows."

"What did he say?"

"As far as I know he didn't act like he was too upset about it, but you know how guys are. That is probably just a front he's putting on."

"Oh God. I feel sick." I wanted to cry. What had I done? And now I'll look like even more of a fool when Josh doesn't give a shit. "Ugh! All right, let me go so I can call over there and talk with Tyler or Josh."

"Good luck," she said before we hung up.

I had to be accountable for my actions. I picked up the phone and dialed Josh's number. Lucky for me, Tyler answered the phone.

"What are you doing telling everybody about last night?" I started immediately.

"Whoa, whoa, what a minute." I heard him walking with the cordless in his hand. Then I heard a door shut through the phone. "I didn't tell anybody anything."

"Yeah, okay then how does EVERYBODY know?"

"They all just assumed."

"They all just assumed and you didn't deny it? Then you told them."

"Yo girl, I'm not gonna lie, especially to my boys."

"You're not gonna lie to your boy, but you'll sleep with his girl?"

"Oh so now you're his girl? But … last night you weren't."

"You know what I mean! Stop playing games."

"Listen," Tyler remained calm, "you scratched my back all up, and when I walked out in the kitchen to get my coffee this morning, Josh and Jay saw it. They both knew it was you. Josh thought he was looking in the mirror for a minute." He managed a slight chuckle.

"It's not funny, not even a little bit."

"I know. He's my best friend. I'm the one who has to live with him."

"Oh please! You are boys and all will be forgiven in two minutes. I, on the other hand, will look like the biggest bitchy slut and you will look like top dog around the house for a while."

"Nah, maybe any other lifetime, or any other girl," he sighed, "but not you."

"Why, is he mad at you?"

"He hasn't said much yet, but I'm waiting for it to come. I know it will. I can see it all over his face. He is NOT happy with me. Right now he won't even look at me. I actually feel bad, and you know me, I don't feel bad about things like this."

"Great, I hurt Josh, I made myself out to be a slut, and now you regret me. This is wonderful!"

"I never said I regretted anything. I had fun."

"Okay, okay, I don't know what I'm gonna do. I guess there's no denying it then."

"Nah, I wouldn't do that and make matters worse," he advised.

"I'll hang up and call back in a minute to speak with him, I guess. Does he know it's me on the phone now?"

"No. I immediately walked into my room as you were yelling at me. You're going to talk with him?"

"I have to. I might as well do it now and get it over with. The suspense is killing me."

"I hear that!"

"Bye!"

We hung up.

A thick black substance began oozing out of my eyes, accompanied by the agonizing crystals ripping through the corners of my lids. A strange howling bellowed through my apartment. The smog of uncertainty encompassed me in my sorrow.

There was only one way to find out what was really going through Josh's head. I had to call him. After the second ring Tyler picked up the phone.

"It's me. Can you put Josh on the phone, please?"

A simple "yeah," was spoken before I heard him hand the phone over to his roommate.

"Yeah?" He sounded as if he'd just attended a funeral. I questioned if this was the equivalent.

"It's Reba."

"What's up?"

I swallowed my tears with a loud gulp. "What's up?"

203

"I don't know. Did you want to talk to me about something?"

"Yeah, you know what I want to talk about. I want to know how mad you are."

"Pretty mad, I guess. Ain't I supposed to be? Isn't that what you wanted?"

"Not exactly. I don't know what I wanted. But I'm pretty sure it wasn't this." There was the most uncomfortable silence I had ever experienced. I was searching through all areas of my soul to find something consoling to say.

"Well, if you don't have anything to say then I will let you go," he finalized.

"No! Wait! I'm sorry." At least I remembered to say that much.

"Sorry? No need. You just proved to me we didn't have what I thought we did. So there is no need to apologize."

His sentiment reached through the phone and tore my heart right out. I stared at it in its multifaceted form. Bright red soft tissue was mostly replaced with the black diamond that was melting onto the floor. Black lava bubbled up, but that was the only movement. I hadn't heard any more beating.

I began sobbing into the phone. "I didn't mean to hurt you like this. I didn't think you cared enough."

"Of course you knew I cared for you. It doesn't matter now. I don't want to talk anymore. You said last night we were still friends right? Fine then. We are friends. Are you gonna be coming over my house to see him now?"

"No, it's not like that," I pleaded as I watched the dagger come bolting through the phone and pierce my hardened oozing heart on the floor.

"Okay, I gotta go." He hung up the phone.

Sometime during my crying session Casey called me back. I gave her a quick run- through of what happened. Then I hung up with her. I continued to wallow in the molten material of my former heart.

Who the hell was I becoming? For the first time in a long time I had no desire to do anything. Every inch of my being was agonizing. My eyes were swollen from hours of bawling. My head was pounding. The hole left in my sternum was aching. I couldn't keep a steady breath.

A cunning defeat
I am the wise
Or am I mistaken
I now realize
A life of deceit
In my demise
My grounds were shaken.

.

Chapter Fifteen

"Revenge is for the Rogue"

Going over to Shonnie and Rodney's wouldn't sustain me through my voluntary exile. Neither would visiting my female friends, who were all mothers. Shonnie's daughter was moving about now, and Sebastian, Danielle's son, was a toddler, talking up a storm.

I needed to go back to Josh's house. A month had passed by so quickly. Tyler answered the phone.

"Wuzuuup?" I said, successfully disguising my tension.

After a chuckle Tyler responded the same. "Wuzuuup? Where have *you* been?"

"I've been here and there, you know!"

"Yeah! How have you been?"

"The question is how have *you* been?" I returned.

"I've been good. Same old, same old."

"Really?" I continued a little more serious now. "Have things been alright over there?"

"*Oh, that*! Yeah. It's okay."

"Yeah, *that*! For real? How has he been treating you?"

"Well, um, he was pretty quiet and distant for a while. But I think he's coming around."

"You guys didn't talk about it? My name didn't come up?"

"Not between us. Sometimes someone would ask where you've been and Josh would leave the room."

"And what would you say? Anybody call me bad names?" I was hesitant to ask but I wanted to know.

"Nah, not about you."

"That's good." I didn't want to ask about Big Dawg or Joe, specifically. My main concerns were Josh and Tyler. "So do you think he would talk to me?"

"Oh, you didn't call to talk to me?" When Tyler exhibited cocky behavior only part of it was in jest. I often wondered if he was delusional enough to think he even remotely measured up to Josh in my mind. "No, I wanted to see how things were with you too, of course. But I definitely want to speak with Josh."

"Yeah, well he's at work."

"That's probably a good thing then. I don't know how he would take it knowing I just talked to you for ten minutes and then you handed him the phone when it was his turn!"

"You're probably right."

"Do me a favor and leave him a message that I called. Tell him he can call me back if he wants but I will call him later."

"All right."

"All right. Thanks, bye." I hung up the phone.

Later on that night when ten o'clock rolled around I knew Josh would have been getting off of work. My belly was full of butterflies as I awaited the phone to ring. By eleven o'clock it had remained silent, and I couldn't wait any longer. Just as I was about to pick it up, it rang.

"Whoa!" I said to myself, "freaky!" I let it ring two more rings as though I hadn't been sitting there listening for it.

"Hello?"

"Hello." It was Josh!

"Hi. So you got my message?"

"No. What message?"

"Tyler didn't tell you I called?" My voice quivered as I said his name to Josh.

"Oh, no, I just got in a little while ago from work. What was the message?"

"Nothing, just that I called and that was it."

For the first time I knew where I stood. It was the same place I presumed him to be for years. And it was the position I had been pressing on to reach. I accomplished my goal. And to my surprise I didn't like it.

He didn't want to talk to me. He didn't want to see me. He wanted nothing to do with me. I had hurt him beyond repair. Yet, I was irresistible to him. As much as he was cautioned when it came to me, he couldn't keep himself away.

While on the phone for an hour and a half the sun was smiling, the birds were chirping, and royal castles were floating by. We went horseback riding and slid down the arcs of rainbows. We danced with leprechauns and sang with flowers.

Out of the blue, he said, "I want to see you. Will you come over?"

After our dreamy chat I couldn't imagine he was alert enough to drive. "Of course I will. You want to me to call a cab?"

"Yeah, but I'll pay for it when you get here. Sorry, I just don't feel like driving now."

"That's fine. I'll see you in like twenty."

"Can't wait."

The cab arrived quickly. I stared out the window, still seeing unicorns and fantastic creatures grazing in pastures. When I finally reached my destination Josh was waiting outside with money for the cabbie. His smile revealed his vulnerability. He touched my hand lightly, leading me into his bedroom where we both lay on the bed gazing at each other. I didn't want to hurt him or anyone again. I finally accepted that I loved him and wanted him to feel the same, but I didn't know what came after that.

I placed my fingertips above his full dark brow and gently traced the contour of his discerning eye, carefully gliding over the thin skin representative of the sensitivity within. Sliding my finger down his nose sloping to his lips, plump and luscious, I patiently waited to connect them with mine. And there it was. It was so soft at first I almost didn't recognize it, but just as it had done in the past, it became louder and faster. My heart was beating again.

This time I was actually grateful when my heart pumped through my chest, proving that I was still human and alive. Following the rhythm of my heart I tasted the man before me. Passionately I gave myself to him and for the first time was sober for the experience.

Just as my heart came pounding through, so did the torment of my insecurities. After everything that had happened between us we *still* didn't discuss it, any of it. Was this ecstasy an attempt to break down my guard so he could surpass my new rank?

Unequipped to handle that possibility I had no other alternative but to flee.

I gave him space to sort through his feelings. Josh called me again after a two-week period passed. I was delighted with the idea that he had contemplated all aspects of our relationship thoroughly and our love won.

Our phone conversation was very much like the last, except this time I was knocking back Molson Ices. We dreamt aloud over an hour before he came to my apartment. We made love suspended in the air by my heart-shaped balloon.

Some time had passed before I realized this courtship was nothing more than a biweekly routine. So far I had been accepting of all I could get. But I knew it wasn't right. When I had drunk up the courage to state the obvious it had a positive effect, though short lived.

"So you're just gonna fuck me and then one of us will leave. Then we won't see each other again until weeks from now?"

"Well, what do you want to do?"

"I want to go out somewhere."

"Let's go."

"That's not what I mean. I mean like during the day when normal people are still awake."

"I thought you liked being a vampire staying up wicked late. So we'll stay?"

"No, I do wanna go now too."

"Okay, then let's go."

We hopped into his van with no destination in mind. While in town driving on the main street I asked, "So do you have anywhere in particular you wanted to go?"

"Yeah," he said as he made a quick turn down his old street.

"Your mom's house?"

"Hell no, silly girl."

He drove to the Point and parked along Narragansett Bay. We got out of the van and walked down the long pier overlooking the Newport Bridge. I could see the hotel across the way, too.

"Wow, I haven't been here since I was a kid."

"Me either."

"Did you ever go swimming here?"

"Of course, didn't you?"

"Only a few times, but not on a regular basis. I was wary of the sea life touching me."

"Yeah, I swam with a few eels before, and you gotta be careful of the stinging jellyfish."

"Exactly what I am talking about. Yuk."

"How about now?" He smirked deviously.

"No thanks," I said, backing away from him.

"Get over here!" He grabbed for my waist but only got a grip on my shirt. He spun me around and around.

Unable to control my laughter I begged him, "Stop! I'm gonna be sick!"

He wrapped his arms around me, steadying my stance. I accepted his appetizing kisses before we proceeded to the full-course meal.

Gradually our meetings were becoming more infrequent. I was miserably in love with a ghost. I mustered the courage to call him on it.

"Josh, I know we have had a crazy relationship and all but this is rare even for us. If this is all it is then we should just end it all together."

"What are you saying?"

"I just told you. This isn't working. It's pointless and I don't want to do it anymore. So we should stop meeting like this."

"I can't never see you anymore."

"Well, this is stupid. You hardly see me as it is. We used to be such good friends."

"You're the one who refuses to come over my house with us anymore."

"You didn't even like me drinking!"

"I'm just saying."

"Is that all there is to do nowadays, drink and fuck?"

"Are you trying to tell me you think nothing of our conversations over the phone? Seriously Reba, I fucking pour my heart out to you. You know me better than anybody. And that is not good enough for you?"

"No, I love our conversations. And I do appreciate our friendship. I just feel like times have changed and it seems weird sometimes. But maybe not."

"I'll make it up to you, I promise."

And he did. The physical aspect was well worth our while, and he called more often. Our late-night rendezvous were at least once a week, until they became more sporadic. When I stopped fighting for more the amount of time passing in between meetings grew to unpredictable lengths.

My twenty-first birthday was approaching. I had been working my behind off for years and decided it was high time I had something to show for it. Danielle took the bus with me out to a few car dealerships. We drove home in my new Chevrolet Corsica. It was a green four-door sedan that would fit my niece and nephew's car seats with ease. After all, with two kids Amber needed it as much as I did. Since she finally got enough sense to get rid of her abuser, I was free to take the kids as often as I liked.

I took Shonnie out for a ride around Ocean Drive in my new car. On the way back home we saw Kevin and Dan walking downtown. I stopped the car and rolled down the window.

"Hey, what's up," I yelled.

I received a big smile from Kevin and Dan as they excitedly approached the car. "Hey! What are you doing?" Kevin asked.

"We were just about to head back to my place and get our drink on. What are you two doing?"

"We're drinking with you at your house." Kevin replied. He opened the back door and he and Dan hopped in.

There were instant sparks between Kevin and me; so much so that I was not the least bit apprehensive about inviting Dan to my house. They were talking among themselves in the back seat. As I neared a convenient store they asked me to pull over.

"I'll be right back." Kevin said. "I just need a pack of cigarettes and a condom."

"A condom?" I laughed. "For what?"

"For you!" he said as he shut the door and started towards the store.

"You're kidding!" I yelled after him.

Shonnie couldn't stop giggling.

"What is so damn funny?" I finally asked.

"You know what! Reba's getting busy. Reba's getting busy …" she sang.

"Shut up. He was just joking."

"Did you see the look on his face, mommy, 'cause I did. He was not joking."

"Don't be ridiculous. You don't even know what happened the last time I saw him. I'm surprised he's even talking to me right now."

"You told me what happened." She was still giggling.

"Yeah, but you didn't see his face that night! I did."

"Quiete, here they come," she warned.

The guys got back into my car.

"All set?" I asked.

"Yeah," Kevin replied.

"So, what did you get?" Shonnie asked as I drove toward my house.

"I told you. I got a pack of cigarettes and a condom."

"Stop playing," I said in disbelief.

Shonnie whispered, "Told you."

"Of course he did," insisted Dan.

"I'm serious." Kevin pulled a condom out of his pocket and showed it to Shonnie and me. I was happy to be driving so I wouldn't have to face him at that point. I stopped at Dan's to pick up their twelve-pack before driving to my house.

I needed the alcohol to keep my wits about me, so I suggested we play Black & Red as a quick boost. I wondered if Kevin had moved on or harbored any ill feelings.

Throughout the next few hours we played card games and drank almost all the beer. My curiosity got the best of me and I asked more than once if there was another female in his life. He denied it every time.

I had forgotten how attracted I was to him. This time I was ready to put forth an honest effort. The question was would Kevin give me a second chance. His actions suggested so.

We went to use the bathroom at the same time.

"Go ahead. Guests first!" I waited on the stairs.

"Your turn," he came out smiling.

After I came out, I started back down the stairs but noticed him in my bedroom. I backtracked and peeked my head in. He was meandering about, admiring my photographs and decor. "See anything you like?"

"It's been a long time since I've been here."

"Not much has changed!" I admitted.

"Some of the pictures are new."

"Well yeah."

He walked up to me, taking my hands. "You're still beautiful too; that hasn't changed." He leaned down for a kiss. I was surprisingly hopeful about the possibility of a relationship as the kissing became more intense. One thing led to another and he pulled out the condom.

"I shouldn't even go that route with you since you just expected it from the beginning."

"I certainly didn't expect it. I was hoping it would turn out this way. I wanted to be prepared just in case."

"Uh-huh!"

"Seriously Reba, I know you have a hard time believing that someone other than Josh could actually care about you."

"No, you don't understand …" I started. I'd wanted to explain my actions many a lonely night. I finally had the opportunity.

"There's nothing to say. The past is the past. We are here now, so what are we going to do about it?" Kevin seemed so much more emotionally mature than me that I let him take the lead, and this time I was willing to follow.

Kevin had never seen me completely undressed before. I was without a stitch of clothing with nothing to hide any longer. I wondered if it was a stupid move to pass him up. Lying next to him I was convinced it was. I wasn't going to make the same mistake twice.

It was four o'clock in the morning. Dan, we suspected, was still downstairs. I heard the door a short time ago and assumed Shonnie went home. I wanted Kevin to stay the night with me, but instead he got up and started dressing.

"What are you doing?"

"I'm getting ready to go." He didn't even look in my direction when he spoke.

"Can't you stay?"

"No, I got Dan downstairs."

"So he can sleep in the spare room or on the couch. Better yet, he can go without you."

"Nah, I gotta go." He still avoided eye contact with me.

"You *are* with someone else, aren't you?"

"No, I am not. I already told you a hundred times," he said, frustrated.

"Then why would you leave me like this? I am laying here naked, hello?"

He finished tying his shoes and finally looked at me square in the face. I was lying on the bed looking hopelessly up at him. He was ready to walk out of the door when he said, "Payback's a bitch!"

Kevin left my house that night, and I never heard from him again.

I realized then how I had hurt him, too. I deserved his payback. I was a bitch! I saw Kevin not too long ago with a girl I had been acquainted with for many years. She showed me a diamond ring he gave her as a commitment ring, but not an engagement ring. I was happy for her and told her she had a good guy. I wished her luck. Kevin and I said hello and that was the extent of it. I saw a glimmer of something in his eye, but I ignored it. I knew we weren't meant to be. I respected his girlfriend.

Chapter Sixteen

"Careful Who Your Friends Are"

Temperatures in New England are in the single digits during the month of January. Wind chill factors are below zero. The leafless trees look grey and bare after the holiday lights are taken down. When the decorations are put away it feels like the spirit is as well. The days in January drag on.

By February signs of depression may emerge. Some brilliant mind decided that throwing Valentine's Day in the middle of the melancholy, freezing, life-lacking days of winter was a good way to pick up spirits. And I would imagine a special day set aside honoring your significant other, snuggling with each other for love as well as warmth, might be nice. But that brilliant person didn't think of those losers who don't have sweethearts. That person didn't think of those too insecure and guarded to give love a chance. For them Valentine's Day can bring the real threat of depression.

Trees look like nothing more than naked death. My skin is so pale after being denied sunlight for long. The extra coating of dry, dead skin adds to the graying of my own natural flesh tone. By this time of year the only colors I may see are the redness of my cold nose or the strange tint of purple frosting my already-cracked hands. The bustle on the streets has been at a standstill for long. More than half of the shops downtown are closed from November to March.

The once very warm and lively, loud and electrifying atmosphere of downtown Newport suddenly looks like a ghost town stripped of any living inhabitants.

This somber time of year did not do my physical appearance or personality any justice. I was like a zombie going through the motions of life even when I was sober. I looked forward to my night visits with Josh. We were still in each other's path, despite the lack of effort. It gave me the false sense that we were meant to be. And it made me angry that I didn't know how to make it work with us.

I wound up developing another nasty habit of self-destruction. During a heated argument or an intimate moment with Josh I closed my hands into fists. The mannerism limited the amount of affection I allowed to seep out of myself. Holding hands was not something I was accustomed to.

Josh was not tuned in to my safeguarded tick until this period of our relationship when I was grossly at a loss for understanding. I rubbed my pointer finger up and down the inside of my thumb in a rapid movement. My anxiety was bursting through, but I didn't know how to contain it.

Josh heard the scraping of my skin in his ear while we lay there in his bed silently. He asked, "What are you doing?"

"Nothing," I replied. Suddenly self-conscious, I stopped.

"Come on, what were you doing with your hand?" he asked again, and my response was the same.

He grabbed my hand still clenched in a fist. Instantly I felt threatened. I was half naked in his bed, with his body semi on top of mine, we were alone and talking, and now he wanted to touch my hand. It couldn't get much more intimate than that. My heart was deflating and I grew extremely uncomfortable. I tried to pull my hand away from him.

"Let me see!" he said with a giggle, as though we were playing another game of "hard to get."

"See what?" I said, yanking my hand. "I gotta go. It's late and I'm tired."

By the look on Josh's face I knew he saw that the inside of my thumb was irritated. I didn't acknowledge what he'd seen. I got dressed and went home like I had done so many nights before. He didn't speak a word of it that night or ever, although he did express his concern in other ways. During the rendezvous following, Josh would grab my fist without looking and try to pry my hands open. If he was successful, the holding of hands didn't last more than sixty seconds. But it did stop me from scraping the skin off of my thumbs.

I saw Joe on the couch in his house when I was leaving.

"Hey, blast from the past! I knew I would eventually run into you here again," he said.

"Wow, I didn't know anyone was here. Hold on. I'm gonna go start my car and then I will come back in to chat with you."

Back inside I sat on the couch beside him. Josh was falling asleep in his bed.

"So what have you been up to?" I asked.

"Same old shit, girl. What you think everything changes just 'cause you ain't around no more?"

"Course not, but I didn't think the parties were the way they used to be."

"You're right about that. Party central really died down since you left. It's only us, but you know that's how I like it. Would like to see you more often though."

"Things just aren't the same, ya know?"

"So, just because things aren't the same with you and Josh you gonna leave us all hanging?"

"Sorry. Just one of those things, I guess."

"Yeah, I see how you are."

"Don't be like that, Joe."

"Well, I am, 'cause that's who I am. But I won't hold it against you. You're still the baddest chick I ever knew."

"Thanks, Joe. Maybe I'll see you again soon!"

"I don't think so."

"Alright then, bye!" Though I found his response rather odd, I refrained from probing into the meaning behind the words and actions of Joe Fisher.

To my surprise Josh called me the following day. The question as to how Joe was out of jail earlier than expected and seemingly daring the cops at times to arrest him was finally answered. Josh's house had gotten raided while he was at work. Tyler, Jay, and Craig were arrested and in jail for selling drugs. The strangest thing was that Josh's room was free of any paraphernalia and there were no charges brought against him.

It came to be common knowledge that Joe had hidden cameras on him at times. The police have video footage of all of us at the house. I often try to remember things that were done and said and try to determine which of those things were seen and heard by the police. What a lost soul I must appear to be. I wondered why Josh wasn't involved. He would've been the biggest catch with his history.

Because the video footage and other findings were so minimal, our friends Craig, Tyler, and Jay were only in jail for a few months. The fact is, for the average person, three months is long enough to put a damper on your entire life. Their record will be forever tainted. I couldn't imagine how someone could rat out a friend like that, especially Craig. He took Craig to prison but not Josh. It didn't make sense to me.

Now that Tyler and Jay were in the state penitentiary the landlord advised Josh to get a new apartment immediately. He didn't look kindly upon the apartment getting raided. Josh grew frantic trying to find something for the two of us.

I thought it was fate that brought us back together in times of need. I was grateful that we were communicating as if Tyler and I never had an affair. I gave the housing authority my notice to vacate my apartment, and I was packing my belongings. Josh was scouting the city for a vacant, affordable rental. It was a more difficult task than anticipated. At the end of the month I had just days left in my place.

"Josh, maybe I should renege on my intent to vacate."

"No, don't doubt me now. I think I am onto something. Relax; I'll get it in time."

"It's not a big deal. We'll just keep this one another month."

"My landlord reminded me today to be out by the first of the month. No offense, but I can't stay in the Hill. Not after this. Your crib is in a bad spot too. You know that."

"I know. Good luck, then. I'll talk to you later."

The weekend came and went and I was expected to hand my keys in on Monday.

Josh was ecstatic the next time I spoke with him about it.

"Shorty, I got something! Load up your car with all the boxes and I'll be by to put the big shit in the van."

"Are you serious?"

"Yeah, girl. Go hand your keys in before those snakes get another month outta you."

"Alright. I'll see you soon?"

"Yeah, baby!"

I did as he asked and waited for him to meet me at my place. I finished packing and then rested to have a cigarette. I waited for Josh to come by and then waited longer. It was after dusk before he arrived at my house with the bad news. Typical of Josh, he didn't give me details of what went wrong. All I knew and all I needed to know was that I had to keep my apartment.

The next morning I called out of work to square things away with housing and hopefully get my keys back. I begged and pleaded, then resorted to yelling, but no matter what I did, offered, or said they wouldn't give me back the keys. It had been less than twenty-four hours. Why were they being so damn difficult?

Amber said that Josh and I could stay on her couch as long as we needed to. I put my stuff into storage and Josh paid for it. We said it would only be for a few weeks tops and took Amber up on her offer. That few weeks turned into six months in no time at all.

Chapter Seventeen

"Some Moments in Your Life May Remain Lost Forever"

Josh couldn't visit any of our incarcerated friends because he was an ex-con himself. I chose not to visit any of them. I had seen all I wanted to see inside the prison gates. I wrote letters to the fellas explaining how I couldn't bring myself to that place anymore. I was a supportive friend, but I had enough of driving for forty minutes to sit at a cold, dirty table in uncomfortable chairs, being treated like a prisoner myself by the guards while the other inmates undressed me with their eyes. It was a sense of relief that they all understood. I would never step foot into that place again. And Josh vowed the same.

My sister, Amber, found a new boyfriend. I was tremendously protective at first. But soon enough the kid I called Willis stole my affections as a little brother. He was a wonderful and caring person. He was good with my niece and nephew, and they adored him. He and Josh got along very well too. It was no wonder the months flew by so fast since the rapport between the housemates was so fantastic.

Josh crashed his van one night while out of town. He called his grandfather to come pick him up and have the van towed to a repair shop back on the island. He spent the night at his grandfather's house and was at Amber's the next morning telling me what happened.

Fortunately, the order of occurrences left me no time to be worried. He was standing before me telling me about the accident and the damage to the van. I could see that he was unharmed. The van, on the other hand, was in bad shape. But he insisted on fixing her up. The repairs took over a month, so in the meantime I allowed him to use my car when I wasn't. I was glad to return the favor. I didn't like being in someone's debt, and he was no exception.

I spent all my free time in the Hill at Amber, Shonnie, or Danielle's. Unfortunately, Josh spent the majority of his time there, too. At first he maintained a legal lifestyle. He didn't spend too much time with any group of people for too long, to help keep him out of the loop. But naturally old habits creep back in when you surround yourself with all of the outside factors.

Josh and I spent many nights drinking at Amber's house with Willis and on occasion Willis' friend, Robert. We kept it quiet at Amber's because of the children. It was a safe haven for Josh. None of Josh's thug friends or acquaintances knew of my younger sister. But alas, that didn't last long either.

One peaceful sunny afternoon there was a knock on Amber's door. I went to answer it. I saw a tall, thin, light-skinned black man standing before me. I had never seen him before. He was apparently older than Josh and me by a few years. He was thugged out in oversized FuBu wear with Timberland boots on.

"Yeah?" I asked in my usual uninterested manner.

"Hello, is Josh here?" His conduct was very polite, easing my suspicion slightly.

"Yeah, who are you?"

"I'm Martinez. You must be Reba," he said slyly.

"Do I know you?"

"Nah," he laughed, showing a side I more expected. "I try to keep it low around here."

"Uh, huh." I left him at the door, leaving it open just a crack.

Josh came running downstairs. He walked right past me, and I watched him walk out, shutting the door completely behind him. I couldn't hear any voices so I went to the window. They were nowhere in sight.

Soon enough Brown showed up next at Amber's. I finally got the opportunity to speak with her about it.

"Amber, what is up with all these people coming here?"

"Well, Josh asked if he could let some of his friends know he was staying here."

"And you said yes?"

"Well yeah, I don't mind."

"I do! I don't wanna a bunch of fucking thugs up in here where my niece and nephew sleep."

"No, he said that."

"He said what?"

"Josh said he wouldn't let everyone know. He wasn't gonna blow up my spot or anything … just like one or two people. He said he would keep it tight for me and the kids."

"He better, and YOU need to make sure of that."

"It's fine."

My twenty-first birthday finally arrived. The day started off like any other workday. This time I drove my car to the liquor store afterwards. I bought my first twelve-pack of Molson Ice myself, and for Amber and Willis I bought a bottle of E&J. I'd never felt so liberated.

Shonnie and Danielle came up to my sister's house to celebrate with us. Amber and the kids made cupcakes. Even Josh and Willis sang happy birthday. It was simply sweet and full of love.

Shonnie, Rodney, Josh, and I planned to go to a club called Senior Frog's in downtown Newport. After we put the kids to bed Danielle went home. We prolonged our stay at Amber's as long as possible before heading out. We left at half past eleven.

Josh paid my cover charge, and my drinks were on the house the entire night, since it was my twenty-first birthday. It was awesome. Most of my time was spent on the dance floor with Shonnie and Josh. He really proved that I was the only girl for him in the room that night.

I don't remember leaving the club or who drove my car home. I don't remember anything from the dance floor to my sister's couch where Josh was happy to give me my private birthday present. Overall I was pleased with the way I spent the milestone birthday.

Shonnie, Josh, Rodney, and I went to Senior Frog's often after that. I remember dancing in the amazing light show. Every so often Josh danced with me. Some time while out on the dance floor I blacked out again. I don't remember going home or how or when. But sure enough I woke up the following day on Amber's couch.

I promised myself I wouldn't drink so much the next time. Towards the end of the night a black man started dancing with me. He appeared to be a college student. I knew most of the people around my age group and had never seen him before. He was properly dressed, with his shirt tucked into his khakis. He kept his distance as he danced in front of me, so I had no qualms. I smiled at him and continued dancing.

Suddenly Shonnie came up behind me and grabbed my arm. She swung me around and for a second I expected to see Josh's face, even though I was surprised he was displaying jealousy. We danced with other people all the time, keeping boundaries. But when I turned around and saw Shonnie's face I was even more stunned.

"Mommy, what are you doing?" she asked as she led me off the dance floor.

"What? I was just dancing. Why, you think Josh would get mad? 'Cause he shouldn't."

"No. You mean to tell me you don't recognize him?" My expression was of complete bewilderment. "Reba, take a good look at him. You don't remember him?"

I looked at the guy who was still dancing, and struggled to recall anything about him. I sorted through my brain of links and links of people and friends that might lead me to him somehow. I couldn't figure it out. He was a short black man who looked as though he had a decent appetite. His clothes were fashionably preppy and fit him well. He was a complete stranger to me. "Should I?"

"Oh my God, I can't believe you don't remember."

"Enough already. Are you going to tell me who the hell he is, or do I have to ask him?" I said frustrated with the riddle.

"That's the guy I was telling you about last week. He was dancing all over you and you kept walking away from him. But he kept following you. I had to tell him to leave you alone and he still tried following you so Rodney and Josh had to step in and tell him to back the fuck up!"

"That's him? Why didn't you tell me? I'm out there dancing with this freak. No wonder he was all smiling in my face and shit."

"I didn't know you were dancing with him until I just looked over and saw you. Then I told you."

"YUK!"

"Oh, Oh! Look at him. He just realized he was dancing right next to Josh. Look at him—he's scurrying away." She started laughing.

"Alright, well come dance with me then and keep him away from me," I said.

We headed out to the dance floor. As soon as we started dancing Josh came over to join us. We stayed away from the club for a couple of weeks after that. From what Shonnie and Rodney relayed the guy was a real stalker type. That was the last thing I needed in my life!

As usual our blissful period was short-lived. Brown was smoking with Josh, Willis, and Amber every so often and I couldn't shake the bad vibe I kept feeling. If he was smoking it, then it was in his possession and so I wondered how. And if he had enough to smoke large amounts and still had plenty to spare then I assumed he was selling it again. It all came about rapidly. The lifestyle was second nature to him.

More and more during our conversations he mentioned Martinez.

"Who the hell is this guy anyway?"

"I told you he's from New York, like you."

"So his ass couldn't hang with the big boys in the city so he decided to come to our little spot and demand top-dog position around here?"

"It ain't like that."

"Oh really? Why the hell else would someone like that come from New York to here?"

"You don't know what you're talking about, man!"

"I know that this conversation should not even be happening. You're just looking to go back to jail."

"You're right. This conversation shouldn't even be happening."

We were growing further apart. The tension grew in Amber's house.

Josh displayed certain behaviors I'd learned to expect when he was feeling inadequate. It was only wishful thinking that we had moved on from this chapter. I was leaving the house without telling him where I was going or even that I was leaving. Sometimes he would catch up with me at Danielle's. Other times I was in town with Shonnie. I purposely didn't want him to know where I was and intentionally kept my life more secretive. It was my way of saying, "If you can't behave you won't ever have me 100 percent," without ever saying a word.

It was my silent ultimatum. I was secretly wishing he'd choose love and quietly praying he'd choose me over that lifestyle. Only a fool would think I had shown him what life was like without the thug role. Not that I had the self-worth to know that I deserved more, but the mere fact that I was getting bored with the whole thing told me that circumstances would not be like they were for much longer.

Josh continued to page me, but this time I didn't call him back. The "1-4-3" pages of "I love you" changed to "1-8-7." I knew what it meant; I listened to 2-Pac and Biggie too! I ignored the threats.

Then he went on a hunt looking for me. He was a human time bomb and a moment further without hearing from me or finding me he would explode. But the sight of me defused it all. Of course he couldn't show me how much I meant to him and how not hearing from me even when we were not happy with each other ate him inside out.

I knew enough not to push anyone too far. After a second page of "1-8-7" or a "666" page I called him back. I knew he was the culprit of the idol threats. I held back accusations. He never admitted to them either. Though on occasion he did say, "If any girl ever hurts me again, I'll kill her."

Josh was making mention of a girl out in Providence to Willis. He would say it softly as if to whisper but loud enough so I could hear him. I don't know how fictional the female character was. It was disturbing at any rate. After a week it really tugged on my heart-strings.

As a result we played a silent game of who could come home the latest. It was tricky for me because I wanted to win, but at what cost? I couldn't wait to come home until the next day because then I would be labeled a slut. But when the arrival time got increasingly later, I wondered what was considered the next day. When I came home at four o'clock I knew it was getting out of hand. It was hard enough trying to keep my other friends awake that late. I concluded anything after five o'clock would be considered the next day. The latest I came home was 4:38 A.M. Ironically, we got home at the same time. The game was over after that.

Suddenly, the air seemed a little lighter and he no longer mentioned his supposed mistress's name. Whether the affair was over or he gave up trying to convince me that there was one because he wasn't getting the desired reaction from me didn't matter. It was enough to raise my spirits.

Chapter Eighteen

"There's a Thin Line Between Love and Hate"

I was asleep on the couch one night at half past eleven. I was exhausted due to the lack of sleep I had gotten the previous week. Josh came in and sat on the couch beside my head. He gently woke me.

"Reba, are you awake?"

"What?" I answered, not fully awake and with no intentions of becoming so.

"Can I use your car to go to the store?"

"Yeah, go ahead."

"Where are your keys?" he said a minute later.

"On the kitchen table," I grumbled. I noticed the clock on the VCR. It read 11:36 P.M.

I fell back asleep. An hour later I woke up double-checking the clock, which now read 12:22 A.M. "Hmmm," I whispered to myself. He must have dropped the car off and walked over to Brown's, I assumed. I tried going back to sleep, but I wondered where he was, as it was apparent that he wasn't home. My curiosity got the best of me, making my attempt to fall back to sleep futile.

I glanced at the clock: 12:39 A.M. I got up to search for my keys on the kitchen table. They weren't there. I took a peek outside the window to find the driveway vacant. In disbelief I went to the front door to look outside as if the transparent window was impairing my ability to see what was actually in front of me, or in reality what was not, which happened to be my car. I took a walk out to the curb, thinking perhaps by some chance he may have parked it along the street due to the possibility that the driveway was blocked when he came home. Still I saw no sign of my car.

My internal alarm began to buzz, "What do I do?" The house phone was shut off earlier that week because Amber forgot to pay her bill. I checked my pager for messages, but there were none. I rechecked my pager and triple checked my pager, but no matter how hard I tried no new messages appeared. The house was still, and the entire street was oddly quiet. I began to feel like I was in the twilight zone. I crept upstairs unsure of what to expect, but I saw Amber sleeping, nothing unusual about that!

I went back downstairs and stood in the middle of the living room taking in all the clues. My left arm was wrapped around my waist with my right elbow resting on it as I bit my nails in my usual worrisome stance.

"Where is he?" I said aloud. "Did he get arrested? Is my car impounded? Did he get into another accident? Is he in the hospital?"

I decided to sit back down on the couch and catch myself before I jumped overboard. The anxiety was building in my chest. I looked at the clock again: 12:48 A.M. "It's almost 1:00 A.M. It was eleven thirty, wasn't it?" I started to doubt myself and used that as an opportunity to relax and contemplate the actual events and precise time line.

In gathering myself I lay down, trying to picture the numbers on the clock from the exact position. I was lying on my side, watching the numbers trade spaces: "12:54, well he shouldn't be past one anyway. He's probably over at Brown's. He'll be home any minute," I assured myself.

I got up to smoke a cigarette and promised myself not to check the time until I was done, and by then he should be back. "I mean where's he gonna go at this hour anyway?"

I lit my stogie and inhaled the smoke deep into my lungs. I held it for a minute as if it was laced with something more than tobacco and nicotine before I exhaled. There was a distinct odor that crept through my nose. I had read about this peculiar scent that apparently only I can sense even when I am in the presence of others at the time I travel into this strange dimension. This aura pierced my nasal cavity and tingled my nose hairs, giving me the sensation that I have to sneeze; yet I never do.

I poured a glass of Kool-Aid, using all my energy to remain calm and unaffected. But I couldn't stop the "What ifs" dancing around in my head. Finally I took my last drag.

"It's after one," I gasped as if that was literally a deadline. The electricity in my brain suddenly ceased like a frozen mist had penetrated my skull. It added pressure on my brain from all directions. Pounds of pressure increased with every minute, weighing me down as I watched the clock. The pressure squeezed my temples together, making me completely aware of my pulse.

The icy wave lingered within and next impaired my vision. With a subconscious crinkle in my forehead and a squint of my eyes I could see tiny stars of flashing lights through the haze before me. These specks of bright lights anxiously danced in an unstructured choreography.

I stepped outside into the night for fresh air and a change of scenery. Walking down the street I was hoping to run into someone, Josh in particular, but any form of life would do to help me contain my ever-growing anxiety. The sound of silence commenced to ring in my ears, leaving all other sounds somewhere in the distance.

On my way back to Amber's I walked behind the units. "As if he could drive through the woods in my car!" I muttered to myself.

I went back into the house and couldn't help but check the time again: 1:16 A.M. Anxiety had taken its course. I lit another cigarette. One minute I was in deep, heavy thought and the next minute I was at a complete loss for any cognitive brain function. I was unaware of the world around me, like I was in a new dimension, though one that is very familiar to me because I have frequented it much in the past.

Despite my efforts, I began to feel the flutter of the stars in my chest. The attack was undoubtedly under way.

As I expected the boa constrictor slithered underneath my rib cage. With his extraordinary muscular strength he tightened my internal tissue. My breaths involuntarily became short and quick as it hurt to breathe, and I felt like I wasn't getting enough air into my lungs. I could feel a lump in my throat from the lack of oxygen passing through my windpipe, and my heart hardened to a heavy rock against my sternum.

I became extremely weak. The boa was becoming visible, merging with the outside of my body as his belly increased in size. His tremendously painful hold had my life clutched in his coils. At that time I noticed that my extremities were shaking. I tried to hold my hands steady, but to no avail. I tightened the muscles in my thighs, yet they continued to quiver. I began to pace the floor, but my efforts were futile. He had me in under his spell.

I had reached the climax of my attack, but the extent of its visit was always unknown. I do believe I have tried every tactic from ignoring it to contradicting it with happy thoughts to fighting this oncoming cycle of rage and confusion within myself, but nothing ever worked. My only choice was to deal with it and accept it, and I always did, with as much grace as possible.

I lit another cigarette and decided I would drag my serpent over to the pay phone at the mini-mart. I figured I could start by calling the police station and confirming if there were any accidents or arrests. I opened the closet door and pulled out my change jar. It was a Snapple bottle Josh had drunk from one night when we were only late-night lovers. I opened the bottle and poured the contents into my pocket. I was obviously dazed because I should've just taken the bottle with me. I threw on a coat and looked at the clock: 1:28 A.M. "Please let him be okay!" I said as I grabbed my cigarettes and headed for the door.

Just then headlights shone through the kitchen window. "Oh, thank God!" I exclaimed. I lit another cigarette and sat back on the couch. I started to empty the change back into the bottle when I heard the car door shut. I jumped up to meet him at the door. My intention was to hug him. I was so relieved he was okay; I just wanted to feel him close to me. But when I saw his nonchalance I had a quick flashback to what the last hour was like for me. So instead of hugging him I jacked him up against the basement door.

"Where have you been?" I was scornful as a parent towards her absent-minded teen.

He pushed me off of him. "What the hell is wrong with you?" He was furious that I rushed at him like that.

"I have been worried sick wondering where you are. I didn't know if you got into another accident or you got arrested or what. You said you were going to the fucking store."

"You are so lucky you are you. Don't ever touch me like that again. You're so fucking lucky."

I actually felt a little remorseful for approaching him the way I did. It was the rush of emotion when I saw his face. I was stunned by his anger for a minute. He had never been that truly angry with me before in my presence.

"Gimme the keys."

He put them on the table and walked out the door. I slammed the door and positioned my back up against the wall. I never anticipated that kind of reaction. The incident replayed in my head over and over again. On the one hand I was uplifted by the breakthrough in allowing my emotions to speak, but I was regretful due to his response. I noticed my cigarette had burned down to the filter in the ashtray, so I walked over to put it out. Then there was a knock on the door.

"I want my sweatshirt," he said when we were face to face.

"What sweatshirt?"

"The purple one. It's on the back of the chair."

Disheartened that there was an actual sweatshirt, I walked over and picked it up, awaiting a comment or for him to walk into the house. I was anticipating an apology so we could make up, but his silence proved me wrong, invoking my anger. In retaliation I threw it outside, and the ugly purple sweatshirt landed on the dirt in front of the stoop. I slammed the door shut.

It was the same sweatshirt that the crack head gave him a couple of weeks earlier. I had pulled up to Shonnie's house to talk to her and I saw Josh. He approached the car to greet us. When he saw that I was cold he tried being chivalrous by lending me his button-down shirt. A few minutes later he started shivering and demanded that the crack head walking by give him his sweatshirt. After a short deliberation the crack head unwillingly complied. Then the sweatshirt stayed in my trunk until the day before, when he finally took it out.

Asking for it was just a ploy to get me to the door and to open the lines of communication. He expected me to break down and hug and kiss and make up. I expected him to do the same. We were both way too obstinate for that. He was as mad at me for not breaking down as I was at him.

Ten minutes later he came knocking on the front door again. This time he yelled at me, "Why are you throwing my shit out the door like that? Why are you disrespecting my shit?"

"It ain't even yours! Don't act like you give a rat's ass about that damn sweatshirt, 'cause you don't!"

"Of course it's mine. I can't believe you're treating my shit like that. I should slap you in the face for that." He backed down the stairs.

I accepted the invitation and stepped outside. "What are you talking about? I was there when you took that thing from the crack head."

"This ain't even the same one."

"Yes it is. Don't fucking lie to my face." At that point I could tell that he was pretending to be angrier than he was. The drama energized him. I despised feuding with him and so I had to walk away from this ridiculous quarrel.

"You're lucky you are you. I should slap you!" he repeated, trying desperately to keep me outside by provoking my confrontational side. If I continued to walk away it would've shown I truly didn't have a place in my heart for him. But I did. I fell for his game and decided to call his bluff.

"Hit me then! Go ahead and fucking hit me with your lying ass!" I said with my arms outstretched, inviting the fight. I was facing him, standing still in the front yard waiting for his reaction. He stood there blankly.

"Whatever, man!" I heard him exclaim as I went back into the house.

I was in the house smoking another cigarette and thinking of how out of hand the entire ordeal had gotten so quickly. I was too angry to cry. He was acting so childish. I had never seen behavior like this from him before.

About thirty minutes later, just when the situation seemed to be cooled down, there was another knock, but this time from the back door. I opened the door to see Josh's face.

"I thought we were done!" I said.

"We are. I just wanted to tell you not to talk to my grandfather anymore."

"Don't be ridiculous," I said. "I have a relationship with him beyond 'us.' You can't ask me to do that. It's not fair."

"I told you if you and me is nothing then you can't talk to him anymore."

"You're so fucked up. That is the dumbest thing you've ever said."

"I'm serious. Don't let me catch you talking with him," he threatened.

"Or what? You think your grandfather would agree to this? I don't."

"Just keep away from my family. Don't talk to my mother, or my grandfather. That's all I'm saying."

"I don't think I can do that. And I think you're wrong for even requesting such a thing." I tried to remain calm. He was pulling at all angles trying to hit a nerve. His tone had gotten louder, so I shut the door behind me and walked down the back steps into the darkness of the nearby woods. He started to walk away from me, so I called out, "That's it?"

"I told you, there's a thin line between love and hate," he started.

"Come on!" I almost laughed.

"I hate you!"

I looked at him in utter amazement. What can be said to something like that?

"I hate you!" he said it again. My face involuntarily expressed sorrow, and he felt he'd finally hit the nerve he'd been trying to find from the start. So he repeated it twice more, "I hate you, I hate you!"

He turned around and walked away. I stood there in disbelief. It was nearly three in the morning and all was quiet around me. The woods in front of me were suspiciously still, for there was no breeze. The sky was black as a hollow. The streetlight shone above me where the woods curved in their peninsula shape, rounding their way towards Hillside Ave, the same direction in which Josh walked. I walked around the bend but couldn't see him. I peered through the trees and brush in the woods to see if he was spying on me. It was rather dark for me to catch sight of him if he was there. He didn't knock on the door anymore that night.

I went to work the next morning, depressed all through the day. My mind was busy reliving the previous night with clarity in the detail, because I hadn't had a drop to drink. The pounding in my head was a sharper unyielding pain due to the stress I was under. I wondered how the argument would've gone down had I been drinking as usual. It's strange how things have a way of coming about.

It was a miserable day for me, so I took my time cleaning. I figured I had nothing to go home to, no one to get all dolled up for, and no one to try to make jealous, and no one of importance would be around for me to conceal my insecurities with a little veiling. I didn't finish cleaning my rooms until after four in the afternoon.

I drove my car to Amber's house with my stomach in knots. I was struck with worry about what might happen if I ran into Josh. I didn't want him to publicly humiliate me. When I got home, I was greatly relieved to find he wasn't there. But before I had a chance to relax, Willis came downstairs with a warning.

"Yo, I don't know if you should be here," he said.

"Why?" My brain was too tired to be any more confused.

"Because Josh came by here looking for you."

"Was he mad? What did he say?"

"He was pissed. He said he was going to kill you."

"What?" I said with a sense of sarcasm.

"For real. I don't know what he was talking about. He was talking so fast. He was definitely on something. He said he was going to pound your head in with a rock after he shoots you. He said something about you disrespecting him." Willis was very nervous and anxious to get me out of the house.

Under normal circumstances I would've dismissed the threats as idle. He was a hothead who lived to get people's attention. But since he was suspected to be on drugs there's no telling what he might've done. I was aware of the fact that I'd hurt him immeasurably in the past; after last night he was capable of anything.

For the first time in my life I feared him. I heeded Willis's advice and called Stew from work. I kept it honest. I told him I needed a place to hide out for the day. Stew rented in town and Josh had no knowledge of him, let alone where he lived. I was grateful that he was more than willing to accommodate me for the evening.

I hurriedly took a shower. I told myself I wouldn't allow him to unnerve me enough not to. My sister came home just as I was ready to leave.

"Can you take me to get the kids?"

"Of course." Their needs always came first.

After we put the children into the car my emotions got the best of me. Fear was an emotion I was unfamiliar with, and at that magnitude it was eerily uncomfortable. I felt a complete lack of control over my existence. What was done was done. I had hurt this young man immensely, and he was mixing his emotions with drugs.

I couldn't stop the tears from streaming down my face as I headed back to the Hill to drop Amber and the children off. She knew why I was upset.

"Don't let the kids forget me!" It was my only request. "Let them know how much I love them. Please don't let them forget me."

I could see from the corner of my eye that Amber was crying too. She didn't say a word. I was able to drop Amber and the children off at her house without running into trouble. I gave the kids a great big hug and kiss before I drove into town. I stopped at the liquor store and bought a twelve-pack.

Stew and I discussed the scenario as it had occurred. He was a little taken aback after hearing Josh's threat.

"What can I do?" he asked.

"You're doing it. I really appreciate you letting me stay here for the day."

"Yeah, but darling, then what?"

"Well, I am hoping he will cool down after today. And after the drugs wear off, he'll be less of a threat. If you get involved it would only feed his rage. I can't have you taking any hits for me. And I don't want to piss him off any more."

Stew drank his Bud Light and listened to me ramble on as I drank myself drunk, emptying the entire twelve-pack. I had nothing left to do. It was time for me to go home despite the early hour of nine o'clock. I felt cowardly hiding out. I felt defeated. I had procrastinated long enough and was ready to face whatever was coming my way. Stew tried to convince me not to go, but I didn't want to give him any ideas by staying. I figured the best thing was for me to drive home.

On the ride I was too intoxicated to let my emotions get the best of me again. As I turned onto Hillside Ave I felt the knots in my stomach again. Even alcohol couldn't subdue that feeling. I drove down the street carefully, watching my speedometer as I tried to keep a lookout in case I saw Josh or a police cruiser.

As soon as I turned onto Cowie Street just before my destination, my headlights shone on Josh looking directly at my vehicle. He was talking to someone in a parked car on the side of the road. From the look on his face I was instantly relieved. "He didn't look psychotic!" I thought to myself. "Let's get this over with."

Josh disappeared into the shadows between the houses as the car he was leaning into drove away ahead of me. I pulled over, remembering to put the car in park, got out, and started after him. I looked behind the houses and saw no sign of him, then looked back at my car. I gave one more stare into the darkness down towards the next street and saw no one. Convinced that he vanished intentionally I drove home. I slept well that night. The doors and windows were locked. He didn't have a key. I gave him the opportunity to "get me" and he turned it away. It's a liberating feeling after a courageous move, a great confidence boost, even if I was drunk!

I saw Josh the next day outside Amber's house. We didn't speak. He didn't try to take my life. It was as if we didn't know or see one another.

Chapter Nineteen

"Our Choices Determine Our Fate!"

Two weeks after the threat on my life there was an unexpected knock at Danielle's door. Accompanied by only a six-pack, we hadn't anticipated an eventful night. I was making a conscious effort not to overdo it with alcohol. When Danielle opened the door she was even more surprised to see my sister Amber.

"Oh, hey girl! Come on in," Danielle said, holding the door open wide.

"Is my sister here?" I heard Amber ask.

"Yeah, she's on the couch."

"What's up?" I called to her. "What are you doing here?"

"Brown just came up to my house and told me Josh just got arrested." Amber said in a chaotic fashion.

"What?" Danielle, Casey, and I said in unison.

"I'm not really sure what they got him for, but what I heard was that his van got pulled over for whatever reason. Then, you know they knew who he was so they searched the van. Brown called Josh's grandfather on the phone. His grandfather was able to go down there and see the whole thing. Then they arrested Josh. Josh told Brown to go up to my house and tell you what happened." She finished it all in one breath.

"Josh told him to run up and tell me?" I asked.

"Yeah, he told him to bring his clothes and CDs up to my house to give to you and let you know what went down." Amber loved the drama. She was happy to be in the mix.

"UGH!" I was basically speechless.

"You knew this day was coming," Danielle said.

"Yeah, I tried telling him," I sighed. "You know how he is. He knows I don't like dealing with this shit. That's why we haven't been talking. Now look!" I finished my beer and went home. The last time he'd sent me a message years ago that he'd gotten arrested I was so upset. Feeling helpless I went out drinking. He was disappointed with me for drinking while he was in jail. But when I asked what he expected me to do he had no answer.

I stayed awake talking with Amber and Willis long after the bottles ran dry. If there was anyone I was comfortable enough to be around while sober it was Amber. We went to sleep at about two in the morning.

I woke up to my beautiful niece tapping me on the leg. "Josh is here, Aunt Reba." I suspected I was dreaming. She said it again and I heard my sister's voice outside. Then I heard Josh's voice.

I slowly opened my eyes and looked at the clock on the VCR. It read 8:48 A.M. That was too early on my days off work. It was a bright sunny July morning. I jumped up and fervently brushed my fingers through my hair. I rubbed my eyes, hoping to get all of the sleepiness out. He was standing just outside the door at the top of the stoop with my sister. I continued to hear their voices but was too much in a morning fog to comprehend any of it as I walked over.

"I thought you were in jail?" I interrupted.

"I just got out this morning." His entire disposition was very casual.

"They let you go so fast?"

"Yeah. I'll let you know everything later. I gotta go to my grandfather's right now and straighten things out with him. I'll be back later. I wanted to see you first thing," he said as he prepared to leave.

He was smiling at me as brightly as the sun shone. I was relieved to see him out and happy. I let the specifics go for the time being. He could fill in the blanks later. "Okay, see you later. I'll be here."

Amber just looked at me and shrugged her shoulders as Josh drove away.

A few hours passed before he returned. He was the calmest I'd ever seen him in my life. He wasn't jumpy. He wasn't itching to go anywhere even with nowhere to go. He wasn't speaking wildly about the mischievous incidents that may or may not have occurred. He wasn't pacing the floor back and forth. He wasn't asking to use the phone. His pager was silent; as a matter of fact I don't think he had his pager on him.

He briefly told us what happened. Brown actually gave us more description than Josh did. When it came to the reality of dramatic events in his life it was ironic that he suddenly became vague. Usually his storytelling was very vivid; that's one way I knew a story was at least somewhat fabricated.

"Well, I gotta keep it low around here," he said, acting mysteriously. "I'm going to my grandfather's where nobody can find me."

"Alright. You know how to get me if you need me. I'll be around here."

"Well, I'll be back later."

"I know. I ain't going nowhere!"

"That's fine," Amber added. "We'll be here." She said referring to Willis and herself.

I went over to see Danielle to tell her what I knew, which was nothing more than the previous night. I stayed there for a bit while the girls gossiped about this one and that around the neighborhood.

I returned to Amber's for dinnertime. I decided to eat a meal that night with my niece and nephew. We had hot dogs and macaroni and cheese with a can of mixed vegetables. Conversing with them was one of my most treasured pastimes.

Josh came over in the evening. Amber, Willis, Robert, and I were watching *Scarface* when Josh knocked on the door. He sat with us and watched the rest of the movie. Afterwards he gestured for me to follow him to the unoccupied corner of the house.

"Yo, I got a plane to catch in two days."

"Plane? To go where?"

"Hush, keep it down. I'm going down south. I gotta get outta here."

I didn't know what to think, let alone what to say, aside from, "Really? When?"

"I leave Monday morning."

"Really?" I was completely dumbfounded.

"Don't be mad at me and don't take this the wrong way, but they made me make a deal. It was the only way I could get outta there. You know I can't do that so I have to go. There's no choice. I can't tell you exactly where I'll be because I don't want you getting caught up in the mix."

Part of me wanted to discount the whole story. How many times did we talk about getting an apartment together? How many times did he tell me he was grown up and done with that lifestyle? How many times did we talk about leaving the state together? Although his calmness still didn't fit him especially in his current dilemma, I was speechless.

"Okay? Don't tell anybody."

"Yeah, I know. Not even Amber?" I asked.

"Well, you can tell Amber and Willis. But don't go telling your girls nothing. And don't let Robert hear you talking about it with your sister." I was sure to respect his wishes. He stayed at the house for a bit longer waiting for Robert to finally leave so we could speak frankly about the current situation.

Josh asked candidly, "Can we have a goodbye party? Ya know just the family … tomorrow night?"

"Yeah, what do ya think, Amber?" It was her house, so she had the final say.

"Of course." She turned toward Willis, "You gotta keep Robert outta here then. You know how he's been up your ass lately."

"Yeah, man, I know!" Willis replied.

The next day was a quiet day. I didn't see much of Josh until nightfall. The daylight hours seemed to drag on forever. The heat was uncomfortably humid, leaving yet another reason to look forward to the sunset.

At least I had work to occupy my time. During my break out in the receiving area my faithful security guard, Bill, gladly accompanied me. He had proven to be a real confidant. He was a true sense of security and a great listener. This time I spilled my heart out about Josh's planned departure, although I left out the details of the cause.

Bill knew of Josh only through the words that had come out of my mouth during our cigarette breaks together. Up until then he never spoke of his disapproval of him, but he didn't have to—every inch of his body did at the mere mention of his name. I learned to ignore it. I was surprised that Bill decided this was the time to voice his opinion of Josh, but the words revealed what I already suspected.

When the Josh bashing was over, Bill said, "Hey, I got this place in the city; in New York City. You should come with me. It's a nice little place on the corner. It'll do you some good."

My stunned silence tipped him off to my puzzlement. He continued, though digressing a bit and speaking of a woman he used to care for. He described the sassiness and hard-ass nature of his long-lost beloved and didn't hold back his admiration for her. She was no longer a part of his life, and he wanted someone again. Then returned to his invitation.

"It's a nice spot down there. You could help me with things, and I would provide you with a resting place. I like to have hearty meals and a clean house. A real hotshot like you would satisfy me just fine. Of course, I'd pay for everything and give you some extra on the side."

The expression on my face changed from puzzled to offended. And he reluctantly rescinded his offer, "Well, you stay here then and continue on like this. I would've paid you good." With that he took his last puff and disappeared through the receiving entrance. That was the last time I ever saw Bill.

I tried not to be too offended by Bill's advance. Every other man in my life had disappointed me, and most of them through their fantastic sexual ideas. Why should Bill be so different? I'll just never understand it.

As it turned out Robert was at Amber's when Josh arrived with liquor and weed ready for his sendoff party. I was also anxious after enduring the agonizing boredom throughout the day.

Amber kept giving Willis the eyes as if to say, "Tell Robert to leave." Willis was in a tough position. He was afraid he'd hurt Robert's feelings. I gave Amber a consoling smile, and Josh decided to make the best of it. Robert was delighted to see us drinking and wanted to participate as well. It was a shock to us all when he pulled out a bottle of E&J from his baggy jean shorts. He wasn't normally a contributor.

Robert was an unattractive character. He was black kid younger than myself with lips that looked swollen. His eyes were round and wide, spaced somewhat close together, giving him the appearance of someone with little intelligence. In his case it wasn't just the appearance—Robert was not brightest crayon in the box. He spoke very quickly and seemed to salivate quite a bit more than the average person, and in doing so he slurred his words occasionally, spitting or spraying his ideas. He was unappealing to look at, to talk with, and to sit next to. On a normal day I'd rather he not be there, so naturally I didn't want him there for our special family party.

His attendance began to irritate me. Josh didn't feel as though it was his place to ask someone to leave. Willis felt bad, and Amber didn't want to fight with Willis about it. Josh wanted to light a blunt. Trying to keep his paraphernalia concealed he secretly pleaded for someone to get Robert to leave.

I decided not to put the burden on Amber or Willis. It was long overdue, and Robert was wearing my patience thin anyway. He hadn't gotten the hints we'd been throwing out. I don't know why any of us expected him to.

I finally asked him outright, "Hey, Robert, ya know we wanted to have a family party tonight. I don't mean to be rude, but would you mind hanging out somewhere else tonight?" I was polite as I could possibly be.

"Oh, alright Reba. If that's what you want," Robert replied, feeling slighted. Willis shook his head at me. Amber's eyes were wide in trying to hold back her laughter. Josh walked to the kitchen with a satisfied smirk on his face.

"I don't mean to be rude," I elaborated. "But we kinda had this planned for just the family. I'm sorry."

"Nah, I understand. Just the family; that's cool. I'll catch you tomorrow," he said as he gathered his cigarettes and lighter and walked towards the door.

He gave daps to Willis and Josh as he passed them respectively. I got up and locked the back door. Josh locked the kitchen door behind Robert, then came back and sat next to me.

"Yo, you are cold," Willis said, feeling guilty for throwing his friend out.

"What do you mean? I was nice to him."

"That was pretty rough," Amber said in accordance with Willis.

"Well listen, he wasn't supposed to be here. I asked him to leave after a while. I wasn't rude. I said it was a family affair … why? Do you think he's really upset?"

"Probably. You know how he's afraid of you!" Willis said.

"He is not. I just speak my mind. He knows I don't play around, and so he chills when I ask him to chill. That doesn't mean he's afraid of me." I didn't like to think that people feared me. I never wanted anyone's fear, just his or her respect.

"Yeah, okay!" Amber replied sarcastically.

"Anyways …" I dismissed the subject.

"All right. Who's smoking this?" Josh digressed, lighting the blunt he'd finished rolling.

"Are you hitting it tonight?" Willis asked me.

"Yeah, she's getting in tonight. She has to; I'm leaving tomorrow," Josh answered for me.

That's when it hit me. He really was leaving. Life was unfathomable without him. Even when we went through our bouts of silence for months at a time there was always a glimmer of hope he would surprise me with a call or visit. Now the chances of that happening were next to nothing. Some sixth sense was telling me that when he got on that plane the next day it was the end of us forever. Because I didn't want to think about it, I did what I knew best. I got inebriated and smoked whatever was handed to me.

Josh and I were very cozy next to one another on the couch. When I was sitting upright he was reclined back into the couch caressing my back. When I was sitting back into the slope of the cushion he leaned into me, our legs stuck together like glue. We laughed and told stories, enjoying everyone's company for the last time.

By one o'clock in the morning every one of us was drunk beyond comprehension. Amber and Willis inconspicuously retreated upstairs and Josh and I were left downstairs alone together with a strange sense of emptiness. He turned all the light switches off, leaving one dim light on the stove overhead before joining me on the couch.

We whispered solemnly about his nine o'clock plane the next morning. The he began kissing me. I didn't hesitate to relish the moment. The idea of not being a major part of his daily life and vice versa was the strangest feeling I'd ever felt. I hadn't a clue what life would be like without him. His existence had somehow managed to influence most of my decisions all my adolescent and adult life. Who would I be thinking of while getting dressed every day? Who would I be trying to impress while styling my hair?

He had to have been in some serious shit if his only way out was to flee so abruptly, leaving me behind. Part of me certainly wanted him to get away and start off fresh. I knew it would do him some good to distance himself from these old habits. He was better than this bullshit he lived.

We made love for the last time. I lay there, quietly reflecting, contemplating if it truly would be the last of us. He whispered, "I love you," and kissed me gently on my lips. He said it again, "I love you," before kissing my cheek. He put his pants on and lay down on the other couch quietly.

Suddenly it dawned on me. I couldn't recall him pulling the condom off. We always used a condom, *always*! I reached down and felt my belly. It was dry. I felt the couch underneath me and to the sides of me. That too was dry. I was too embarrassed to ask where he had ejaculated, so I ran upstairs to the bathroom. That's when I found out, because in between my legs felt gooey.

"Yuk!" I whispered, totally disgusted and petrified of my findings. I ran to the sink and I started throwing water on myself. I filled a cup and splashed the water in between my legs, hoping to rinse everything inside out. I cleaned myself as long as I could until the gooey substance was completely gone, finalizing the process with a strong pushing urinating as if my life depended on it.

By the time I went downstairs Josh was asleep. His Cheshire was still gleaming though he was snoring. I decided not to bother him and went to sleep on the opposite couch, happy that he was still smiling and grateful that I could still see it.

When I awoke the next morning I sensed my niece telling me Josh was at the door again. I slowly opened my eyes, expecting to see her silhouette in the bright morning sunlight shining through the opened front door the same as I did the other morning. When my eyes were opened, it was dark inside the house. The opaque drapes were drawn. No one was awake. The house was desolate space. The couch Josh had fallen asleep on was unoccupied.

I was able to focus on the clock; it read 9:12 A.M, and after a few blinks to double-check my vision there was no change in the time. The vacancy of the couch was that within myself. The lost sense I had a hint of last night was reality now. I peeked outside the window curtain to find the grey and quiet morning surrounding me. My life up until that moment seemed like a dream.

"This is it," I said aloud. "He's gone."

Chapter Twenty

"These Days Were Unseen from Child's Sight"

Child's Sight

The view caught in existence
Lies reality at hand
Once so far in the distance
That's why I don't understand
Time flew with no resistance
That time that was never planned
Life's clock had such persistence
Leaving the past to expand

Now; an unrewarding scene
A picture not to be proud
The present here is obscene

A vulgar mind became loud
Envy is the color green
And so is the tainted crowd
Pray a smile to intervene
It fails through the twilight cloud

Every foot the steps outside
Needs the eye to stay alert
Trust is only self relied
Precautions not to feel hurt
Feelings fatal not to hide
Remain buried in the dirt
Kill or be killed; you decide
A consequence not to flirt

Rainbows only shades of grey
Their arcs under the streetlight
Stars above don't show the way
Fools in doubt would think they might
Trust in heart leaves you the prey
Heated blood will guide the night
Brings you just another day
These days unseen in child's sight

Less than two months have passed, yet it seems like a lifetime ago. Already things have changed dramatically. I found out I was pregnant three weeks after Josh left. For my "safety," he had left me no address or number to get in touch with him. When people in the neighborhood began noticing that Josh wasn't around the rumors started.

Martinez had only been around here for less than a year, and already the natives were in fear of getting on his bad side. Josh befriended him, maybe even became his protégé. A week after Josh's secret escape, the rumor was that Josh had ratted Martinez's name out to the cops. He was arrested and in prison, and some say Josh is to blame.

Since Josh left town, reneging on his deal, there is currently a warrant out for his arrest. But that wasn't convincing enough for those he left behind in the Hill. There were a few people who harassed me about Josh's whereabouts. Because Josh wasn't here to defend himself, even his faithful friends began to turn on him. I reminded them how he went to prison before for some drugs that weren't his.

"He wasn't a rat then and he isn't one now," I proclaimed. That much I knew was true.

After two weeks of living my life in melancholy, I missed my period. I figured it would come the next day, despite the fact that my cycle was like clockwork. Alas, the next day came and went without any sign of my cycle beginning again. When my period was a week late, I knew I was pregnant because I had been stressed out before without it affecting my cycle. I went to Visiting Nurses with Shonnie by my side.

I was sent to the bathroom with a little plastic cup from one of the nurses. Following the directions, I cleaned myself thoroughly with the wet wipe provided and then held the cup under the stream as I urinated over the toilet. It's an odd and uncomfortable process. The nurse was waiting with gloves on for me to hand the half-full cup to her. Slightly grossed out, I sat with Shonnie in the waiting room.

We read the magazines, commenting on each page with mindless chitchat. Minutes passed by, seeming like an eternity, before the nurse returned to call me back to her office.

Before I even sat in the chair, the nurse stated, "The test is positive."

She continued speaking with absolutely no hint of emotion. It was as though she was asking me what I was going to do for the day, not the possible options I had to contemplate about the growing fetus inside of me. But I hadn't made any decision, even though I was well aware of my options. The nurse offered the agency's assistance in handling any decision. I was grateful that she didn't put more pressure on me than she did. She didn't insist that I decide anything that instant or what avenue I would take in following through with that decision. Baffled as I was, I still managed to thank her quickly before I left.

I knew all along. I had never been late before. I remembered the gooey substance I'd found when I went to the bathroom, and there had to have been a really good reason why the cigarettes were suddenly making me nauseous. I just needed confirmation.

When I told Josh's grandfather about my pregnancy, he was disappointed but supportive. I also sensed a hint of sorrow. I insisted on telling Josh myself rather than place that burden onto his grandfather. After all, it wasn't his responsibility. Nonetheless his grandfather scheduled calls from Josh during my visits several times, but I was working two jobs one right after the other and always missed the call.

When I told my mother I was pregnant her reaction was cryptic, unjustified, and unsupportive, as it lacked any advice.

"I think you're falling into feelings of inadequacy," she solemnly stated and added nothing more.

Just the mere fact that she implied that I had done this to myself on purpose put me over the edge. "Does nobody know me anymore?" I wondered. Josh would know I didn't do this to myself on purpose. Why isn't he here to help me?

Writing usually helped me put things in perspective and gave me a release of pent-up emotion. Unbeknownst to him a letter was being composed in his name. I knew the letter would never reach him, which enabled me to write openly. The sentiments expressed ranged from sorrow and loneliness to missing him with understanding as to why he'd left to hating him for not only leaving me but for treating me badly in the past and then resenting him because I couldn't hate him. All the while I was at a complete loss as to how to handle my current situation.

All of my friends look at me so differently now. Everybody I know has suggested in some approach or another that I should get an abortion. It seems like the simpler choice, but is that the right decision? If I get an abortion, whom would I be making the decision in favor of? Is an abortion the best thing for me, or is it the best thing for the baby? And how could killing a baby be the right choice for the baby? Or does it even count? When is the fetus actually a baby? Is it when the heart starts to beat or is it not a baby until there's brain function? The spinal cord is one of the first things to develop. It stems from the brain. Is that considered brain functioning?

But will I only be doing a disservice to this child by raising it? In all honesty, I have no education, no career, no money, and up until two days ago I didn't even have a place to live, so what the hell do I have to offer someone else? Will it really be better if I don't go through with the pregnancy?

I don't recall giving up on anything before, especially if someone tells me I can't do it. I am quite the tenacious individual. But then again this is unlike anything I have ever faced. Someone else's well-being is at stake here. Will I only be doing the child an injustice by plunging into something I am by no means equipped to handle? If I go for the challenge simply to prove that I don't give up but yet mess up royally will it make the decision to keep the baby a selfish one?

What do I have to offer a child anyway? I have nothing to offer a guy in a relationship. I couldn't even break down my guard to trust someone that I loved. Do I have love to give? Is it enough for a baby with only one parent? Is it fair bringing a child into this world already so many steps behind the rest? He or she will have no money, no father, and an uneducated mother.

This baby doesn't have a chance in today's world. Look at how ugly this world is. Why on earth would anyone want to hurt an innocent beautiful creature by raising it on this hideous place we call earth? And this child is already going to be labeled a bastard. There is no hope for Josh and me. He is in no shape to raise a child either.

Even if he could come back, he isn't ready. He'll be in and out of the house, in and out of a relationship with me, and in and out of the baby's life. That won't be fair to the child. I will not do what so many other single mothers do. Part time dads leave the children to suffer burning questions as to why daddy doesn't love them enough or even like them enough to stay. That decision is easy to make. How ironic that it takes a baby to finalize things between us. And it's his baby at that!

My Soundproof Dimension

Half of me still walks this earth
Traveling in steps of stomps
My presence is known
To none but my own
My bites are no longer chomps

The road behind zigs and zags
The edges of razor blades
Been slashed with a knife
Through this scorching life
Sometimes I yearn for the shades

Myself is pieced in puzzles
A million pieces been chewed
Undefined jigsaw
My past is a flaw
For now my journey's subdued

Yet the remembrance of sin
Sings such a sweet melody
And the sun does fall

And then demons call
Every night in memory

In pain I scratch at the door
Drooling in this redemption
So at night I scream
My boiling bloodstream
For my soundproof dimension

"OH," I gasp, taking in a hardened ball of air that feels lodged in my throat. The one person I cared about, the one person I thought cared for me, doesn't want me. My mother is disgusted with me. Josh's grandfather is disappointed in me. Everybody is looking down on me.

"LOOK AT ME!" I yell in the mirror. "What a fucking mess! You're ugly and getting fatter by the day. You're a fucking housekeeper, for Christ's sake. You're nothing. You clean other people's shit and get paid shit for it. You're a nobody. Even an asshole loser like Josh doesn't want you!"

I look up into the mirror again and see the veil vanish before my eyes. What's behind is ugly, and I quickly turn my head to the window next to my bed. It's dusk and the sun is finally descending, but that's when the demons come out.

I break down into a howling cry. I hate myself. I am completely alone. I have to handle this and think everything through without the aid of substances to ease the pain or distort reality to make things less severe. I can't do this. The howling is piercing my ears. My head can't take the pressure any longer. I think my brain is going to bust right through my skull.

A wave of anger rushes over me like a blood-red blanket. I can only take so much hurt and sadness. It usually manifests itself into anger and hatred. I let out a gigantic roar, "I hate this. I hate this. I hate this." I jump up, too frustrated to sit any more, and pace the floor back and forth. Another roar sounds through my bedroom. I want to hit something, but what is there to hit? I turn around and pick up my trash barrel full of clothing, for it's the only item available. I toss it across the room.

I feel no better, instead left completely unsatisfied, so I pick it up again and toss it at my mirror. The headboard breaks the throw before the barrel has a chance to smash the mirror. The hideous clothing will reap my pain as I begin flinging them all across the room until I collapse onto the center of my floor. The daggers of blackened crystals have torn through my fingertips. My clothes have been ripped to shreds.

Sitting on my knees the rage is still strong within, so I start pounding the floor, watching it crack beside me. The blood is flowing through my body, seeping out of my fingers, dripping from my lips, oozing from my ears. The black lava is pouring out of my eyes as I continue screaming and wailing. This temper tantrum has its claws dug into me. It ceases when I keel over in defeat.

I lie there quietly, breathing deeply. The entire perimeters of my eyes feel as though they are housing tons of sand bags, yet I can finally appreciate the silence. There is nothing going through my head any more, and I become comatose in the fetal position on the floor surrounded by debris. My eyes remain wide open, as I lie there unaware of everything in the world.

Over an hour of time is lost before I come to. I scope the room around me, catching sight of the evidence of my fit that lies all over the place. I don't move for a moment to collect my thoughts. Then I remember where I left off. I remember the sorrow and confusion and then I remember the hatred, which leaves me hollow.

"I can't do this," I say aloud in a painstaking whisper, because I just don't have the energy to bring my voice to its full capabilities. "I can't do this. I have no one to turn to. It's just me and I hate me."

The sensors in my nerve endings begin to revive themselves and I feel the hardness of the tiles beneath me. I slowly climb up the side of my bed, clawing my way onto the mattress. Directly in front of me is my reflection again.

"What the fuck? What the fuck is going on? How did I get here? Who the fuck are you, you ugly fucking bitch?" My words are spaced and sound as though they are physically difficult to push out, "You're a useless piece of shit. And that's it!"

I change the scenery to the night sky outside of my window. It's elegant, honorable, and peaceful. How I envy it; I wish I knew how to be exactly that. The sky is a perfect color of ebony with a glowing ball suspended in its beauty accompanied by countless cheerful twinkles. Who would miss little old me? I gaze into my view of the universe much bigger, more powerful, and more significant than me. My mind takes me to a place inside myself I have never before visited. It's bleak and stuffy, resembling the day I've had.

My imagination takes me to the driver's seat of my car. I am anxious to go for a ride to find the sensation I see above me. Such tranquility is foreign to me. I reach up to it but I can't touch it, so I keep driving heading towards the Ocean Drive. I cherish the ocean. I can smell its inviting aroma. The salt taste as I lick my lips gives the implication that I am so close I could touch it.

The stories the waves reveal to me are heaven sent. Throughout my existence I have felt their pain and their frustration. Unfortunately, somehow I have lost their determination despite my possession of the will they exude. I dream of obtaining it all on the waters before me.

I am well aware of the curve just ahead on the road before my view. If I just keep the wheel straight … I could slam the pedal down to the floor and fly straight off the edge into the rocky waters below. I could become one with the ocean, finding strength in the waves. I could soar to the moon and be free from the world, with the ocean and the night sky as my only counterparts. With their power I wouldn't need anything else.

It's all bliss except for one tiny oversight—the baby. I'd be killing the baby to free myself. I could never be free if I have the unfair death of this baby tainting my soul. If that's not the express train to hell, then I will be sent to purgatory for the rest of eternity. And what would become of the baby's spirit? Will it be with me in purgatory? Will it have the chance to go to heaven? Who will be there for it? Who will care for it? Who will console and comfort it? I can't kill a baby—what the hell am I thinking?

"Wait a minute," I come back to reality still lying in my bed staring out the window, "I can't kill a baby!"

In that instant it all becomes clear to me. I can't go through with an abortion. I must face whatever comes my way. I have to be strong for this baby. Nobody else is here for this child but me. This baby is depending on me. I've made it this far on my own … I can do this!

"I can do this!" I say aloud. "I have to! It's not about just me anymore. It's about this beautiful, precious, innocent spirit growing a body inside of me. And I will do the best I can. The baby needs me with the will and determination I have but forgotten. I've found my meaning. Mother is the most magnificent title to be held. A child is the greatest gift on earth. What the hell was I thinking? I'll just have to change. It's high time for that anyway."

I place my hands ever so lightly against my belly. I take a few minutes to reflect upon my new resolution. Satisfied with my decision, I whisper, "I won't fail you."

Chapter Twenty-One

"As One Door Closes Another Opens"

Now that I am able to face life with a clear mind and an open heart it seems simpler to me. I am more focused with the knowledge of what I have to do. I go through an OB-GYN office that was highly recommended and choose to see the midwife, which turns out to be a favorable decision. My apartment is furnished with my belongings within a week's time, with Amber and Willis' help. My family and friends are more supportive and respect my decision.

All I hope for beyond hope is that I am producing a boy. I am so unsure of how to become the woman I want to be. I know I'm finally on the path, but I have so much to learn about womanhood as well as myself. I am confident I will be able to do well by my baby. But if I have a girl I will be presented with an abundance of issues I'm not yet willing to face. From my own experience, I am certain how to raise my boy to treat others properly, especially females.

At five months pregnant I finally have the opportunity to talk to Josh. His grandfather informs me of his plans to come into town for the holiday.

I had come to conclusions that completely excluded Josh from my life. I had come to certain realizations about him and his personality flaws. I had lost respect for him, and with that went the deep affection. I am as nervous and tense to see him as I ever was in the past.

Will all the love I once had for him come back the moment I lay eyes on him again? Will he welcome me into his arms, or at least his house? What kind of response will I receive after I tell him? I am sick with unanswered questions as the anticipation eats away at me, bringing me to an insensible state.

For some reason I'm under the impression he has been in town for a full day without contacting me. I remain patient, awaiting a knock at my door or the phone to ring or even my pager to go off, yet all is quiet. I go to sleep after my shift ends at midnight, furious that I am still hurt by him. The following day I can't take the suspense anymore. It's worse than when I made the biggest mistake of my life. I have to see him and get it over with. I remain patient enough for my day shift to end, grateful that I have work to occupy half of my day.

With my stomach slightly bulging and entangled in knots I drive straight to his grandfather's house. To my surprise Josh answers the door. He welcomes me as though I had just seen him the day before. I am taken aback by his nonchalance as we exchange simple hugs with minimal physical contact. It's not enough for him to notice the protrusion underneath my oversized sweatshirt. His grandfather walks into the room and invites us to have a seat.

"Why haven't you called to tell me you were here?" I ask with only a hint of the anger I feel in an effort to hold back my negativity in the presence of his grandfather.

"What do you mean?" Josh asks.

"We just got in," they say simultaneously.

Oh, the humiliation yet again! Now I am completely thrown off course. The knots in my stomach tighten and twist in odd directions as I sit in the chair on the opposite side of the small room from Josh. Josh is sitting in his chair obviously as uncomfortable as I while his grandfather's in his chair honorable and upright.

"Well, go ahead and tell him," his grandfather expresses with impatience.

That introduction leaves me with no other option than to say what I came to say. There is no room for small talk first allowing time for me to build up the courage. There is no time to be apprehensive and chicken out or postpone the inevitable. I have to just say it and be done with it. If what is underneath my baggy sweatshirt doesn't speak for itself, I have to. With no hard feelings about the introduction I am glad that I can finally alleviate my wonderment of what his reaction might be.

So I blurt out, "I'm pregnant."

Josh doesn't say anything. He lets out a record-breaking exhale and a hint of a smirk, which reminds me of my question about his intentions during our last encounter. It is at that point his grandfather leaves us with some privacy.

"Well, how far along are you?"

"About five months now."

"Do you know if it's a boy or a girl?"

"Not sure yet."

"You're gonna keep it?"

"Yeah."

Josh seems so aloof. The enormous amount of pressure released from inside of me makes me dizzy with light-headedness, which then brings about nausea.

"Well, I gotta get to work."

"I thought you just got off?"

"I did, and now I have to go to my other job." I start towards the front door.

"Am I gonna see you again?"

"Call me."

I leave without a hug or a kiss or any sign of affection. I'm able to sleep after my late shift, grateful that the hard part is finally over. The next day I only have to work my day job. Josh pages me a couple of times and we plan to meet again after work.

I drive to his grandfather's and we sit inside the spare room to talk with privacy.

"Will you come down south with me?"

I stutter, at a loss for words.

"You'll like it there," he continues.

"I have already been making plans to go to CCRI." (Community College of Rhode Island)

"Well, you can change your school and it won't affect the federal grants."

"Maybe, but I will be needing a babysitter. Danielle's mom already said she'd do it for me."

"They have a daycare right at the school you could go to."

"I don't like daycare. It's better if I know someone to watch the baby. I know nobody down there."

"You know me."

My pager interrupts the conversation.

"Do you need to use the phone?"

"No, thanks. I am just gonna go."

"You got a replacement for me already?" he asks concerned.

"No, it's Amber. I'm just gonna go see her."

"Oh how's she doing?"

"Good. She's still with Willis. They're good."

"Well, you think you could find me a dime or even a nick?" Josh hands me thirty dollars.

"You want it tonight?"

"Yeah, if you don't mind."

"Well, I am sure I can find that easy enough. I'll see you in a little while."

As I drive away I become more and more disappointed that he is able to talk about a baby one minute and smoking the next. It just proves I came to the right conclusion before seeing him again.

Later on that night I return with the dime bag of weed he requested. He tells me to keep the change.

"Alright. Well, I gotta go."

"Why so early?"

"I got some shit to do before I go to sleep. I am working my ass off at two jobs, ya know?"

"Yeah, I know. But I only got a little time here. I thought you would want to see me."

"I do. That's why I am here. But I got a lot of shit going on. Shit you left behind."

"Well, can you just take me for a ride so I can smoke this?"

"Alright, but I gotta get going soon."

We go for a boring drive through Middletown so no one will recognize him in my car.

"Ya know, if you moved down south with me I could help you out. You wouldn't have to work so hard."

"Josh, I got no one down there. You know how hard it was to get everyone around here on my side about this whole thing?"

"Yeah?"

"I finally got my mother talking to me like a normal person again. My girls don't look at me funny anymore. I got plans and goals, and I am working at them. How can I just get up and leave all that?"

"But you can have a good life in the city. You're the city girl. You love the city."

"It's not gonna work."

"Oh here, can you stop at Cumby's so I can get a soda?"

I wait in the car this time. His presence doesn't seem to have the same effect on me as it has in the past. I have yet to see his captivating Cheshire. I wonder if he has lost it altogether. Part of me is looking forward to leaving him for the night.

Back in the car, he asks, "Can I see you tomorrow?"

"I gotta work during the day 'til four then I gotta work at six."

"Damn, girl."

"I told you, this shit ain't no joke."

"I know. I'm not saying nothing. I'm just like ... Damn! That's all."

"What time are you leaving?"

"Early."

"I am gonna go back now. I will try to see you in the morning, but I ain't much for mornings. I usually get real sick, so I can't promise anything."

Back in front of his grandfather's I keep the car running while we say farewell. He leans over for a kiss. I feel my stomach knot up. I listen for the beating of my heart, anticipating the future torment of uncertainty to come. But I hear nothing.

Our lips meet and I'm expecting my heart to jump through my chest again. But it does not. I cut the goodbye short. "Safe trip, if I don't see you."

"Of course you will, but thanks anyway. Bye."

At the time I don't fathom the infinite length of time that will extend through this separation. This is the last I will ever hear from him. While driving to work the next morning I see his grandfather's car approaching in the opposite direction. Josh and I catch each other in passing. I merely smile as he looks like a lost puppy dog. In my rearview mirror I see the brake lights on the car. My foot remains steady over the accelerator. Then they continue down the road and I continue off to work.

The rest of the gestation period flies by and I have no complications in the pregnancy. Amazingly I go into labor the night before my due date. I am up most of the night in my bedroom, where so many thoughts and ideas haunted me in the past, where unsightly tantrums were thrown and transformations were made, and where significant final resolutions were conceived. When the sun rises I take a shower and call my mother, with whom I now share a respectful relationship. I call my sister and Shonnie next with news that I am going to have the baby.

Together we go to the hospital just after eight in the morning. My midwife, Paula, arrives approximately an hour later. I am more than halfway into the labor, at 6 cm dilated and 80 percent effaced when she first checks me. Throughout the spread of the next several hours my sister brings me ice chips, my mother rubs my back, and Shonnie talks to me about non-related issues to take my mind off of the pain. Paula spends a considerable amount of time in the room with us, involved in the process of comforting me.

Paula demonstrates confidence in her ability, which allows me to relax. She is diligent with her demands of the nurses' assistance as well as their sensitivity while in the room. I never doubt her, and in return she never doubts me. Having delivered hundreds of babies as well as birthed more than a few of her own, my midwife is truly an amazing woman.

During active labor when it comes time to push, Paula is by my feet urging me on. She is ready for my son to be born. My mother and my sister are on either side of me, holding each leg respectively in position to aid as much as they can in pushing. Shonnie has a cool washcloth draped over my forehead and chants encouraging words. It all boils down to my efforts.

Just then I see the image once reflected in the mirror before me now charging at me. I grumble, "Why am I bringing a child into this fucking ugly world?"

It jumps inside my vessel and wrestles its way out. Meanwhile I am grunting and pushing with every ounce of everything I have. Finally I see what the hardened tigress is struggling with. It is my heart and I can hear it beating. It is bright red and full of life, except the part that is in the clutch of the monster before me. There it is, the glistening ebony of the diamond substance. They fight for some time and I see the pumping muscle change from black diamond to soft tissue. Finally the tigress is flushed away, and a bright light penetrates me, returning my beating heart.

My son is born six hours after our arrival that morning. I have pushed his head out and the shoulders are through. Paula persuades me to pull him out onto my chest. There I hold my beautiful and perfectly healthy baby boy.

He looks up into my eyes immediately. Such divinity, such purity and innocence held so much meaning, as though this tiny creature sent by God knew of the excruciating path leading up to this very moment. He looks at me with angelic eyes as if to say, "We did it! You did a good job, Mom. Together we will be alright!"

"That was the most beautiful birth I have ever witnessed." Paula exclaims. "Good job, everybody."

"Thank you!" I say for the compliment. "Thank you!" I add for the gift.

Printed in the United States
213967BV00001B/6/P